SIN CITY GODDESS

For Susi,
librarians are
a special kind
of magic!

Barb

ALSO BY BARBRA ANNINO

The Stacy Justice Series

Opal Fire
Bloodstone
Tiger's Eye
Emerald Isle

More

Gnome Wars
Every Witch Way But Wicked
My Guardian Idiot

SIN CITY GODDESS

BARBRA ANNINO

Published by Thomas & Mercer, Seattle

www.apub.com

ISBN-13: 9781477849279
ISBN-10: 1477849270

Cover design by Kerrie Robertson

Library of Congress Control Number: 2013911790

Printed in the United States of America.

For the goddesses.
You know who you are.

Chapter 1

Life in the Underworld had its perks, and poker night was one of them. Ever since I could remember, on Thursday evenings, Bill and I would meet by the river, appoint one of the newly dead as our dealer, and play until one of us busted out of the game. Occasionally, others would join in for a hand or two, but Bill and I were pretty good, so not many challengers could outlast us. Tonight was poker night, and we had been at it for several hours now. I was waiting for the next sweet hand before I made a push to go all in with my coins. The hour was late, I was tired, and the air would grow chilly soon. Furies were not fans of the cold. Not to mention, I needed desperately to stretch my arms, legs, and wings.

The dealer shuffled the cards and flipped three over onto the table. The flop was a jack, king, and ace of spades, all suited. When the dealer flipped the fourth card over (the turn), I eyed my opponent. I was relieved to see that it was an ace, because 70 percent of the time, Bill had pocket eights or pocket aces. He was prone to dead man's hand. But since I was holding one ace and there were two on the board, that meant he might have one, but he couldn't have a pair of them. Then again, he could have been holding jacks, kings, or something else entirely.

I set my gaze on him, trying to ignite a flame in my violet eyes. He hated when I did that. Said it gave him the heebie-jeebies. So naturally, I fired up the lights. There was a tiny bit of heat that accompanied the spark, but it felt good, like a massage.

It worked. A bead of sweat bubbled on Bill's forehead, breaking his poker face.

I smiled. He was holding eights. Had to be. If it had been a pair of jacks or kings, he'd have been cool as granite.

I was holding big slick, an ace and a king. In Texas Hold'em (a game I wasn't nearly as fond of as Five-Card Draw), you shared the cards on the board with the other players at the table. Which meant that it could be anyone's game until the final card was dealt—the river. That was the one aspect of this game I enjoyed. The excitement. The thrill.

The danger.

Right now, I had a full boat, aces over kings. The guy across from me with the wild hair and the floppy ears best kept under a hat narrowed his eyes. There was one card left to deal.

I collected my breath and steadied every muscle in my body, which came easily to me. A little trick I picked up on the job, policing humans. I had noticed—ages ago—that if I was calm, they would be too. I leaned in ever so slightly and pushed the rest of my coins forward.

"All in," I said.

Bill raised his upper lip and snarled at me, but he pushed his coins in too. If he was holding what I thought he was holding—a pair of eights—then he couldn't beat me. That would give him a full house, aces over eights. Or he could have the queen and the ten of spades, which would give him a royal flush, kicking my full boat out of the water.

Even a straight flush would get my ass handed to me on a silver platter.

But I was here to gamble.

The dealer flipped over the last card, or the river, as it's called.

Ace. Combined with the other two aces on the board and the one in my hand, that gave me four of a kind. Only thing that could beat it would be a royal flush, and the cards were showing that was a possibility, but it was a long shot.

Bill grinned at me wickedly and spit a chunk of cigar onto the black slate patio. A flutter of doubt ruffled my feathers, and I sat taller, hoping he wouldn't notice. I still had trouble controlling my wings when I was tense.

He flipped over pocket kings, sat back, pleased with himself, and twiddled that ridiculously long mustache. Then he blew a ring of smoke across the table to circle my head like a halo.

"Well, I'll be damned," I said, intending the pun. I widened my eyes, feigning surprise, toying with my prey like I used to in the old days.

Bill grunted and reached across the table to claw at my coins, assuming his full house—kings over aces—was the winning hand.

I slapped at his meaty paw. "Not so fast, Hickok."

I turned over my hole cards.

Bill took one look at my hand, cursed, and kicked a rock that sailed into the river Styx. It landed with a splash that startled a black swan, who squawked violently at us.

I smiled at my opponent, stood, and scooped up my coins.

"That's the bitch of it, Bill. That damn river will get you every time."

Bill pounded his fist into the table, throwing a temper tantrum. The dealer, a wispy shade still getting used to its surroundings, jumped.

I stood there, patiently waiting for Bill to finish his outburst. After he had kicked a few more rocks, toppled a chair, uprighted the chair (because the last time he hadn't, Hades had not been pleased), crinkled up a card, and laced the air with a stream of obscenities, he removed his weathered hat with the bullet holes, ran his fingers through his too-long hair, and said, "Same time next week, Raven?"

I would never understand human emotions.

"Absolutely, Hickok. And stop calling me that. You know I hate it."

He had given me the nickname because my hair was a stream of black curls and that was the only color I ever wore. And also because of the wings.

He smiled sheepishly and bowed, and the onetime lawman lumbered off to meet up with his love, Jane.

I stood up from the table. The shade stood too, and I said to it, "Put the cards back in their place."

The shade nodded, the inky blackness of its shape bobbing in the moonlight as it collected the cards, trying to unwrinkle the one Bill had crushed. Finally, after a few clumsy attempts, the shade gathered all the cards in its less-than-solid hands and whispered off to the den, where gaming supplies were stored in the Underworld.

A few minutes later it was back, wandering around the ebony table, wondering what to do next.

I stopped it on its third pass.

"You've done well in serving the gods." I plucked a few coins from my winnings and placed them in the shade's hand. "Here, give these to Charon and tell that greedy bastard that if he doesn't allow you passage, he will have to deal with Tisiphone, and I will not be in a generous mood."

The shade nodded and rushed off toward the ferryman, Charon, to pay for his ride across the river.

I'm ashamed to admit that our system for transferring souls to their final resting place was embarrassingly outdated. I and my sisters, Alecto and Megaera, had tried to convince Hades that Charon's work as the ferryman was no longer needed. That since we three did not police humans with the same tireless intensity with which we once had, our time was free to help deal with matters of the dead. Especially the lost souls who needed guidance. As daughters of the dark, we thought it only fitting that we be put to work in such a capacity. The ferryman objected, of course. He enjoyed his position of wealth and power, so naturally he argued before the court that his role was vital to the process. Hades agreed, insisting, "Tradition is tradition."

Personally, I believed it had more to do with family squabbles and politics than with tradition. Otherwise, why would Hades have allowed me to interact with the shades at all? I should explain that "shades" were what we called the newly deceased who haven't yet gained access to Hades's realm. Souls who had lost their corporeal form in death but had yet to obtain their Underworld body. Humans, I had heard, called them ghosts.

Such an odd word.

Once the mortals completed their burial process, the souls arrived here, at the river's edge, carrying only their shades and their valuables. Long ago, humans knew to place coins or jewelry in the coffins of their dearly departed to pay Charon to escort them across the river and into the Underworld, but that practice had slowly faded over time. Even though many were buried with heirlooms or trinkets that would satisfy the fare, for reasons not related to our system, some souls arrived with nothing of value—the homeless, helpless, familyless, and victims of foul play whose bodies were never discovered on the outer plane.

The Lost, we called them. They were the shades that wandered the riverbanks, searching for a purpose, a plan, some guidance on what to do in the After. It was through no fault of their own that they had nothing to offer Charon. Cold reptile that he was, he simply didn't care. Rules were rules. Coin was all he cared about.

But I had never been one to play by rules that served no purpose.

For what was law without justice?

I stretched my legs and released my wings to their full, six-foot span. I shook them once, limbering up, and drank in the night air. Patches of clouds drifted over the water, which sparkled like black diamonds. The gentle lapping of the current relaxed me, and I listened for a moment, meditating, absorbing the perfume of the blooming night jasmine. A few minutes later, I calmly tucked all the coins from my winnings into my feathers, making certain they were secure and prepared for flight. It was brisk, but I preferred the heat, so I would welcome the exercise.

I took a running start and leaped off the river bank, soaring high into the velvety-black sky, past cliffs made of ebony and marble, and up, up, up, until I was just beneath the moon, looking for the lost ones.

There were pockets of them along the hillside, in the dark fields, and at the water's edge. I released the coins from my thick feathers as I flew above them, one by one. I could see that some shades were afraid at first, until they spotted what had fallen from the sky. Some of them looked up and waved, while others collected the coins and passed them out to confused ones. The river was choppy this evening, and I could see the waves crashing into the jagged granite, sending up fresh sprays of seawater that coated my long hair.

After I had dispensed all of the coins, I landed on top of a gray cliff twinkling with fool's gold. I flapped my wings, shook out my hair, adjusted my pants and top, and watched as Charon was approached by dozens of souls waiting to gain passage, coins in hand. He lifted his cloaked head and raised a gnarled fist at me, his face twisted into a rage.

"Tisiphone, you spiteful hellcat! I'll get you for this!"

How very original, Charon, I thought. I smiled and waved at him. "Nice to see you too, you overinflated rhinoceros scrotum."

I watched for several minutes as the shades formed a polite line. Then I turned, expanded my wings, and lifted my head to bathe in the moonlight, my best source of energy. When I felt refreshed enough for the journey home, I turned to walk through the dark forest, a smile on my face. Before I could take a step, however, I bumped into Hermes, messenger of the gods.

"Tisiphone, I'm so happy to have found you."

The small god fluttered his winged sandals and landed before me. He strained his neck to look up at me as he spoke. He was a twitchy little thing by nature, but he seemed unusually antsy tonight.

"What is it, Hermes?"

"Hades requests your presence immediately."

Perfect. Charon had complained already, and now I was going to get a tongue-lashing. Honestly, gods could be so sensitive. I bent over at the waist and cracked my neck. Then I tucked my wings away and faced him again.

"Why?"

"I'm not supposed to say," the messenger god stammered.

This piqued both my curiosity and my suspicions. Hermes was well known around Olympus for his practical jokes.

I narrowed my eyes. "Why not?"

Hermes looked around nervously. "It's top secret."

I bent down, stared Hermes right in the eye, and lit the fire in mine.

He tried to snap his eyes shut, but it was too late.

You see, my little ability, which I had mastered over the last millennia, could function as a simple parlor trick, as with Mr. Bill Hickok, but it also had the power to coax a god to tell the truth. It didn't always work on one with more strength than I had, like Zeus, but on minor deities it worked quite sufficiently. I still hadn't perfected the trick on humans yet, but I was working on it.

"He wants you to go back," Hermes blurted out.

"Go back where?"

Hermes bent his head, shifted his eyes to the right.

"You know... *there.*"

I shot up to my full height of six feet.

Now it was my turn to be twitchy. I had vowed never to return. Not after what had happened last time. Not after what I had done.

It was too dangerous. *I* was too dangerous.

Chapter 2

I had come a long way since that time, but still. The thought of slipping back into what I had once been terrified me.

As a Fury, I was born with an innate sense of law and order. It was once my duty to police humans. To drive them to understand their crimes against humanity, decency, compassion, truth, and society as a whole. I was to coax them to repent, to show remorse. Humans being humans, you can imagine this was not always an easy task. I and my sisters pursued the cruel, the wicked, the conscienceless, sometimes mercilessly, until they had seen the errors of their ways.

Unfortunately, some souls were black as coal and could never be enlightened.

As a Fury, I was also born with a temper. So a stubborn mortal who refused to repent—or, worse, committed another offense on my watch—was my worst enemy. I'm afraid I didn't always handle those cases well.

The forest floor was damp, and I could feel the heels of my boots sinking into the thick mud as I walked faster and faster, trying to think, trying not to recall my last assignment.

Trying to escape Hermes's high-pitched, incessant chatter.

"Please don't do this, Tisiphone." He was fluttering next to me, attempting to keep up with my stride.

"Hermes, you gnat, go away. I need to think."

The woods were growing darker, thicker. Every so often a set of glowing eyes popped out through the boughs of the trees.

"There's nothing to think about. You must at least go and talk to Hades. He's called a meeting with Zeus and Poseidon, so there's no avoiding it. He'll send someone else to find you eventually, and then I'll be blamed for failing to complete a simple task. I hate it when they're angry with me."

He said that last part with the pathetic whine of a kitten who hadn't been fed in a week.

I sighed. I didn't want to see Hermes scolded. He had enough trouble trying to gain his father's respect. Zeus was quite proud of most of his children, yet Hermes seemed to be an utter disappointment to the king of the gods. Granted, Hermes wasn't gifted with wisdom like Athena, or the musical talent of Apollo, but he had his charms.

I stopped walking. "I suppose it couldn't hurt to talk," I said, although I wished I had time to think of a thousand excuses that would prevent them from sending me. Perhaps I could break a wing. What good was a Fury with only one wing? She'd be half as powerful. Not very effective.

Hermes clapped his hands and tipped his hat. "Excellent."

We made our way out of the woods in silence as I chewed my bottom lip, wondering what could be so urgent that they would take such a risk in sending me back after what I had done. After all, I could no longer be trusted—the Fates had made that abundantly clear. I had broken a high law, a moral law, and I could have put us all in danger.

Hermes said, "You still haven't forgiven yourself, have you?"

I glanced at him sideways. His white tunic was bright against the backdrop of the Underworld landscape.

"Could you?"

He nodded. "Absolutely. If you ask me, you did your job properly."

I clicked my tongue, disagreeing.

Avenger of murder was my official title. Human societies were not as civilized millennia ago. They were fragmented. Corrupt. Dysfunctional. Barbaric. And when a person sinned against another or against a populace, it was the duty of the gods to ensure that the person be punished when mortal law failed to do so. Sometimes the humans handled things well on their own. Sometimes not. My sisters covered lesser crimes—thievery, assault, societal violations, moral codes, falsehoods—while I had the big one. Murder.

As societies developed, laws became more enforceable, courts became more judicious, and we were needed less and less, until eventually the gods decided it was time to allow humans to police themselves except under the most heinous of circumstances.

Unfortunately, humans being humans, those circumstances did arise from time to time.

It was just such a circumstance that had led to my exile.

"You were found not guilty, Tisi," Hermes said.

It was an arduous trial, and the Fates were furious with me, especially Atropos, since it was her mess to clean up. They wanted to bind me to the Underworld forever, and I couldn't blame them. What I did disrupted the fabric of both worlds, but no punishment could be as severe as my own shame. My own withdrawal from my people. If it weren't for Hades's and my sisters' constant encouragement, I doubt I would ever have left my cavern.

Hermes said, "Sometimes we are forced to choose between the lesser of two evils."

We were approaching Hades's palace. But instead of the excitement that usually flushed through me at the sheer majesty of the sleek stone walls encrusted with garnet and hematite, I was filled with dread.

What was this task? Where would I have to go this time? Europe? Asia? America? Africa? Lords, I hoped it wasn't Alaska. Too damn cold.

But more importantly, whom would I be there to punish?

Because, gods help me, if it was another man who had shed the blood of children, I just might kill again.

I looked down at my hands, the murder weapons, and stepped forward.

Chapter 3

When we reached the stone steps of Hades's palace, I looked up at the gaping mouth of the gargoyle that framed the gargantuan gray door and hesitated. What if they wanted me to hunt another serial killer? Would they listen to my protests? Would they accept the fact that I was not up to the challenge? Perhaps they would consider sending one of my sisters, Meg or Alex. Or perhaps they would be too stubborn or prideful to hear my concerns. Wouldn't be the first time. The highest gods in our pantheon, while often fair, did not like to be questioned about their decisions—although, rumor had it, we were better off than the subjects of the Norse gods. Thor, I'd been told, could be a real hard-ass.

Hermes asked if I was ready. I took a deep breath and nodded before he swung open the heavy door. I stepped over the threshold, the messenger god floating behind me, both of us expecting to be greeted by Hades and his brothers in the parlor, but the palace was dark and quiet.

"Where do you suppose they are?" I asked, scanning the hall and the parlor. The rich-indigo walls were lit by firefly sconces, their fluttering wings zigzagging around the crystal glass. The sleek piano that anchored the receiving area beckoned for Apollo's skilled fingers, while a silver sideboard overflowed with delicate pitchers of wine and glass bowls filled with fresh plums, blackberries, and grapes.

Hermes said, "Perhaps they're in the war room."

The war room was where the gods met to discuss policy, strategy, and laws. It'd been updated in recent years, thanks to Athena's inventive mind. The walls were now covered with large screens that transmitted information to the gods about the goings-on of all of Olympus, as well as areas of the human plane. I had no idea how it worked, nor did I care to learn. Technology did not interest me. All those lights, bells, buzzes, and talking machines made my head want to explode. I preferred the dark, the calm, the quiet.

"I'm sure you're right."

I turned left toward the hall that led to the war room but stopped dead in my tracks when I heard a deep, menacing growl.

Uh-oh.

I couldn't see him, but I heard him coming. I was about to release my wings, when he came hurtling at me full speed. I put my hands out in a feeble attempt to slow him down. "Cerberus, no! Easy, boy!"

Too late. He crashed into me, all three heads and 250 pounds of him. He was a massive beast, taller than I when he stood on his hind legs. He knocked the wind from my lungs for a second. As I struggled to free myself from beneath the muscular frame of Hades's hound, I was glad I hadn't opened my wings, or surely he would have broken one. On second thought, perhaps I should have. It would have been a graceful way to decline the mission and still maintain my reputation. Dammit. Why couldn't I think more like a deviant?

Hermes hovered over my prone body, concern coloring his face. "Are you all right, Tisi?"

"Eh," I choked, still trying to catch my breath as Cerberus coated me in licks from head to toe. Much faster to accomplish with three tongues. I could feel his hot breath frizzing my hair, but I couldn't see much beyond his watermelon-sized heads.

I really wished Hades would send him to obedience school.

A familiar voice shouted down the hallway then. "Cerberus! Off!"

It was Artemis, Apollo's twin sister. Thank the heavens. The goddess of the hunt had a special knack for taming beasts.

Immediately, the dog leaped off me and I felt the breath fill my body once again. I gathered myself, with the assistance of Hermes, and stood, straightening out my clothing. Cerberus slunk over to the golden goddess, remorse dripping off his frame. He hung his heads low as she scolded him. She whispered something in his fourth ear a moment later, and he gingerly walked over to me and extended his paw. I shook it and told him he was forgiven. Artemis tossed him three bones, and the big black dog caught each one and trotted down the corridor and out of sight.

"A thousand pardons, Tisiphone," Artemis said. "I have tried to instill propriety in that canine time and time again, yet Hades refuses to correct his bad habits." She flicked her blue eyes to where Cerberus had trotted off, and finished with "I'm afraid the poor beast is terribly confused about etiquette."

"Don't give it another thought, Artemis," I said.

She smiled, her bright teeth lighting up the room, and motioned with her suntanned hand. "Come. We've been expecting you."

Hermes and I followed Artemis down a wide passageway. Her gauzy robes grazed her curved hips as her sandals clicked against the marble floor. We passed gilded portraits of the gods, vases of black dahlias, and chairs carved from jet, until we reached the massive room filled with screens, knobs, buttons, type boards, speakers, cords, and various other electronic devices that I could not identify. The war room had changed since I had last stepped foot in it. Gone were the welcoming stone walls, replaced with a smooth, shockingly white surface from which the screens now hung. The whole place was offensive to my senses. I was forced to shield my eyes for a moment.

A gentle hand covered mine.

"Tisiphone, remember your breathing exercises," Athena said.

It was Athena who had shown me the power of mercy, forgiveness, and meditation. She had taught me how to gain peace and strength from the natural surroundings that appealed to me, like the water and the moon. In other words, it was Athena who had taught me how to subdue my fury.

Her gray eyes gazed into mine as I took a few deep breaths, imagining all the noisy electronics fading away, gently lapping waves taking their place.

"Feel better?" the goddess of wisdom asked.

"Yes, thank you."

I turned to find Zeus and Hades deep in conversation. Zeus's thick, snowy brows kept crashing into each other like two caterpillars fistfighting as he listened to his brother with intensity. Hades tugged on his black beard as he spoke, the dark skin on his bald head wrinkling with his movements. I spotted Poseidon at the opposite end of the room, sitting in a chair that was too small for him, his long, thick legs propped on a far table, remote in hand. His back was toward me, trident at his side, green robes pooled around the metal chair. A tiny trickle of seawater dripped from his seat as he watched that movie the mortals had made about him.

Hermes flickered over to Zeus, said something quietly, and shuffled from the room. Zeus and Hades exchanged a few more words. Then they both stood and faced me.

"Tisiphone!" Hades boomed in that roaring voice of his. "Wonderful to see you." He smacked his hands together to emphasize his point.

I felt Athena and Artemis slip to the side.

"My lord." I bowed my head.

"I suppose you're wondering what led us to request your presence."

"As I understand it—"

Then I stopped, remembering what Hermes had said about this being a secret.

Zeus rolled his eyes and grumbled under his breath.

Snake spit! I hadn't intended to get Hermes in trouble. I quickly tried to cover. "It has to do with Charon."

Zeus's sky-blue eyes sparkled at me. He didn't believe my explanation, but he seemed to appreciate the effort I had made to cover for his son.

Hades waved a bejeweled hand. Poseidon rose to join his brothers. He had to tilt his head to the side to avoid hitting it on the ceiling. He was the tallest of the brothers, although all of them were impressive in stature.

"No, I'm afraid it's more serious than anything that old bag of bones has to whine about," Hades said.

I stood there expectantly, dreading what was to come. A dozen alternatives ran through my mind. Perhaps Artemis could go? She was skilled in the hunt. Surely she could train her beasts to help her find mortals. Or Ares? He was the god of war, after all. He had more skill than most in battle and strategic planning.

The bright lights were hot on my face. *Steady breaths, Tisi, steady breaths.*

Hades glanced at Poseidon and nodded. The ruler of the seven seas raised his remote and aimed it at a large screen to my left. He clicked it once, and an image filled the rectangular frame.

"This is a land in the mortal realm called Las Vegas," Hades said.

The backdrop of the picture was a night sky void of stars and moon, but that was the only darkness. Endless stretches of bright lights in every color covered the landscape, blinking, twinkling, and chasing each other in circles. The speakers in the war room screamed out horns, bells, jingles, and endless shouts of humans who had clearly consumed too much wine and were spilling all over the streets and the sidewalks. Flashy automobiles crawled across the roads, with people hanging out of the windows in various forms of dress, and it seemed there was a talking machine every few inches across the screen.

It was garish. It was vulgar. I had once had an assignment in a restaurant called Chuck E. Cheese's, and this was more obnoxious than that place. It was unlike anything I had ever seen, mortal or immortal. Granted, I had not been to the outer plane in years, but had things really changed that much?

"This is what the humans have succumbed to?" I asked, incredulous. "Is the species now ruled by machines?"

Zeus chuckled. "Not exactly. This place is, for lack of a better term, a human playground. It's where they holiday."

I widened my eyes. "Holiday? I cannot imagine a less relaxing place to holiday."

Poseidon clicked the remote again, and the image changed. I stared at the screen as giant animals stumbled across the walking paths, bottles of liquor in hand.

"Those creatures. They don't seem real."

Hades said, "They aren't. They are people in disguise. They are a part of the games."

"I don't understand. Are they hunted for sport?"

Zeus said, "No, Tisi. They provide entertainment and souvenirs to the visitors in the form of pictures."

That was the dumbest thing I had ever heard. "Why would anyone want a portrait of a stranger dressed in a giant mouse costume hanging on the wall?"

Humans. I didn't get it.

Hades said, "It's not our place to question; it's our place to observe. Keep watching."

Poseidon hit another button on the remote, and the scene changed to a fountain spouting water into the air in tandem with glaring lights and symphony shouts set against the backdrop of a most uninspired building. I cringed. I found the melodic song of water in its natural state to be beautiful. Dressing it up with lights and trumpets was blasphemy. Like drowning a steak in ketchup.

I had the sickening feeling that this outrageous human playground was where they wanted to send me.

I wouldn't last a day.

The next image was indoors. A grand lobby of some sort, with creamy marble floors ribboned with swirls of darker colors that met acanthus-leaf rugs. A long reception desk hugged the back wall in an oval shape, and there were huge paintings depicting Olympus behind it. Centering the area was a likeness of the three Graces, the party girls of Olympus, surrounded by a gazing pool. Some mortals referred to them as the three Charities. It was a common misconception that the Greek and Roman pantheons were separate entities, but that wasn't so. We were one and the same; it was just that different mortals called us by different names. Artemis, for example, was also known as Diana.

Hades spoke. "You are looking at a lodging house called Caesars Palace. It's more refined than other inns of the village, but it does have gaming and public water holes within its walls. It also has bathhouses and is quite popular with the mortal elite."

Again, the sea lord clicked over to another scene. More talking machines, more bells, whistles, flickering lights, and humans wandering about aimlessly like sheep without a shepherd.

I rubbed my temple to stop it from throbbing.

"This is one of the gaming arenas," Zeus said.

Another click, another image. This one revealed a ridiculous representation of sea horses lined up behind a liquor dispensary with a glass-ensconced water tank filled with floating fish. More gaming tables too. They seemed to be everywhere. Quite profitable, I imagined.

"Caesar must be an aristocrat. Is he a descendant of the great statesman?" I asked.

"The lodging house is named after Julius Caesar, but his descendents do not own the palace," Hades said.

That seemed silly. Why would anyone name a modern facility after an ancient general if he wasn't a relation?

The next image showed another public house, lined with bottles of elixirs and revelers gathered around tables, enjoying a dance performance. The silhouettes of two women, each behind a white screen, moved in a graceful rhythm, gyrating their curves and swirling their arms overhead. There was a sign off to the side that read SHADOW BAR.

Hades turned to me. "This is the reason I called you here, Tisiphone. Several women have gone missing from this establishment. We've been monitoring the problem as of late because the police seem to be at a loss for answers. There is no apparent link between these females, and the baffling part is that their companions don't seem to realize the women are missing until days later."

Missing women? That was the top-secret mission? Women went missing all the time in the mortal world. True, the perpetrators did not always meet justice, but we had resolved not to get involved with this class of crime long ago.

I looked around the room from one god to another. Athena was smiling at me, while Artemis twirled a lock of hair through her fingers. The three brothers stood in silence. I didn't know where Hermes had gone off to.

"I don't understand. This seems not to be a matter for a Fury. The new law states that only under the most heinous of circumstances should I return to the human plane to seek retribution for a mortal sin—acts such as enslavement, matricide, infanticide, genocide," I said. There were more, but just saying those words brought up painful memories that boiled my blood.

Hades said, "You're correct. Normally, we wouldn't send you or anyone, wouldn't even be monitoring the humans, but this is an important case."

I looked at the screen. I would rather dig out my own eyeballs and feed them to a raccoon through a straw than go to Las Vegas. I had to think fast. "By order of the Fates, all missions of duty by any god or goddess must be approved by them. Surely they would never agree that I, a daughter of the night, travel to such an aesthetically offensive locale. They would fear that my decision making would be compromised." I didn't add, *Like last time.* To this day, I cannot look at a clown without wanting to strangle him with my bare hands.

"The Fates have offered their full support," Zeus said. "It has to be you."

I snapped my head toward him. "Why me? Why not Athena or Apollo?" Athena smiled at me patiently, shook her head. Heavens help me, this was not going well. "We don't even know if the women have been harmed. And why, for the love of Gaia, would the Fates approve of this cause?"

"Because I asked them to." It was a woman's voice, coming from behind me.

I spun around to see my sister Megaera step into the room.

"Meg? What are you doing here? I thought you were on holiday."

"I was. I'm home now." She sniffled and looked down for a moment, then steadied herself.

I rushed to her. Meg rarely showed emotion. She was a rock, a Fury. I grabbed her hands.

"What is it? Why would you request that I complete this task?"

Her stormy eyes met mine. She said, "It's Sister."

"Alecto? What about her? Is she all right?"

"She's... gone."

Chapter 4

It turned out Meg and Alecto had been on holiday in Las Vegas.

"We knew you wouldn't come, Tisiphone—you never travel with us to the outer plane—so we didn't bother asking you to join us. It was to be a short excursion anyway." She was right. I left home only if I was forced to.

Meg went on to explain that they had both posed as mortals enchanted with a hazing spell designed by Hecate the sorceress. You see, humans cannot gaze upon the gods in our natural state—it would blind them—so we use disguises to protect their tender eyes. We still generally look like ourselves, but our normal attire is altered, our skin dulled, and our coloring toned down to match that of the humans. My hair was actually blue-black with threads of pure silver running through it, my skin a shimmering white, and my eyes a vibrant shade of purple, but no mortal had ever seen my true colors, so to speak.

Shortly after arriving in Sin City, as Meg called it, my sisters had met a man who offered them work as dancers (a job for the Graces, if you asked me, but my sisters were more free-spirited than I was) at the Shadow Bar.

"He said his girls never showed up that night. We were there having a blue cocktail, and the next thing I knew, we were behind the screen, performing for patrons. It was actually quite exhilarating." She smiled feebly; then her emerald-green eyes flashed red, and I could smell the anger like lava bubbling beneath her skin. And...something else. Regret? Guilt?

"Then what happened?" I asked.

Meg looked at me sincerely. "I honestly don't know. We ate, drank, and danced for a few days, and then one night she just didn't show up in our suite."

I sat back in my chair and stared at her, my knee bobbing up and down so frantically it rattled the table. I stood, paced, trying to control my anger, but I was losing patience with my middle sister.

"Well, do you think someone took her?" I shouted. "Was she cross with you? Did she take a lover?" I slammed my fist down onto the table, shattering its leg. Somewhere, Cerberus barked. "Think, Meg."

Hades stepped forward and gently squeezed my shoulder. I took a deep breath and dropped my head into my hands. I could feel my wings vibrating in my back with utter frustration.

Meg said quietly, "Yes, I think someone took her."

As Furies, we all had tempers. We'd learned to control them over time, but Alecto—the youngest of us—was the worst of all. Her name actually meant "unceasing anger." I could not imagine anyone's trying to kidnap her and getting away with it. In fact, I was willing to bet that whoever had her was sorely regretting his decision.

"How could this happen? How is it even possible?" I shouted again. "Was it another god? A human?" I rushed forward, shook my sister. "Who?"

Meg twisted her arms free, stood, and screamed back as smoke billowed from her ears. "I don't know, Tisiphone! Curb your fury, or, I am warning you, I will curb it for you!"

We glared at each other.

Zeus stepped forward then. "That's enough, ladies. This is not helping."

I spun around and kicked the wall. None of this made any sense.

"Athena," I asked, remembering something, "did you not invent a device that monitors the gods and goddesses while in the mortal world? Can you not track Alecto through your machine?" Shortly after my crime, thirty-five years earlier, the Fates had insisted on a tool to better watch over us while we performed our duties.

Athena nodded. "Yes, there are measures in place to track goddesses who travel through portals, but we don't track them on holiday unless they plan to be gone a full moon cycle. Your sisters planned on being away only two weeks."

"So can't you try?"

"We have, Tisiphone, but the signal that was trained on Alex has been compromised. Whether by accident or intentionally, we don't know for certain." Her eyes softened as she tried to reason with me. "Believe me, we've exhausted all the options, run through all the scenarios. We wouldn't have called on you otherwise."

"And we cannot waste time arguing," Hades said. "You have less than a week to find Alecto and bring her home."

"And why is that?" I asked.

Athena shifted uncomfortably. "Because when the new moon arrives under the earthly cycle, her tether will break. And we may never be able to retrieve her. It's the law of the Fates, I'm afraid. No unplanned absences."

I raised one eyebrow, looked at Meg, and said, "Well, that's just brilliant."

My sister threw her hands in the air and said, "I'm done listening to this." She started for the door.

"Oh, no you aren't."

I reeled her toward me, and in a fit of rage her wings snapped open. I unlocked mine as well, and we stared each other down.

"This is your mistake. You fix it, Meg." I looked at Hades, pointed to my stubborn sister. "Send her."

Hades said firmly, "We can't. Whoever the kidnapper is knows what she looks like. We cannot risk it."

"It has to be you, Tisiphone. You're Alecto's only hope," said Athena.

I flapped my wings to think, and a gust of wind blew several papers to the floor. Then I had it. "She can inhabit a mortal form." I looked at Artemis. "Aphrodite did it on one of her quests. What was the name of that mortal?"

"Norma Jeane Baker, or Marilyn Monroe after Aphrodite's transformation. But that takes weeks to prepare. And it didn't have the outcome we had hoped for."

"There's no time, Tisi," Athena said.

Meg retracted her wings. "I had every intention of going back myself, Tisiphone."

I studied her eyes. She was telling the truth. I flicked my gaze to Hades and tucked my wings away too. "What difference does it make if they recognize Meg? She could be the bait that leads directly to Alex." It made sense. She had been there only recently. She knew the land. I didn't. She was versed in the people. I wasn't. And, most importantly, she could tolerate the mortals. She hadn't killed a single one.

I continued, trying to convince them that this was a better plan. "Athena can monitor Meg. Should the kidnappers try to take Meg, she'll resist and track them back to Alecto. She frees our sister, and together they rush to a portal, and both of them are home, safe and sound." I snapped my fingers.

"Or," said a deep voice behind me, "she could be kidnapped, taken to God knows where for God knows what, *away* from Alex, and you could be minus two sisters."

I turned around. The god standing before me was one I did not recognize, although there was something frustratingly familiar about him. He was tall, taller than I was, with hazel eyes and chestnut hair and a build that rivaled Apollo's. His hands were stuffed into jean pockets, and his T-shirt was the color of Poseidon's robes. Hermes fluttered next to him just above the floor.

Zeus said, "Tisi, meet your partner."

I took in the newcomer's cocky grin and thought, *Over my rancid carcass.* There was no way I was going to get anything accomplished with a god around. Most of them had one thing on their minds, and it wasn't duty but rather their next conquest. And I was no one's conquest.

I took a deep breath and centered myself, plastered a smile on my face, and turned to the three brothers. "All right, my lords, you win. I'll go to Las Vegas to retrieve Alex. However"—I glared at the interloper standing in the doorway—"I work alone."

Zeus stepped forward. "Not an option, I'm afraid." He motioned to Hermes, who whipped out some maps and papers and went about spreading them across the table. Poseidon got busy with the remote control, and Athena bustled around the room, adjusting monitors. Everyone took a seat around the large conference table, save the stranger and me.

The god I had never seen before said quietly, "By the way, great hand earlier. Hickok never saw it coming."

I widened my eyes at him. How could he have known about that? The weekly poker game I had with Bill Hickok was our little secret. Bill knew better than to tell anyone, especially a god, for his place was not the river Styx but the Elysium Fields, where heroes rested. And Hades did not like the dead to leave their resting place. I never understood that rule. It wasn't like they could get any deader.

Wait. Was he the shade? The shade that had dealt the cards for the poker game? That would explain why I didn't recognize him.

As if he had read my mind, he pulled a coin from his pocket and wove it through his fingers, smiling at me like a man with an ace up his sleeve.

No. There had to be some mistake.

"My lords, you must be joking." I crossed my arms. "You cannot possibly think that I would work with a mortal." I could hardly hold back my laughter. Aside from being absolutely ridiculous, it broke all protocol. The Fates would never allow it.

The king of the gods bellowed, and a bolt of lightning struck the floor near my feet. "My patience is spent, Tisiphone. Sit down and hold your tongue. It has already been decided."

My mouth fell open. So they had just been humoring me this whole time? I wanted to take that lightning bolt and shove it up Zeus's pompous ass. Honestly, I wished the three of them would just retire. Hera, Persephone, and whichever sea nymph Poseidon was poking this week could rule better than these three untrained monkeys.

This was the worst idea ever. Even worse than sending me to that carnival the humans called a town. It would never work. How could they even conceive it would? Surely they wouldn't be so careless as to strap me with a mortal. It would be like assigning a fox to guard a henhouse. Preposterous.

The man in the jeans leaned over and whispered in my ear. He smelled of clover. "You didn't actually think you had a choice, did you?" He winked at me.

I'd like to say I handled the situation with all the grace and aplomb of a wizened queen. I'd like to, but I can't.

I punched him in the face.

Behind me, I heard Hades say, "That's right. Get it out of your system now, Tisi."

Chapter 5

I had to sit through a forty-five-minute lecture Athena gave on the workings of the latest modern technology, the sources of power in and around Las Vegas, and the special requirements of the portals as they pertained to Caesars Palace. Only through those portals could we return.

As if I had just received my wings yesterday. I hated being spoken to like a child.

"So, to recap," Athena said as she clicked through her slideshow, "your whereabouts will be monitored at all times with the tracking device that Artemis has installed in this moonstone ring." She held it up. It was huge and spherical, with a bronze clasp wrapped around the center. "Should you need to speak with us, the statue of the Graces in the lobby will be your closest point of contact. You just lift open the ring and aim it at the eyes, and the signal will be sent. Remember, it could take some time for your request to travel to Olympus, so be patient. Then the god or goddess will slip into the statue."

"Excuse me, Athena, but I thought you said that only the god or goddess who represents the *form* can enter the sculpture," I said.

"That's correct," said Athena. "It's the water surrounding the statues that provides the conduit for the charge."

"What use would I have for a Grace? They are not warriors, lawmakers, or leaders. They have no talent save for debauchery and shenanigans."

Zeus growled at me.

I rolled my eyes.

Still icing his jaw, my "partner" said, "You just described Las Vegas in a nutshell. They may come in handy—you never know."

Athena smiled at him. I bit my tongue.

"Tisi, as I pointed out, there is another portal. In the market area, you'll find what is called the "Talking Gods" show. Aphrodite, Dionysus, and Apollo can be reached there. Just remember, because the city's energy is highly concentrated, you get only three chances per moon cycle to reach us via the portals, so use them wisely. Otherwise, we won't have enough power to transport all three of you home."

She had explained earlier that because the city of Las Vegas drains so much energy, the signal to Olympus was quite weak, much like a radio station loses its clarity the farther one travels from the broadcast tower. For the transportation of one or two goddesses, it worked adequately, but with the added burden of the reanimated shade and his cloaked human vessel, the strain would be great.

Although I had no problem ditching his ass if it came down to it.

Zeus stood and said, "Now, Tisiphone, there is a very good reason I've asked Hades to allow this mortal to accompany you on your mission." The sky lord nodded once to the man on my left.

He stood, extended his hand. I took it grudgingly, squeezing so hard, I cracked three of his knuckles. To his credit, he didn't even wince. "My name is Archer Mays. I work…" He caught himself, corrected his mistake. "That is to say, I *worked* for the FBI. That's the Federal—"

"I know what the FBI is, Mr. Mays," I interrupted. "It's an organized form of law enforcement the American humans implemented to supplement the incompetent lower levels of law enforcement for the peace of mind of the populace."

He smiled. "I'm impressed."

"Don't be. Because it's been my experience that the FBI is just as incompetent as the local police."

I heard Hades whisper to Poseidon, "It's a good thing he's already dead, because she'd kill him."

The smile faded from Archer Mays's face.

"Okay, look, I let that little sucker punch slide because you're a woman and because I'm still a little freaked out."

I stood to face him. "I am not a woman. I am a goddess."

He looked me up and down and said, "Not in my book, sweetheart. I'd say you could use a few pounds."

I was about to hit him again, when Hades grabbed my arms. "Remember what this is for, Tisiphone."

Mays held steady, his jaw firm, angry, and, you know, bruised.

Hades was right. Alex needed me. And I needed to keep my temper in check. I was shocked, to say the least, that the man I would be working with was a modern-day American lawman. I had seen firsthand the mistakes his type and the courts had made. Cleaned up the messes they left behind—messes that led to criminals' roaming free to rape, murder, and molest again. It sickened me to my very core. That hadn't happened in Hickok's day.

But that wasn't what this was about. This was about my sister.

I swallowed hard and said, "My apologies, Mr. Mays."

He nodded. "Call me Archer." He looked at Zeus. The god waved his hand.

"So, as I was saying. I was an FBI agent. I was just beginning to investigate the abductions. Five women. All taken from the Shadow Bar within a five-week time frame, including your sister. That's one per week. No one saw or heard anything. In fact—and this is the part that baffles me—some of the women weren't even reported missing until a day or more later. Their friends, family members, boyfriends completely forgot they were with the victims at the time of the abductions. By the time they recovered their memory, the trails were cold."

How odd. I looked at Meg. "Dark magic, perhaps?"

Meg, who had already told us everything she knew from the moment they had arrived to the exact point in time when she had last seen Alex, a few days ago, said, "It's possible. Hermes, please check with Hecate regarding all mortal spell casting that pertains to the moon cycles. Particularly those of the dark arts."

Hermes said, "As you wish" and dashed off.

"Is there a connection? Are they related? Same age? Race?" I asked Archer.

He hesitated, just for a moment, but I caught it. He shot a glance to Athena and said, "Can you please link to my computer and pull up the file titled 'Shadow Disappearances'?"

We could link to mortal electronics? Athena must have forgotten to mention this. Not that I would understand the intricacies of the process.

Athena's slender fingers manipulated a device that linked to the monitor, and within seconds, a yellow picture of a folder appeared on the screen.

"Go ahead and open it," Archer said.

Immediately, the photographs of four women swooshed into view. Archer explained he didn't have one of Alecto, for obvious reasons.

Next to me, Meg gasped. I floated toward the screen in shocked awe.

All of the victims, my sister included, looked exactly like me.

I slowly turned to face the gods, the soft buzz of the monitor the only sound in the room.

"When do we leave?"

Chapter 6

Athena explained to Archer Mays the various rules to follow when you're the animated dead walking around on the outer plane. Things like "Don't break the skin of this body, or the area will rot and fall off" and "If your true corpse is discovered, we'll need to get you a new frame ASAP." Then she jotted down the room number of the hotel at Caesars Palace where the high gods always stayed and handed Archer a card that apparently served as a key.

I sighed. So it was all set. Not only did I have to work with this mortal, but it looked like I might have to share space with him as well. I couldn't help but think how cruel the Fates could be. They had to have seen this coming and hadn't bothered to warn me. Figured. Those wrinkled old bats could sure hold a grudge.

You see, the Fates controlled the birth, life, and death of a mortal. Clotho spun the thread for birth, Lachesis measured the string that determined one's life span, and Atropos cut the string that ended a life. Once that happened, they drew up a report on the individual. It included things like what his station was in life, where he lived, what he had accomplished, what he had failed to accomplish, and, of course, his sins. Once the soul traveled across the river Styx, Hades received that report. So when Archer Mays had showed up in Hades's realm, the dark lord must have known that the FBI agent might be important in finding Alecto. Unfortunately, from what I gathered, Archer had been killed before he'd had the chance to locate any of the missing women. I listened as he explained to Hades that he did have some leads, and that was where he intended to start once we arrived in Las Vegas.

Artemis got busy cloaking me for travel through the portal so that my appearance would be subdued immediately upon my entering the mortal world. She cast an invisibility spell over my wings, the source of all my power. Hecate had created the spell. I could tuck my wings away whenever I wanted, but the bones where they met my spine still protruded from my back. Hecate solved that problem.

"You simply apply the potion directly over the cartilage," she explained.

I crinkled my nose. "That has a foul odor. What's in it?"

"Virgin tears and cloud ether."

Archer was looking on in amazement. I wasn't sure if it was the virgin tears or the cloud ether that had him more perplexed.

"Virgin tears," Meg said. "You best keep your distance, Hecate. Tisi might burst into flames where she stands."

I shot her a hard look. "Who are you today, Megaera, the pot or the kettle?"

Meg said, "Need I remind you I am a mother now?"

Meg had given birth to twins a few years earlier. It was the reason she no longer looked as similar to me as Alecto did. Mothers gift their children with slices of their own attributes. Her hair, once as blue-black as mine, was now the shade of a coffee bean, with hints of pomegranate threaded throughout. Her eyes had faded to a mossy color, except when she was angry.

"Another reason I should take the mission, I suppose." I was being sincere, not sarcastic, but she looked miffed anyway.

Archer, the lucky bastard, didn't have to cloak himself at all. He would be returning to the mortal realm wearing a copy of the same vessel in which he had left it.

"Are you sure this is a good idea?" he asked Athena. "I mean, won't it look pretty strange if I show up and whoever murdered me sees that I'm walking around?"

She shrugged. "Whoever seems most surprised by your animated form will be the murderer. Would that not please you?"

The look on his face indicated he had not considered that possibility. Then he wrinkled his brow and asked, "So when I return, everything will be intact, correct? I mean, say I was shot in the head—it won't show, will it?"

He didn't know how he had died, and that was not something the Fates tracked. Carrying the negative energy of a violent death into the Underworld could lead only to chaos and heartache, especially in the case of the tragic passing of one so young. When the mortal life is shed, it is a chance for the souls to renew and move on, not cling to the old.

Artemis sighed. "For Hera's sake, man, do you think we're amateurs?"

"Sorry," Archer mumbled.

"All vessels go through a cleansing process when a shade arrives in Hades. You were essentially wearing a replica of your original body when you got here. That gets stripped before you're even aware of it. Then, once you cross the river, your new shell is prepared and perfectly adequate to wear."

"Adequate?" he asked, glancing down.

Artemis raised an eyebrow, shot a look at Archer's crotch, and said, "Adequate for a mere mortal, that is."

Meg, Hecate, Athena, and Artemis all snickered.

"Ladies, stop teasing the human, will you, please? He'll get enough grief from Tisiphone while he's working with her."

"I only hit him once," I protested.

"Yes, well, don't make a habit of it," Hades said. Then he motioned for me to join him in the hall.

Archer was frowning at me when I passed him.

"Yes, my lord?" I said.

"Walk with me, my dark daughter."

I wasn't actually his daughter. My sisters and I were born from the union of Gaia and Uranus, but he thought of us as his daughters since we had served him so faithfully.

I followed him down the hallway and out the front door. He called to Cerberus, and the dog built like a teenage black-bear cub came barreling across the threshold. Hades silently approached the thick black gates and creaked them open.

The moon was still high in the sky, as always, its light reflecting off the threads of silver in Hades's robes. He stopped to pick up a stick and tossed it for Cerberus, who couldn't decide which head to use to retrieve it.

I would have asked him what he wanted to tell me, because there was something, I could sense it, but one did not interrupt a high god while he was deep in thought. They got distracted so easily.

We walked in silence for some distance. Finally, I heard the flow of the river.

Cerberus set his sights on a flock of crows and ran off to chase them while Hades watched.

After a moment, he turned to me. "Look at them." He swept his arm ceremoniously across the embankment. "The Lost. Look at how they scramble for answers."

I didn't say, *I have been looking. For ages. It's you who is blind.* Rather, I did as he asked.

We stood side by side, gazing at our subjects.

He said, "I know what you've been doing, of course. Paying their passage whenever you can. I know, too, how you're getting the coins."

I swallowed hard, hoping against hope that I was not going to be punished. Punishment was Tartarus duty, the realm that lay beneath the Underworld—the gloomy pit of nothingness where only the most depraved, vile, unconscionable sinners were locked away.

Hades glanced at me sideways. "Are you surprised, Tisiphone? Surely you don't think that much happens in my kingdom that I am not aware of. I realize that our system is not perfect, that there is room for improvement, but these things take time. They take resources. They take strategic planning and must be in accordance with our laws. Which means they also take getting the Fates and the upper pantheon to all agree. And you know how frustrating siblings can be."

"My Lord, I—"

He held up his hand. "I am not here to scold you, child. I am here to remind you that these are the people you will encounter on your mission. These souls—the ones you have such compassion for after they die—are the very kinds of souls in life who test your temper. Do not let their flaws cause you to lose sight of your task." He looked at me. "Understood?"

"Yes, my lord." I bowed my head in honor.

He was smiling, pleased. "Excellent." Then the smile transformed into a grim line. He placed his hands firmly upon my shoulders, his jaw hardened, and said, "Now go get my Fury."

Chapter 7

We made our way back to the war room, where Hecate was fiddling with the moonstone ring that would be my point of contact with the gods. There was a bandage on her pinky finger.

"Tisi, I've enchanted the ring with a receiving spell using a drop of my blood. I'll look into the possibility of a dark-arts ritual that utilizes the mortal moon cycles. If I find one, I'll send you a signal. It will look like this."

Hecate licked her finger and smeared the saliva across the tattoo of her goddess symbol on her right arm—a three-pronged wheel with a star in the center—and the tattoo bubbled. After a moment, the ring lit up and a swirl of tides and clouds intermingled in its milky-white depths.

The sorceress said, "Tap the ring."

I did, and words floated to the surface of the ring:

Stand by for a message.

Hecate looked over my shoulder and said, "Perfect. It works."

I asked, "Will this work with other gods? Will Meg be able to send a message?"

Hecate said, "Artemis and Apollo will be able to correspond with you, since we are bound by blood, but I'm afraid that is all."

The twins were Hecate's cousins.

I thanked the witch. She nodded and vanished in a spray of blue smoke.

Athena said, "Are you ready, Tisiphone?"

I told her I was, and she looked at Archer, who nodded.

"Very well. Mr. Mays has a key and all the information you should need for lodging and currency. Hera often travels there with her servant Iris, so the room should be fully stocked with anything you may desire, as well as a map outlining the location of the portals around the city for transport back to Olympus. I've supplied Mr. Mays with a list of other gods visiting the mortal plane at this time and their contact information. His files from his investigation on Alecto's disappearance will all be copied to the computer at the inn, so that should give you a head start on locating her. Any questions?"

I said, "Yes, I have a question. Who the hell put him in charge?"

It was bad enough that I had to work with a mortal. Now they wanted me to follow his orders?

Athena sighed heavily. "He isn't in charge, Tisiphone. He simply came up with a plan while you were speaking with Hades, and we think it's a fine idea. Now, there's no time to discuss. Just trust that he is on our side."

I trusted no one. Everyone knew that, but I held my tongue.

Athena escorted us to the corner, where the tall, glass cylindrical portal stood. "Once you enter the portal, you'll experience a flash of white light, perhaps a dizzying sensation, and then, after a few moments, you'll be transported to Las Vegas, directly in front of the city sign. You'll need to lock hands."

Archer and I stepped inside the chamber ,and he grabbed my hands. I grunted.

He said, "I'm sorry I couldn't help your sister."

I said, "Just stay out of my way."

Athena slapped a large, silver button. Then a bright light nearly blinded me, accompanied by a piercing, scraping noise, before everything went black.

It was hotter than Hades's closet in Las Vegas, and brighter than a Zeus-fueled lightning bolt.

After what seemed like days of walking, I couldn't take it anymore. My leather pants were melting into my skin, and my skin felt like it was on fire. I liked warmth, but this was ridiculous.

"Where in the blazes is this place we're to stay?" I said. "How much longer until we get there?"

Archer cocked an eyebrow at me, and the tiny lines etched around his eyes danced. "We've been walking for ten minutes. We've got quite a ways to go, so I suggest you suck it up."

"And I suggest you watch how you speak to me, before I blacken your other eye."

A nerve in Archer's neck twitched. "That's not funny. Athena said I can't take any chances. I can't bleed."

"I won't make you bleed. I'll only make you wish you were dead."

"Don't you mean 'wish I weren't dead so I wouldn't have to put up with your crap'?"

I ignored that last comment. The sun was beating so hard on my face, I could have sworn I was frying. I had never felt such immense heat. I gathered my long hair and wrapped it in a knot, waving a hand at the back of my neck. "You know this town. Is there a river or lake nearby? I have to get some water. I feel as if I'm burning."

He laughed. "You're in the desert, sweetheart. No water anywhere. You can wait until we get to the hotel. You're tough. Besides, I thought you'd be used to this heat."

"It never gets this hot in Olympus, except in Tartarus. And I avoid that like I would a snake pit, because, well, it is."

My tone must have signaled I didn't want to talk about the belly of the Underworld, because Archer didn't ask about it and kept quiet for a while. Several loud, annoying cars blasted their horns at us while we trudged along the walkway. We passed the WELCOME TO LAS VEGAS sign, patches of dead grass, and a few tall lights that Archer explained directed traffic.

Then I met the first mortal I wanted to kill.

I was following Archer Mays across a paved road when I heard the motor of a noxious car engage. The vehicle made a braking sound, but before I could turn to see what was taking place behind me, I felt an intense pain on my backside. The impact was so harsh, I was certain my pants were permanently implanted in my ass.

At first I thought perhaps I had violated some pedestrian law and had been hit by the vehicle. Then I saw a middle-aged man with a potbelly and a hairy arm hanging out of a convertible, waving his hand. The driver next to him said, "Yeah! Smack that ass! Hey, baby, what's shaking?"

I was hot and I was thirsty, and the blinding power of the sun had incapacitated all sense of logic. He was too far away to grab, so I used the power of my voice to punish him. I narrowed my eyes, zeroed in on my target, opened my mouth, and screeched.

Immediately, both men covered their ears, and the car came to a jarring halt. The glass fixtures on their automobile burst, followed by their mirrors. Then the drinks in their hands imploded, showering them with foamy amber liquid.

Somehow, they knew I had caused it all to happen.

Archer was several steps ahead of me. He wouldn't have heard the screech—only my targets could. He turned around just in time to see the men circle back, shouting profanities at me.

He was confused, but he quickly realized what had happened when the older, fat man said, "You fucking bitch!"

Then the driver, a young man with spiky blond hair, said, "If you don't want your ass slapped, don't dress like a whore. You better have some money to pay for this shit, lady."

"Gentlemen, is there a problem here?" Archer asked calmly behind me.

The driver, who I realized was a great deal younger than his companion, said, "Mind your own business, fucko."

Archer smiled widely, reached into his back pocket, his bicep flexing just for emphasis, and pulled out something shiny. "See, fellas, Officer Hot Pants is my business. Now, if you don't mind, she's working undercover today. So if you don't want to go to jail tonight, I suggest you keep your heads down and your mouths shut."

The two men looked dumbstruck.

The younger man spit on the street, inches from Archer's foot. "Dude, she trashed my ride. I'm not going to let that go."

Archer craned his neck, making a show of examining the car. "Really, and how did she do that?"

The older man swallowed hard and looked at his friend.

The driver was either too stupid or too stubborn to back down. "I don't know, man—she screamed or used a whistle or something."

Archer pretended to consider this. He rubbed his chin, then turned to me. "You must have quite a set of lungs on you to cause that kind of damage."

I knew the ploy. My sisters and I had played Good Fury, Bad Fury many a time.

"Sure do," I said. "After all, this is Vegas. Couldn't have been a machine making all that racket."

Archer said, "Or missile testing in the desert." He looked pointedly at the older man, who licked his lips nervously. "Or other kinds of activity that may take place in a desert. That may involve, oh, I don't know…flying objects?"

I had a feeling I knew where Archer was going with this. The stories of little green men were as ancient as civilization itself.

I fired up the flames in my eyes, just for a moment, and both men looked at each other, jumped in their broken car, and sped off. I thought I heard the younger guy say, "Man, I told you aliens exist!"

Archer looked at me after the car was out of sight. "Well, hell's bells, is that a smile I see on your face?"

I had rather enjoyed toying with a human who misbehaved, but I wasn't about to let Archer Mays know that. I set my mouth into a grim line.

Archer said several minutes later, when I was certain my skin had cooked right into my flesh, "Admit it: we make a good team."

I stole a sideways glance at his stubbly chin and sturdy shoulders. "Don't push it."

"You want to tell me what you did back there? It's probably not a good idea to attract too much attention to ourselves, you know."

"He needed to be punished. I used my wail."

"Your wail?"

"My voice."

"How?"

I clenched my fists, growing irritated with all the questions. Just because we were a team didn't make us friends.

"Can we not talk? I'd like to keep all the saliva in my mouth until we get near a watering hole," I said.

"Suit yourself," he said stiffly.

I knew we needed to share information eventually, and that I was being spiteful, but I didn't care. I needed to reserve all my strength. The force of my screech had drained me. I could feel my energy slipping with each step. What was it about this city that so instantly infuriated and exhausted me? Why did I feel as if my power was fading?

Is this what had happened to Alex? Had my sister been so immersed in having fun that she hadn't realized this town was stealing her force? Was that why she had been taken? Because she simply hadn't had the strength to fight?

Or was it something else entirely that was siphoning my power? Something darker and more deadly?

Because, after all, the gods are immortal only in Olympus. Here, we are vulnerable. Just like humans.

Chapter 8

He was aching to kill again. It had been so long since he had felt the soft flesh of life being snuffed out beneath his fingers. The ones who were so surprised, they couldn't even scream. Those were his favorite. Sometimes, after he cut them, he would dip a finger into their open wounds and taste the blood. It was like sweet wine to him. And the thrill! Once, when he had been drunk, he had told a friend there was no greater pleasure in life than death. Of course, he'd had to cover up, had to pretend as if he was only joking, but he had meant it. The satisfaction of watching an innocent human being die at his hand aroused him. It was the only way he could achieve that kind of pleasure anymore. And a man had needs. It wasn't his fault he was wired this way.

He felt as if he had been under a trance, a spell of some kind, for far too long. Going through the motions of acting normal. But who among us was truly "normal"? Show him a man without sin, and he'd show you a man with a secret. All the great ones—Jack the Ripper, Ted Bundy, Jeffrey Dahmer—all led perfectly socially acceptable lives until they got caught. Then the judgments came. The punishments. Now, he would dole out his own punishments.

He looked around the darkened room, feeling alive again. His playmates were all fast asleep. None of them had seen his face. None of them knew what he was planning. Their cries, their pleas, their tears wouldn't save them. Women were more emotional than men, sure, but what he hadn't expected was the way they smelled when they were afraid. Like feral cats emitting an odor of protection. They smelled metallic, earthy, sweet, and tart all at once.

He wanted so badly to take one of those fragile necks in his hands and squeeze until her eyeballs popped. They didn't actually pop all the way out, in his experience. At least, they hadn't with the others. He'd like to see that, though. Maybe he could try something new. An experiment.

But no, he had to wait. He had to have patience.

It wouldn't be long now.

Chapter 9

We navigated the city like rats in a maze. We had to cross over streets, go up and down moving staircases, and still it seemed we were no closer to our destination. I couldn't understand how everything seemed within reach when it was actually miles away.

Occasionally, I would point to something and Archer would identify it. He explained that a pawnshop was where people exchanged valuables for currency. I couldn't help but feel a bit sad thinking of all those lost treasures. Humans used to value ancient artifacts. It seemed now that everything was disposable.

We passed open markets, eateries, and a few of those characters in animal costumes that Hades had shown me back in the war room. As the lord of the Underworld had said, people were posing for pictures with them, libations in hand. I saw a few women walking around in elaborate head-dresses, with little covering anything else. I couldn't blame them in this heat, but those things on their heads—and the sparkling, painfully high heels dressing their feet—looked unbearably uncomfortable.

And then I spotted her. An angel with wings. I tugged Archer's shirt and said, "Look, she must be a goddess. Perhaps it would be all right to use my wings. We can fly to our inn in no time!"

There was a shiny pyramid to the right of her.

"That's the Luxor. It's a casino and hotel, and she's likely in costume, handing out two-for-one passes to a show."

"You mean the wings aren't real?" I asked.

He said, "Nothing in Vegas is real."

I couldn't hide my disappointment.

"We're not too far. Hang tight," Archer said.

We passed another casino—which I learned was the term mortals used for gaming houses—that looked like the New York skyline, and Archer explained there was another farther along the path that resembled the Eiffel Tower of Paris. All of them were lit up more brightly than the sun. Why did they need all these lights in the daytime?

By now, the sweat was pouring off me, and Archer didn't look much better. His cheeks were flushed, his hair damp, and he adjusted his jeans now and then, as if he wished he could take them off. I briefly wondered what his legs looked like. Were they strong and athletic-looking, like his upper body?

I pushed the thought out of my mind. The sun was making me delirious.

We passed a small man with skin a few shades lighter than Hades's, slapping some papers in his hand. He handed me one, and I stopped to read it.

Archer snatched it and said, "You don't want to look at that."

I wrestled it back and said, "I can think for myself, Lawman."

It was a glossy photograph of a beautiful, red-haired woman. The caption read: *Cherry. Delivered to your room in twenty minutes. Discreet. Reasonable rates.*

"You can order a woman delivered in twenty minutes?" I asked.

"Faster than a pizza." Archer looked uncomfortable.

I pulled him aside and asked quietly, "Could this have something to do with the missing women?" The photograph was still in my hand.

He said, "I checked that angle. I don't think so. Come on, let's keep moving, and for God's sake, don't take every flyer someone passes to you in this town, or we'll be here all night."

I scanned the streets and noticed there were quite a lot more young men trying to give away more flyers, as Archer called them. I tossed mine in the trash bin, and we continued on.

We had to travel up one more moving staircase—escalators, Archer called them—before we got to the sidewalk that led to Caesars Palace. There was a young man in a red T-shirt with a mouse on it. The man was sitting on the ground with a sign that said ANYTHING HELPS. Next to him was a brightly colored bucket with coins in it.

A lost one.

"Archer, give him something."

"I don't have anything."

"You have that shiny thing you showed to those men in the car. That seemed valuable. The sign says anything helps."

Archer looked at me as if I had snakes growing out of my head, like Medusa. "You want me to give him my badge? Are you crazy?"

At the mention of the word "badge," the young man sat up straighter.

Archer pulled me aside, bumping into a young woman as he did so. He apologized, and she smiled at him. To me he said softly, "Look, this isn't what you think."

"He's a lost soul. He needs help. I recall once upon a time you were lost and someone helped you." I crossed my arms.

Archer ran his hand through his hair. "You're right. And I never thanked you for that, so thank you."

I nodded.

"Now, take a look at that kid."

I did.

"You see that shirt he's wearing? It cost more than my watch. And his shoes? Cost more than my car. The bucket next to him is from the MGM Grand. It still has condensation on it from the frozen drink he ordered. Strawberry, from the looks of his lips."

I studied the boy again. Everything Archer said seemed accurate. His hair was quite kempt for being out in this heat. The two of us looked like we'd traipsed through a rain forest.

I asked. "So, he's a thief?"

"Basically."

I marched over to the young man, who averted his eyes. "Leave now, and you won't be punished."

"I didn't do anything," he protested.

I leaned in, grabbed his cheek, and forced him to look into my eyes. I didn't light the flame, but the Fury in me had been engaged. When that happened, my true colors could emerge if I allowed it. And I did, briefly enough to be safe.

The boy scuttled to his feet, left the bucket, and ran.

I stood up, rather proud of myself.

Archer did not look so pleased.

"What? He needed to learn a lesson," I said.

Archer shook his head. "Tisiphone, if you insist on punishing every sinner in Las Vegas, we'll be stuck here until the end of time."

I picked at a nail. It was in my nature to encourage people to behave better. It was the only thing I was born to do. I didn't know how to turn it off, and even if I could, I wasn't sure I wanted to.

"That many?" I asked him. Could this city really be that full of immorality and lawbreakers?

"More," Archer said. "That's why they call it Sin City."

Archer was right, and that irked me. I couldn't get sidetracked. We had a task to complete. The sooner it was done, the sooner we could all go home.

"I hate this town," I said.

"I know," said Archer.

We turned and began walking toward the entrance of Caesars Palace.

Chapter 10

I followed Archer through a wide passageway. We stepped onto a mobile sidewalk that carried us to another escalator, which led down to a large, carpeted room. There were giant electronic video screens on the walls. Men and women were lounging around tables with pens and notebooks in their hands, their eyes glued to some sporting event on the video boxes. Some were hooting and hollering at the players, while others appeared dejected.

"Keep your head down. Try not to attract too much attention. I don't want to be spotted by the manager until we have a plan in place." Archer looked tense. Worry lined his face, as if he hadn't quite thought everything through yet.

"I need water." My mouth felt as if I had swallowed a sand castle.

He hurried along past gaming tables and people shouting out numbers. I kept pace behind him, feeling weaker with every step. I wished I hadn't disciplined that boy. It seemed to drain even more of my strength, though it was a minor effort.

What was happening to me? Was it the sun? The city?

The noise inside the casino was deafening. People were shouting, lights were blinking, and machines were clinking. It was like being trapped inside a pinball machine. And I thought Chuck E. Cheese's was an obnoxious assignment. This was a million times worse.

Archer paused to check the card that was a key and said, "We'll be in the room soon, and you can have all the water you want." He looked up and said. "The elevators are right there."

I followed his nod, but something else caught my eye. The Shadow Bar.

I poked Archer. "That's where my sister was taken. That's where all the women disappeared, isn't it?"

Archer glanced at the establishment. "Yes. Let's get to the room first and—"

I held up my hand. "I have to go in. Not an option."

"Tisiphone, wait!" Archer hissed, but I was already up the few widemouthed steps and through the entry.

There was a long, sleek bar on the left. A tavern host who reminded me of Adonis acrobatically flipped bottles into the air, to the oohs and aahs of three young women in tight dresses seated in front of him. Several tables cupped with oversized chairs were scattered about the room, all pointing to the wall-to-wall screens behind the bar. A vast array of liquor bottles in front of the thin screens held liquids in every color imaginable. The screens were lit from behind, a pinkish hue highlighting them, and two women—or, rather, the silhouettes of two women—danced behind them.

I walked around the space, trying to conjure the energy of Alecto. Trying to feel the remains of her presence. Any living thing leaves traces of itself wherever it travels—goddesses even more so. I tweaked my nose to turn up its ability to full power. Alecto always smelled like jasmine. It was her signature scent.

Not a trace of it.

How was that possible? She had only just been here.

Someone grabbed my arm from behind me, more forcefully than I would ever allow. I turned to head-butt the perpetrator, but it was Archer. He was lucky I wasn't functioning at full capacity, or I would have broken his nose, and I told him so.

"We have to go. Now. Before he sees us." He quickly glanced behind him at a middle-aged, stout man with black hair in a shiny suit.

The man was talking to someone, but he spotted us and practically ran over.

"Dammit," Archer hissed under his breath. He glared at me, and I rolled my eyes. Honestly, what was all the fuss?

"Relax, Lawman."

He wanted to say something more, I could tell, but he bit his tongue. The man in the suit motioned to the tavern keeper on his way over to us.

He pointed one finger to Archer, another to the far wall, and Archer and I followed.

The man flicked his eyes to me, raised one brow at Archer, and waited.

Archer said, "She's with me. Clyde, this is Tisi."

I stuck my hand out, and Clyde bent to kiss it. I didn't like that one bit. His lips were cold and slimy, like a serpent's.

"A pleasure to meet you, Tisi." He paused and walked his eyes all over me, which I liked even less, and said, "Has anyone ever told you you look like Liz Taylor?"

"No."

"A little skinnier, little lighter in the boob department, but yeah, you do."

I gave Archer a look that warned I might strike Clyde at any moment. And what was it with humans and breasts? They had practically smacked me in the face everywhere I'd looked the entire walk over here. Which reminded me: I still needed water.

As if summoned, the tanned barkeep with the Adonis eyes presented me with water in a V-stemmed glass. He handed one to Archer too.

"Thank you. I'm parched," I said.

"No, don't," Archer said, right after I downed it in one gulp.

I handed the glass back to Adonis and ordered another. The water tasted funny here, but at that point I wouldn't have cared if it had been scraped from the bottom of a river. I needed strength.

"Let her have a little fun, Archie," Clyde said.

For some reason, I found that absolutely hysterical. "Archie. I like that. I think I'll call you that."

Archer pulled up a chair for me and ordered me to sit.

I hiccupped in response.

"So who is this, Arch?" Clyde asked. He seemed edgy.

In a low voice, Archer said, "She's my partner."

Clyde nodded. A brief flicker of unease passed through his eyes. Then he smiled and said, "So you need a cover for her."

Adonis brought me another water. This one had an olive. I downed the water, ate the olive, and tucked the toothpick into the front of his pants. He smiled at me and winked. I winked back, ordered another drink, and watched his very firm behind head back to the bar. Maybe he would let me sip the next water from his navel.

I felt worlds better. The thirst was gone, I was relaxed, and even the sounds of the games seemed a million miles away. The water tasted odd, but it suited me.

Archer looked furious, for some reason.

I pointed a long fingernail at him and said, "You know, pal, if we're going to work together, you need to lighten up."

Wait a moment. Did I just say pal*?* I wasn't even sure what that meant. Perhaps I was picking up the local linguistics. That should serve me well.

"So, can she dance?" Clyde asked.

"No," Archer said.

I smirked at him. "How do you know, Mr. Stick-in-the-Mud?" I paused. My voice sounded funny. It sounded like I had said "Schtick-in-the-Schmud."

Adonis, the new love of my life, brought me another tall glass of clear refreshment. It had sugar on the rim and a lemon peel in it. I ran my hands up and down his chest before I took the glass off the tray.

"Watch this," I said.

I took a big gulp of the water and set the glass back on the tray, then gyrated my hips the way I had seen the Graces do a thousand times. I grabbed the glass again and sipped as I danced, shaking my chest in the chiseled face of my young attendant. When I finished the water, I set the glass down, planted my hands on my thighs, and whipped my head around, loosening up my ponytail so that it was just a mass of black waves. I lifted my arms over my head and scooted up to Archer. I hip-bumped him a few times, then straddled him as my torso leaned back, before slowly climbing up him again to nibble his ear. He had a bemused look on his face.

That was the last thing I remembered.

Chapter 11

I woke up in a strange room, my tongue feeling like it was wearing a cotton coat, my head pounding as if a tiny drummer were trapped inside. A man's voice was coming from somewhere beyond the door.

"Yes, I called a little while ago. Better make it two pots of coffee," he said. "You have any Gatorade?" A pause. "Great. And aspirin. Thank you."

Where was I? The bed was plush, with crisp white cotton sheets and a fluffy duvet. There was a window to the right. A wall of windows, in fact. I pulled the duvet around me, climbed out of bed, and shuffled over to the window.

I was high up. There were miles of buildings in sight. Looking down, I saw a cascading fountain with a statue of Pegasus perched in the center. Then I remembered. My sister. The FBI agent. Las Freaking Vegas.

I groaned.

My brain was fuzzy, thoughts jumbled. I wasn't wearing any pants under the blanket, but I did have a top on.

"How did I get here?" I whispered.

There was movement beyond the wide brown door. Then a knock.

"Tisiphone?"

I groaned again and shut the drapes on that garish sun. Didn't the moon ever rise in this vulgar city?

"What?" I snapped.

The door creaked open, and a freshly shaven Archer stepped into the room, hands in his jeans pockets. He was wearing a shirt the color of a ripe plum, with threads of gold throughout that brought out the amber in his eyes. It reminded me of something Apollo would wear—cut to mold his frame, and stylish.

"How you feeling, Sassy?"

"Like I was hit by a truck." I sank into a plush red chair and wrapped the blanket tighter around me. "You're looking well."

Archer smoothed out his shirt. "I think it was Iris who Athena said stocked the suite. She did a fine job on the wardrobe. There should be clothes in your room too."

He handed me a glass of water. "I ordered room service. Once you get some food and coffee in you, you'll be good as new."

The water was cool against my lips. I put the glass to my forehead. "What happened? Were we attacked?"

Archer wove a sly smile. "You don't remember?"

I shook my head. Then I winced at the pain the movement caused. *No sudden twists or turns, Tisi.*

"Well, for starters, you downed three martinis like a sailor who hasn't seen shore for eighteen months."

"What's a martini?"

Archer cocked his head. "What's a martini?"

"Is it a potion?" All I could remember drinking was one glass of water.

"That clear liquid in the fancy glass." He crossed his arms. "What did you think you were drinking at the Shadow Bar?"

"I thought it was water. Just thought it tasted different here." Then I recalled I was holding a cup of the stuff. I sniffed it. No odor. I took another small sip. Tasted like pure water.

Archer guffawed. "Seriously? They don't have vodka in Olympus? Alcohol?"

"Of course they do. Mostly wine. Some mead. A green elixir, made from juniper berries, called gin. Absinthe. And Hermes makes his own beer." I took another slow sip of the cool water and held the glass to my cheek this time. "I've never heard of vodka, though. I haven't been in your world in quite some time, remember."

Then a horrible thought occurred to me. What had I done that I didn't remember? And where were my pants? I stood and faced Archer, still clutching the duvet.

"Is there anything I should know?"

Archer smiled again, and I so wanted to slap it off his face, but that would require swift movement and energy I didn't have at the moment.

"You were fine. You got hammered, promised you'd dance at the Shadow Bar, and passed out, and I put you to bed."

I narrowed my eyes. "Did you unclothe me?"

Archer held up a hand. "Absolutely not."

"Then where are my pants?"

Archer glanced around the room. He scratched his head. The scent of his cologne, which I had found pleasant the day before, sparked a wave of nausea through me. I sat back down. Archer fumbled under the covers of my bed.

"Ta-da," he said.

My leather pants were balled into a knot in his strong hand.

A knock at the door made my head hurt.

"That's room service. Why don't you wash up and come get some breakfast?"

I watched as he let the door slip shut behind him.

I stumbled into the bathroom, turned on the light, and nearly choked on my own scream. My skin was puffy, my hair was sticking out on all sides like a rabid clown's, and my eyes looked like I was wearing some sort of hideous mask.

There was an array of beauty products and toiletries in the bathroom, displayed on a dainty, mirrored tray. Which was one too many mirrors for my liking. The white-marble room was huge, with two sinks, a steam shower, and a two-person soaker tub with jets. I opted for a bar of orange-blossom soap, lavender shampoo and conditioner, and mint toothpaste.

As I washed, something kept nagging at me. Something from last night? Something Archer had said? It was a memory that lay just out of my grasp. I thought of the perfectly sculpted bartender and that Clyde person. There was something about the man I didn't like, but I couldn't put my finger on that either.

This was exactly why I wasn't a drinker—especially in this realm. Liquor clouded the mind, confused one's thoughts, and relaxed one's morals. Too many times, I had seen the aftermath of a human on drink. The laws they broke, the people they hurt, their own lives and families destroyed.

I sat under the scalding water for a long time, washing, lathering, scrubbing, and brushing. When I was finally finished, I stepped out, dried my skin, wrapped a towel around my long curls, and donned a fluffy robe. I wasn't one for perfumes or lotions, although there were dozens of them in every scent on the planet. I did run a clear gloss across my chapped lips and dab a bit of sunscreen on my already-pink cheeks. I was combing the knots from my hair with a silver comb that I was certain Aphrodite must have provided at some point in time, when the words hit me like an iron fist.

I secured the robe at the waist and rushed out of the bathroom. I found myself standing near a banister, next to a set of stairs that dipped into a wide, carpeted room. "What do you mean I promised to dance at the Shadow Bar?"

Archer smirked. "I was wondering when you were going to process that."

He was seated at a round black table, unrolling silverware from a napkin. The aroma of black coffee, salty bacon, and sweet pineapple filled the room, instantly reminding me that I was absolutely famished. When had I last eaten a meal?

"This is a joke, right? You're toying with me?" I said.

Archer pulled out a chair for me, unveiled a plate of scrambled eggs, poured two cups of coffee, and said, "Sit. Eat. We can discuss this after breakfast. I need you at full throttle."

He had a point, but I didn't like to be ordered around. Especially by a mortal. "I'll sit when I decide, thank you very much." I poured myself a glass of some orange juice that didn't quite look like juice made from oranges. I sniffed it. It smelled tangy and medicine-y.

"What is this?"

"It's a drink that athletes and alcoholics use to replenish electrolytes. Try it. You'll feel better. There's no booze in it, I swear."

He busied himself buttering a piece of toast, and I sipped the drink. It wasn't instant, but I did feel better after a few swallows.

"What do you know about alcoholics?" I asked, setting my drink down on the table.

A faraway look fell over his face. "After my wife left me, I went on a six-month bender. I had my fair share of waking up in strange places, not knowing how I'd gotten there."

"You're married?" I reached for a helping of eggs and a piece of toast, just as Archer reached for a packet of strawberry jam. My hand grazed his, and I felt a tingle surge up my arm. I pulled away immediately and sat down.

"Was. A long time ago." He said it matter-of-factly, and I couldn't help but wonder why humans gave up on love so easily. "She couldn't handle the job." He opened the jam, then looked at me cautiously.

At that moment, I wondered how many years he had spent on Earth. He had a few crinkles at the corners of his eyes. His hair was mostly dark, with a hint of gray along the edges. Forty, perhaps?

"What?" he asked when he saw me staring at him.

"Nothing. I was just wondering how old you were when you passed over." I felt awkward asking that the minute the words left my mouth. What did I care? We were business partners, essentially. No need to muddy the waters by asking personal questions. "Forget I said anything," I hurried to add.

Archer sipped his coffee and stabbed a piece of sausage with his fork. "No, it's fine. I was thirty-eight." He bit into his toast.

So young. Of course, I had seen much younger souls pass through Hades's realm.

Archer poured me more of the orange drink, which I was growing rather fond of. I took a huge swig. It truly was replenishing.

"So, what about you?" he asked.

I raised an eyebrow at him. Was he asking about my love life? I couldn't recall the last time I had met a god worthy of more than a onetime physical encounter. I didn't date much. Didn't even get out much these days.

"I mean, you look twenty-five, but I'm guessing that's not right."

The question took me by surprise. I hadn't thought of my

age in a long time. The truth was, I couldn't even recall what it was. "I'm as old as the Fates allow, I suppose."

Archer considered this. Then he said, "So, how does all this work?"

I stabbed a pineapple chunk with my fork. It smelled like sunshine. "How does what work?" I popped the pineapple into my mouth. It was sweet and tart at the same time.

"I mean your boss. Hades. Is he the devil?"

Oh boy, here we go, I thought. *The talk.* I'd had "the talk" more times than I cared to count. With shades, mostly, but sometimes with resting souls and very rarely with living ones. It never came without a hundred questions, a thousand arguments, and buckets of tears. It didn't matter which part of the world a mortal had lived in. All of them were so dangerously devoted to their religion, they wouldn't accept the truth of it even if was wrapped around their neck like a noose. Believe me, I'd tried it once.

Which was why they were constantly killing each other. In the name of this god or that god, or because this man worshipped the same god as his neighbor, but his neighbor had slightly different beliefs—or, worse, *man-made* rules—they fought to the death. Humans were constantly killing each other over the stupidest philosophies, all of them wrong. I found it maddeningly frustrating.

Zeus, on the other hand, thought it was hilarious. He had a twisted sense of humor, that one.

I studied Archer closely. His eyes were bright, curious—dare I say open to the answers? Would he be the one human who just might listen? Because most of them never had the story right, and no matter how many times you explained it to them, they couldn't grasp the truth. They *wanted* to blame demons for the atrocities that plagued their society. It was easier to accept than the truth. But sin didn't come from outside the soul. There was no evil entity that whispered in the ears of men and women to make them commit their crimes. There was help, certainly, for any who sought it. The monsters that plagued all realms, even mine, gleefully aided those who called to them, gnawing on the twisted impulses of a rotten soul, feeding on the pain and torture of that soul's innocent victims.

And once you called to the monsters, they were bound to you. Forever.

I said, "There is no devil. Evil exists only in the hearts of men. And demons."

"Demons?"

I nodded. "Monsters. Atrocities of nature born from the cruel things that mortals and immortals do to each other."

Archer leaned back in his chair, thinking for a moment. "So you're saying that monsters exist, but only because people and, er, gods created them?"

"Precisely."

He looked perplexed. "So everything I learned in Sunday school was wrong. There is no God? No devil?"

"There are many gods, but no devil. Hades is a ruler of the Underworld. He watches over the human souls until they are rested, cleansed, and prepared to return to the mortal world."

He tapped his foot, grabbed a piece of bacon, then put it back. "So there was no Jesus?"

"Yes, there was a Jesus. A passive preacher man, as I recall. Lived in a desert city like this one." I helped myself to another piece of toast. "But you killed him." The bread was crisp and hot; the butter melted instantly.

The FBI man stared at me, slack-jawed. I realized my mistake. "Well, not *you* specifically. You know. People."

Archer was silent for several moments. Perhaps it was all a bit too much for him. I took a few bites of the toast.

"History lesson is over," I said after a few moments. "Tell me more about the Shadow Bar, because there is no way I will be dancing there."

"You have to. Besides you giving Clyde your word, and me trying to convince him that yes, you are an FBI agent who can't handle her liquor, you auditioned for the gig. He loved it."

There was a bit more juice left, and I drank it, feeling the last remnants of the prior evening's debauchery fleeing my skin.

"I can't dance, Archer."

"You did great last night."

Oh, Lords.

"Listen, if you do this, it'll be a great in with the staff, not to mention you can monitor the patrons without them even seeing you watching them. It's the best way to find out what happened to your sister."

It might also draw out the person responsible, since I seemed to fit his preferences.

Archer stood and asked if I was finished eating. When I nodded, he covered up the trays, put them on a cart, and wheeled the cart out of the room.

"You ready to get started?" he asked.

"Yes."

"Great. After you get changed, we'll head out. Then, later, I want to go over the files with you. They've all been transferred to the laptop." He pointed to an electronic machine with a video screen and type board.

"Where are we going?" *Please don't let it be a casino,* I thought.

"To the tunnels."

Chapter 12

He was feeding his newest playmate when the bitch bit him. Nearly bit his goddamn finger right off.

"You bitch!" He sucked his finger to stop the blood flow. Then he slapped her as hard as he could across the face. He couldn't believe it didn't leave a mark. He wanted it to leave a mark, to leave *his* mark.

She just laughed. Then she spit on him, and that enraged him even more. He flipped over the soup tray, and it splattered across the wall, leaving splotchy chunks of noodles stuck to the torn wallpaper. They looked like dead worms in the dim light. He dragged her off the mattress by her hair and flung her against the cement wall, hoping she would smack her head.

His partner wouldn't like that, but he didn't care.

"You think it's funny? I'll show you funny, you fucking bitch!"

He grabbed a knife, the one he was going to use to carve his initials into her stomach when the game was over, and held it to her throat. She squeezed her eyes shut, but he could smell a trace of fear. It wasn't strong like the others'. It didn't last long, and this one's scent was herbaceous, floral, even, though he couldn't identify the plant.

"Look at me!" he hissed.

She opened one eye. It sparkled for a moment. Almost…illuminated. Then she shut it.

This one was harder to break, but he had every confidence he would be able to break her, given enough time. He had broken many. She wasn't anything special.

Then again, he could always kill her and find another. But no, it was too late for that. His partner had promised the plan would be enacted soon.

He pressed the tip of the knife to her swan-like throat, his other hand gripping the back of her head. Her breathing was steady, calmer, and her eyes were still closed.

Then one of the other playmates said, "No, please, don't."

That's when he felt the tension shift beneath his hold on the newbie's head. That's when he learned what her currency was. She actually gave a shit about the others. She didn't just fear for her life. She feared for *theirs*.

He swung his head back, dropped her like a water hose, and made his way over to the one who had interrupted his game.

He dragged that one—the one with the mouth—kicking and screaming, tears running down her face, over to the handcuffs that dangled from the ceiling. He gripped one skinny wrist and then another, binding her to the ceiling. Then he duct-taped her feet as she whispered, "Please, please, not again."

Ignoring her, he watched as she swayed gently, like a side of beef in the Chicago stockyards. *Fresh meat*, he thought. She was firm, well toned. A dancer, maybe.

Then he turned back to the one who had bitten him. She tried to appear defiant, but he saw the emotion when she opened her eyes again. That sparkling was there still, but he saw what she was feeling just the same.

Empathy, remorse, and anger. Oh, yes, there was a lot of anger there. If she had been a man, he might have befriended her. Could have coaxed her to join his team. He could use that kind of piss and vinegar. Too bad.

He said to her, "This is your fault. I want you to remember that. Every plea, every scream, every scar—it's all on you. It should *be* you."

Then the fun began.

Chapter 13

"You're kidding, right?" Archer asked me when I met him back in the common area of our suite after I had changed.

"Look, I don't want to hear it. In fact, I don't even want to think about it. Let's just say I need to go shopping as soon as possible."

I was wearing—not by choice, but rather out of necessity—a much-too-tight orange sequined tube top, jeans that looked to have been painted onto my thighs, and leopard platform heels. I couldn't believe my sisters even owned this kind of garb, let alone wore it out in public. Honestly, what did this city do to all who entered? I had never known Meg or Alex to be caught dead in such attire. It had to be theirs, too, because of the fit. Not many goddesses came close to my height.

"Well, there's plenty of dough in the safe for that," Archer said.

"Why is there dough in the safe?" I asked. "Shouldn't it be in the refrigerator?"

"Money, Tisi, I'm talking about money. Coin. You're going to have to start picking up some colloquialisms if you're going undercover. Which reminds me." He crossed over to the sofa, picked up a fancy shopping bag tied in ribbons, and handed it to me.

"What's this?" I asked.

"Your uniform."

I peeked into the bag. It was rather small to hold much of anything, let alone a uniform.

"Do I get a badge too?"

Archer paused, seeming confused. After a moment, he appeared to understand my question. "No, Tisi, this is the uniform for the Shadow Bar, not the FBI."

I untied the shiny purple strings and pulled out what looked like something one might use to sheath a sword.

"This? How am I supposed to wear this? It's like a pair of gloves."

Archer shrugged. "It's supposed to be tight. Don't worry. You'll be behind the screen." He glanced at his watch. "Come on, let's roll."

Judging by his gesture to open the door, I guessed that meant we were leaving.

I pretended to ignore the men gawking at me as I walked through the casino. This was no easy feat, because I had to walk with measured care so I wouldn't break my neck. How did women wear these things? They felt like ancient torture devices designed by an angry god who hated females.

Archer was pretty far ahead of me when he noticed I wasn't keeping pace. He rushed back to tell me he was going to run an errand, then grab a cab. He disappeared through the crowd.

Halfway through the Pussycat Dolls portion of the casino, I spotted a woman with fiery red hair, wearing jeans and an athletic T-shirt with a cartoon cub in a baseball cap on the front of it. She was sitting in the bar with the sea horse sculptures, trying her best to ignore a pudgy man who was sweating on her and smoking a cigar. He seemed excited about something. She didn't seem too thrilled to be in his presence, however. Something about her made me keep my gaze aimed at her. Her body language, the frown on her face, the way she scrunched into the seat, leaning away from the man and never making eye contact, led me to believe that this woman was in the midst of unwanted company.

Just as I reached them, he grabbed her arm forcefully and she shuddered. Then she said something, barely moving her lips. Her face grew fierce, but she still refused to look at him.

She seemed a woman in trouble. Could this be the kidnapper of the Shadow Bar victims? Was he targeting redheads now?

I rushed over to them, looked her square in the eye, and said, "Excuse me. Do you need help?"

The man puffed on his cigar, ogling the woman lasciviously, but he didn't say anything more.

The redhead, who I saw had grassy-colored eyes, looked at me and plastered on a false smile. "Excuse me?" she said.

"Is this man bothering you?" I asked, glaring at the brute.

The man looked confused, as did the redhead, who narrowed her eyes and said, "What man?"

I pointed. "The one standing in your space, smoking a cigar."

The young woman stiffened. She glanced at the man, then at me. She leaned toward me and said softly, "You can see him?"

The man said, "Who are you talking to? Is there another medium in the house?"

Uh-oh. Either she was crazy or she was an empath to shades. I hadn't run into many of those in my travels. It was a shade who was bothering her, not a living man. That's why he couldn't see me. In this realm, the gods are not visible to shades, for fear of confusion. Until their business on this plane was finished, they wouldn't or couldn't cross to the Underworld. People like this woman often aided them in their quest for closure.

Before I could answer, another man, with bulging biceps, sandy hair, and a wide smile, approached us. "Hey, Stacy." He kissed her. "Got us both signed up for the next Texas Hold'em tournament." He looked at me. "Hi."

Texas Hold'em tournament? If only there was time.

Stacy said, "Um, Chance, this is..."

I blurted, "Sorry to interrupt." It was best not to tempt fate, best not to give her any inkling of who—and what—I was.

By the time she opened her mouth to speak, I was learning to run in heels.

I looked back, just once, and she was staring at me, a gleam of knowing in her eye.

Outside, in the oppressive heat, Archer was impatiently tapping his foot and looking at his watch. He spotted me. "Finally. Come on—we can't be late."

I slipped into the cab and noticed he was holding a couple of paper bags. One smelled of beef and mustard.

"You can't be hungry again," I said.

Archer tapped the bag. "It's not for me. It's for a friend." He winked.

He gave the cab driver an address, and we circled around the parking area and exited down a side street.

I wasn't certain where we were headed, but this road didn't seem as active and bright as the one we had traveled the day before. There were still plenty of casinos and eateries, but not as many people, or people dressed as furry animals.

Where were these tunnels?

It wasn't long before the cab stopped and we got out. Archer tipped the driver with money he had taken straight from his pocket. I noticed he didn't have a wallet, as many mortals carried. Just his badge in a black case.

Had his murderer stolen it? If so, why hadn't he taken the badge too?

We walked a few blocks, turned a few times, and climbed down some steps, until we came upon a cement tunnel large enough to pass through walking upright.

"What is this place?" I asked.

"This is the entrance to the tunnels. We're about to walk under the city of Las Vegas."

That was the best news I had heard since I'd gotten here. "You mean, the city itself has an Underworld?"

"In a way, yes. People live here. Hundreds of them."

If I had the choice between living aboveground in Las Vegas and below, I'd certainly choose the latter. However, that didn't seem like something a mortal would choose.

"Why?" I asked.

Archer said, "Some folks are just down on their luck. Lost a job, a spouse, maybe. Others are struggling with addiction problems. They had no place else to go, so they came here. They make the best of a bad situation." Archer stepped deeper into the tunnel. "You'd be amazed by what they do with so little."

"So if they live here and they don't have jobs, then why were we going to be late?"

"My contact." Archer stepped over a broken bottle, then held his hand out to assist me. "He likes to keep a tight schedule. Many of these people work the casinos in the daytime, looking for chips gamblers may have dropped, ticket stubs left in slot machines, loose change, things like that."

We stepped even farther into the tunnel, and I could feel myself strengthening. It was dark here, cooler too. It wasn't home, but it was better than the desert. Beneath their invisibility spell, my wings ruffled.

Archer led us through the tunnel to a boarded-up passage.

"Looks like it's blocked," I said.

"Not blocked. That's a wall." He knocked. "Jeremy, man, can you let me through? I brought your favorite."

There was some shuffling behind the board. It inched aside, and a small young man in a camouflage jacket appeared through the crack in the wall. He was smoking a cigarette.

He said, in a raspy voice, "What's the pass code?"

"Two all-beef patties, special sauce, lettuce, cheese, pickles, onions on a sesame-seed bun."

"Who's your friend?" Jeremy asked, eyeing me. He blew a ring of smoke out through the crack, and it floated up through the tunnel.

"Agent Ninety-Nine," said Archer.

I didn't know what that meant, but I decided I also didn't care.

Jeremy looked suspicious. "She's taller than I remember."

"It's a new formula. Growth juice. She can fly too."

Why would he tell him that? I stiffened.

Jeremy broke out into a wide smile and opened the wall. "Archer, my man! Great to see you!" The young man wore his hair in a ponytail that trailed to his knees.

"Brought you your favorite." Archer pulled out a sandwich wrapped in paper.

"Extra pickles?"

"Of course."

"No onion?" Jeremy unwrapped the cheeseburger and sniffed.

"You smell bad enough."

Jeremy bit into his sandwich, smiling at both Archer and me.

"You need smokes?" Archer held up a package with gold lettering on it.

"No, man. Trying to quit. I found a weight set someone was tossing out near that shitty apartment I used to live in."

Jeremy lifted his left arm, which was the circumference of a shower rod, still holding the cigarette. "Gonna start working out. Get in shape."

He devoured the sandwich in a few bites and wiped his mouth. "Would you like to come in? I got a new book on tape. Stephen King, man. Traded it for an iPod I found."

"We're just passing through, buddy, but thanks." Archer patted his shoulder. "I'm actually looking for Tommy."

Jeremy thought for a moment and said, "Man, I haven't seen that guy in days."

Archer stood a bit taller. "Oh yeah? Since when, do you think?"

Jeremy scratched his hairless chin. "I don't know, maybe Tuesday?"

Archer gave me a foul look.

"You guys need a flashlight?" Jeremy said.

The frown faded, and Archer smiled at the young man. "What do you think?"

"Right, right, Secret Agent Man." Jeremy looked at me with kind eyes. "Nice meeting you, Ninety-Nine."

"Likewise," I said.

"Let's go, Ninety-Nine. We have a mission," Archer said.

We certainly did. Tuesday was the day Archer had died.

Chapter 14

"Jeremy is a huge *Get Smart* fan. It's an old TV show. Ever hear of it?"

"No." I said it in a way that warned I didn't want to either. Archer dropped the subject.

He was concerned about something—perhaps what Jeremy had told him about the last time he had seen Archer's informant.

"What's troubling you?" I asked.

"I don't believe in coincidences is all. Tommy hasn't been seen since last Tuesday, the day I got whacked. I hope to hell he's all right."

The farther we made our way through the dank tunnel, the darker it got. Archer had a small flashlight to guide our way, but my eyes were used to navigating the darkness. I could feel my energy returning bit by bit. I felt empowered. My cloaked wings twitched behind, begging for flight.

The bags Archer had brought with us contained food, cigarettes, batteries, and packs of matches that he passed out as offerings to various people in exchange for passage through their homes. Archer explained how the tunnels were designed to expel excess water from the city and that occasionally they did flood. They ran, he told me, all the way from Las Vegas to California.

"Some of these folks have been here for years," he said sadly. "These are the real lost ones, as you call them."

We passed through a young couple's "apartment," where I saw signs of a child living there: a teddy bear, a fire truck. When I asked Archer about it, he said, "They keep them hidden. I'm sure they're here, but the local police have yet to find any. It's a tight-knit community down here. Most folks look out for one another."

"And this contact? Why are we searching for him?" I stepped around a bookcase built out of wooden fruit crates. It still smelled like bananas.

"Tommy is my informant. Every city has its underbelly, and I don't mean this." He swept his arm across the tunnel. "I mean the dark side. Drugs, gangs, prostitution, trafficking. And every city has its snitches. He's a pretty good guy when he's clean. He was busted for drugs a few times. The last time, he wanted to strike a deal with the local prosecutor. He'd keep the boys in blue up to speed on any major activity, and they'd reduce his sentence. It's worked out well for both sides. Last year, he got wind of a major drug shipment that was coming in from the coast. That's when I met him."

"How did he know about it?"

Archer slid a glance my way. "He doesn't tell, and I don't ask anymore. I'm just glad he's on our side."

"And the missing women?" I asked. "Did he know anything about the women?"

Archer frowned. "Didn't get a chance to ask him before..."

"I see."

Archer sighed. "Hope he's all right."

After a few silent moments, we turned a corner. There was a sliver of light peeking through a dirty blue sheet.

"This is it. This is where he lives. Hopefully," Archer said. "Yo, Tommy."

I heard the squeak of bedsprings, some movement.

"Who's there?" Tommy's voice cracked as he spoke. Almost like he was afraid.

"An old friend." Archer smiled.

Tommy mumbled. "Go away."

"Tommy, it's me, Archer."

There was a long silence. Then the sheet was flung to the side and a very small man the size of a satyr stood there. He was holding a very large knife.

"Whoa, Tommy, what the hell? Not happy to see me?" There was an edge to my partner's voice. A hesitation.

Was this Archer's killer?

Tommy was visibly shaken. His face turned white as lightning, and he backed up. "No. No, it can't be. You're a ghost, man!"

Then he turned and ran like mad.

Archer took off after Tommy, and I followed. He was weaving around walls of boxes, cardboard, old doors, and plywood, keeping pace with the small man. I was right behind them when a metal rod crashed down in front of me.

I stopped short, nearly toppled over, in fact.

There was a woman standing in front of me with glazed eyes. She swayed a bit.

"Just what the hell do you think you're doing?" she barked.

"Passing through."

"No one passes through my casa without paying a toll."

Was she serious? I thought about Archer's handing out all those gifts he had brought for the tenants of the tunnels. Except now he was gone. And I had nothing to offer.

The woman blew a strand of blond hair from her sallow

face. Her eyes were vacant, bloodshot. She was wearing overalls and a bathrobe. She smelled of gin and sin.

The woman took a step forward, threatening to do something more serious with that rod.

"I'm afraid I have nothing to offer," I said, scanning the space beyond her. The light was thicker here. The exit had to be just beyond her apartment.

"A pretty thing like you? All dressed up in those fancy clothes? You got nothin'? No wallet? Bullshit." She spat that last part out.

I really didn't have time or patience for this. "Look at what I'm wearing, woman. Where would I put it?" Honestly, even my hip bones were visible through these tight pants.

She curled her lip, thought a moment. "Good point."

"Thank you." I stepped forward, and she poked the rod, or pipe, or whatever the rusty thing was, at my stomach.

Mind your fury, Tisiphone, I thought as my blood roiled. *Mind your fury.*

"Not so fast, missy," said the woman. Her face contorted into a map of sagging lines as she thought.

"Can we hurry this along, please?" I really didn't want to discipline her. She seemed as if she'd had her share of punishment.

"Tell you what." She lowered the rod. "Give me them shoes."

"What?" I wasn't fond of them, but they were the only things standing between me and the disgusting ground that was littered with candy wrappers, stale bread, and gods knew what else. Then a horrible thought hit me. Where did these people relieve themselves? I shivered.

"Your shoes!" she snarled.

Oh, for the love of Zeus.

I crossed my arms. "I am not giving you my shoes. There's broken glass, cigarette butts, and Hades knows what else on these streets."

She considered this. "Tell you what, missy. I'll trade ya."

Well, this just kept getting better.

I looked down at her worn pink slippers. Her cracked, rough heels hung off the back. There were brown stains smeared across them that I could only hope were from chocolate, and the left one had a huge hole in the toe.

The woman followed my gaze. "Oh, no you don't. Them's my lucky slippers. Won my first hundred in these slippers. I got something else in mind."

I expected her to pull out two empty shoe boxes for me to slip into. Instead, she rummaged around her space and presented a pair of white leather running shoes that looked brand new.

"Seriously?" I asked.

"What? You don't like 'em? They're perfectly good sneakers. Found them at the Salvation Army. Nickel apiece."

"Why don't you want them?" I mean, really, they were better than what both of us had on our feet.

She glared at the shoes. "No style. I was gonna gussy them up, but I couldn't find any green paint."

I wanted this nightmare of a conversation to end, so I accepted the shoes. I put one on, then the other, handing the woman the leopard platform stilettos one at a time.

The running shoes were two different sizes, each with a different pattern. One was too big, the other too small.

"Nice doin' business with ya." The woman set the bar down and stepped aside.

I rushed out of there as fast as I could and didn't look back.

I heard voices to the right of the cement drain that led to the tunnels. I climbed up the embankment and spotted Archer and Tommy. The knife was some feet away from the men, as if Tommy had dropped it.

"You gotta believe me, Arch. I'm telling you the truth," Tommy was pleading.

The sun was bouncing off Archer's hair as he ran a hand through it. He blew out a sigh and said, "I believe you. Just lay low for a while, all right? Until I get to the bottom of this. I don't want you buying, I don't even want you using."

"Sure, sure," Tommy said.

"And remember, you never saw me. Understood?"

The small man nodded.

"Beat it now," Archer said.

I watched as Tommy scuttled down the cement embankment and disappeared into the black mouth of the tunnel.

Behind me, I heard a screech. I got the distinct sensation that someone was watching me. I spun around to see a huge black bird flap its wings once, then disappear.

Only it wasn't a bird native to this world.

"Did you see that?" I yelled to Archer.

"See what?" He was ascending the hill.

"That bird. Big one." I turned to face the lawman. "Did you?"

"No. Why? What's the big deal?"

I looked to where it had melted into the sky, scanning the endless blue for a slit, a tear, a rip. I didn't see one. Had I imagined it? Perhaps it was a creature of this plane after all.

As Archer and I started walking back toward Caesars Palace, he launched into telling me what he had discussed with Tommy.

But I wasn't listening. My mind was elsewhere.

Because if that thing was what I thought it was, this was far more serious than any of us had imagined.

For the first time since I had arrived here, I wasn't angry. I was frightened.

Chapter 15

He hadn't meant to kill her. She was just so lovely. Her skin so translucent, so pale, it nearly glowed. He couldn't stop cutting it. And her hair! That thick black mass of curls. He could have fashioned a blanket out of it and worn it all around town.

Of course, now there was a mess to clean up.

And he was one playmate short.

No matter. When his partner arrived, they would have to devise a plan to get another one. Shouldn't be too hard. This was Vegas, after all. Plenty of sluts to choose from. He preferred the spot where he had found the others, because of the energy, but if he had to, he could search elsewhere.

He heated up some black coffee on the one functioning burner of the cracked porcelain stovetop. When it was good and hot, he poured it into a cup and sat down.

The others were much better behaved now. They still whimpered occasionally, but they had stopped pleading after they had watched him drink her blood. Not a lot, of course—it wasn't like he was one of those lunatics who believed they were vampires. But he liked the taste of a fresh kill, and he found it enlivened his soul to feed on his victims.

But that other one—the troublemaker—she was still a pain in the ass. God, he wished he could cut her tongue out, carve her eyes out. He cringed. Those eyes gave him the willies, truth be told. The way they sparkled like…like there were diamonds in them or something.

They reminded him of someone.

So, naturally, he had to blindfold her. Gagged her too, because her spitting habit was disgusting. She was tied up good and tight as a reminder to the others that there were fates worse than death.

Fate: what a funny concept. As if fate had anything to do with anything. Were these women fated to cross his path at just the right time? Were they fated to become his playmates, his tools for the upcoming party?

He laughed at that and sipped his coffee. Then again, maybe they were. What were the odds of finding five women who all fit the profile? Not very good, he imagined. Then again, this was Vegas. The house always won.

He finished the coffee, spitting a few grounds back into the cup. He stood up and rinsed the cup out in the sink. The smell of rotten eggs flowed from the loose faucet. He'd have to fix that soon.

Then he smiled. Soon. It would all happen very soon. And once the stars aligned and everything was in place, the real fun would begin. For there was debt to collect. Punishments to dole out.

He lit a candle. Vanilla scented. And waited for his partner to arrive.

Chapter 16

The entire journey back to the room, I couldn't shake the feeling that things weren't right. Every once in a while, I would spot something that reminded me of home. A griffin here, a minotaur there. Just for a second, a flash, and then it would be gone. My feathers were ruffled, my eyes were burning, and my adrenaline was pumping.

It was the same reaction my body had whenever it prepared for battle. A tiny voice inside my head said, *War is coming.*

I shook it off. That couldn't be. It was impossible. There hadn't been an immortal war in this realm in almost three millennia.

No. I banished the thought. Whatever this was, it was bad, but that wasn't it. Still, I could swear I had seen a Stymphalian outside the tunnel. The birds were the worst of the worst. More horrific than a rabid dragon, fiercer than Harpies, even. These monsters were gigantic, with bronze beaks that could pierce armor, razor-sharp feathers, and an insatiable appetite. They ate everything and anything. I once saw one eat a shark and then circle back for its friends.

But their favorite meal was humankind.

I watched as Archer turned on the electronic computer device, wondering how he and I would be any match for a fight with a Stymphalian. I couldn't imagine it ending well.

If the bird was indeed here, we needed help, we needed weapons.

We needed the gods.

Then again, Archer hadn't even seen it. As a reanimated shade, he should be able to see any demon. Even one that had been banished to Tartarus.

Oh, I so wanted to go for a fly. Stretch my wings, feel my muscles.

Archer fiddled with a couple of cords, and the giant screen hanging on the wall fizzled to life.

He turned to me. "All right. Let's go through this." He stopped, looked at me intently. "What's wrong?"

I was sitting on the curved black sofa, a crimson pillow in my lap. I was wearing the same clothes I had slipped into that morning, but the shoes were in the garbage can.

"Nothing. Just waiting for my clothes." I smiled.

One good thing about Vegas, I had discovered, was that besides women and food, one could also order clothing. Some of the finer hotels had personal shoppers. Within the walls of Caesars Palace was something called the Forum Shops—miles and miles of stores where one could purchase anything from handcrafted jewelry to lingerie to comfortable shoes. My personal shopper was on the hunt while I relaxed in our suite, sipping another orange drink. They were addicting. Gatorade, it was called.

Archer narrowed his eyes at me. "No. That's not it. You've been awfully quiet since we left the tunnel. You hardly asked me a thing about Tommy's story, and you didn't even tell me why crazy Maybel seized your footwear."

I sighed. "I didn't want to talk about Maybel because I'd like to just forget the whole thing. And there wasn't much to discuss as far as Tommy was concerned. You explained your conversation quite adequately."

Tommy, it seemed, had heard through the "word on the street" that Archer was deceased. It had taken Archer a few pinches and a few dollars to convince Tommy that the rumor of his demise had been highly exaggerated. True to his moral code, Tommy hadn't divulged where he had obtained the information but had sworn that he didn't know who had committed the murder. In light of all that, Archer had decided it best to tell Tommy and Clyde, the manager of the hotel, that he was deep undercover. That the FBI had faked his death to draw out the criminal. That they couldn't be seen talking together, and that even the Bureau shouldn't be contacted regarding the case.

I didn't know if Clyde accepted this as truth, but there was no doubt that Archer could be quite persuasive.

All of this meant that now, Archer explained, he couldn't access the investigative tools of the FBI, as he had hoped. He had thought that perhaps he could visit his workplace as if he had never departed this plane. But now…now we were on our own. Thankfully, Athena had successfully transmitted the files to the computer in the gods' suite.

Archer walked over to the sofa and sat down next to me. "I have ways of making you talk, you know. I was an FBI agent."

I gave him an *oh, please* look.

Gently, he slid one of his strong arms beneath my legs and swung my feet over to rest in his lap.

"I could do some serious damage to you in this position, Archer."

He grinned. "Well, then you'd be losing out on my magical touch."

"Ah, if only that talisman you carry truly did hold magic," I said.

"Okay, that's it. Talk. We're partners, remember? No secrets."

He ran his hands along my feet, gently massaging my heels.

Hard to say no to that. I leaned back and told him about the Stymphalian.

When I was finished, he said, "So, these things are like the monsters you told me about."

"They're ruthless," I said. "Even for the gods."

Archer sat back and thought a moment. "Didn't you say that demons could come here only if called forth?"

I felt my entire body relaxing as he ironed out all the tension in my toes.

"Yes, but it would take something incredibly powerful, something not of this earth, to call forth that particular demon."

"And why is that?"

"They are bound to Tartarus. I performed the ritual myself."

"So there's no chance that they could escape?"

"Highly unlikely. The belly of the Underworld is tightly secured from both sides. Not even Hades himself can open the gate. It's much like the human prison systems. There are guards. There are duties. And while prisoners may gain compensation through work or privileges for good behavior, it is monitored like a fortress. At least it was many years ago when I had Tartarus duty."

But had the system changed? Was there new technology in place, like there was for this mission?

Archer said, "Well, that's a relief. You know, we *are* in the land of make-believe. It could have been a prop for a show. Maybe even a bizarre kind of glider plane."

"Perhaps." At this point, I would have agreed to anything the man said. His fingers were magic.

A knock on the door interrupted my bliss.

"Must be your clothes." Archer got up and peeped through the hole. "Yep."

Just before he swung the door open, my moonstone ring lit up. I quickly turned around and tapped the ring, as Hecate had instructed.

Stand by for a message.

I heard Archer thank someone as I waited for the message.

The door shut behind me as the ring sizzled and swirled with an iridescent glow. Finally, a note appeared:

I've discovered an ancient dark-arts spell that may correlate to the missing women. It is practiced only by the most notorious mortal warlocks. The end means depend solely on the magician's intent. The practitioner must harness the five moons of Pluto on the night of the earthly new moon for the spell to work, and it can be even more powerful during an eclipse. As far as we have been able to ascertain, this ritual has not been performed since demons walked the earth. Those who have used it were calling forth either monsters or gods, but it could also be used to harness souls. It may be a dead end, but I wanted to let you know.
—Hecate

I sat back in the sofa. Pluto was Hades's ruling planet. Five moons. Five women. Five weeks.

Could there be a connection? And was that why their companions—including Meg—never noticed that the women were missing until it was too late? Had they been bespelled by some kind of potion or magic?

It was an angle worth looking into.

"Archer, can you look something up on your information machine?"

"Jesus, Tisi, for the last time, it's a laptop."

I threw my juice bottle at him. He ducked just in time. "Stop correcting me. This is important."

"Fine, calm the hell down."

He used something shaped like a mouse to work the laptop. An image popped up on the larger screen.

"What do you want to know on the Internet?"

"When is the next lunar eclipse?"

His fingers typed rapidly. "October."

That was a relief. It was June now.

He tapped on the keys some more.

After a moment, he said, "A solar eclipse is coming in four days."

The world grew a little darker, and the room warmer.

Alex, where are you?

Chapter 17

I told Archer about the message from Hecate and went over all the scenarios I could come up with as to what a spell of that nature could invoke. Demons, black souls bound to Tartarus, even the ferryman could be called forth to escort souls back with him.

Or perhaps Hecate was wrong and the sorcerer intended to use it to banish a lost soul or a monster from this realm. There was simply no way to know.

"So what you're saying is, whoever kidnapped the women may be using them to get rid of something."

I grabbed a packet of nuts from a dish on the counter. "What I'm saying is that if there is a connection between the spell Hecate located and the missing women—and that is a big if—then we need to know if someone is trying to open the gate or if they're trying to close it."

"I thought you said the gate was locked up tight."

I opened the nuts. "I meant figuratively. Is someone trying to banish something to the Underworld? A black-souled shade that refuses to leave this plane? Or perhaps a man with the mind of a monster? Or are they trying to draw something out?"

Archer stood and stretched. "Or is it just a maniac with a thing for raven-haired women?"

"There is that possibility as well."

Archer slapped his hands together. "Okay, let's put aside mythical creatures, warlocks, and magic spells for a moment and focus on what we know."

"Do I look mythical to you?" I asked, irritated by that last remark.

Archer slid his eyes along the curve of my neck, down to my breasts, and on to my legs before answering.

"Absolutely not." His voice was deep, suggestive.

He turned to face the computer screen, and I was grateful. The heat in his tone ignited a heat in my body that I was fighting to extinguish.

The lawman clicked a few keys and opened up the files on the missing women. He touched the screen to move the photographs side by side.

"I can't find any links between these girls except their location, physical appearance, and age."

I stepped forward. They all looked disturbingly alike. Black, curly hair; pale skin; bright, round eyes, some blue, others brown and green. No one's eyes were violet, except, of course, for Alex's, which Athena had thoughtfully included in her file transfer. She was standing in front of the statue of the Graces in the lobby of Caesars Palace. Meg must have taken the photograph. She was smiling broadly. Like she hadn't a care in the world. With no inkling of what was about to happen to her. I stepped forward, studying the photograph.

Archer said, "None of the women knew each other." He touched the photograph of one young girl, wearing a red dress, to enlarge it. "Cicely Barnes. Twenty-three years old. Student at the University of Chicago." He touched the second photograph. "Melissa Walkins. Twenty-six. Freshly engaged. She was here for a bachelorette party." He moved on to the next. "Stephanie McPherson. Twenty-one. Just accepted into nursing school." Archer touched the last image. "Yasmine Bloom. Twenty-four. A waitress from Omaha."

Archer then enlarged the picture of Alecto. "Tell me about your sister."

I sighed, missing her. Aching for her to be all right. Had she any strength? Any power at all at this moment? "I'm not sure what I can tell you. She's a Fury, like me. Her job is to punish crimes of morality, especially if they are premeditated or cause harm to any human being. She's the angry one."

"She's the angry one?" Archer laughed.

I rolled my eyes. "We all have our tempers, but Alecto especially so. That's the very meaning of her name."

"So she wouldn't go down without a fight."

"No way. I would wager that whoever took her has battle scars. She once broke the leg of a man who kicked a dog."

Archer's eyes widened. "So how do you suppose she was captured? Is it possible her abductor knew who she was?"

"No, I don't believe so. Because she was on holiday, her powers wouldn't have functioned at full capacity. Like me, she would have been cloaked in appearance, but also—just as my wings are disguised—her power would have been dulled." I cleared my throat and explained, "You see, Furies no longer police humans as we once did. Only under the most dire of circumstances are we permitted to intervene. And even then, it's usually I who is sent. Murder is my specialty. So the cloaking, combined with her rare use of her abilities and the bright lights of this city, likely rendered her incapacitated."

Lords, I hoped I was wrong about that.

Archer was staring at me. "So you punish murderers?"

"Only when the human laws fail to do so."

Archer nodded slowly. "Yeah, the system isn't perfect." He looked like he wanted to ask me something, then stopped.

"What?"

His eyes glimmered like those of a child with a new play-mate. "I was just wondering, and, well, I don't know the rules, but can you tell me any cases you worked on? What was the last one?"

His question threw me. It had been many years since I had spoken of it. Not since the trial had I told anyone the full story, but we had agreed to keep no secrets, Archer and I. As painful as it was to remember what I had done, what *he* had done, it might be therapeutic. That was another lesson Athena had tried to teach me: purging myself of grief and anger through talking or writing about the times that tried me. Perhaps relaying the actions that had led me to be banned from the mortal realm—and the Fates to put me on indefinite probation—to a lawman was just what I needed. I had blamed the mortal police and their incompetence for so long that the anger had turned to hatred, and the hatred had transformed into suffering. And while my fury had served me well over the years, the suffering had only heavied my heart.

I was tired of carrying the extra weight around.

I closed my eyes, imagined the rushing river for a moment, and began.

Chapter 18

"The human records show that it began in 1967. That's when they believe he committed his first sexual assault on a boy."

Archer sank into an oversized chair, listening intently.

"Assault isn't my domain, as I've told you, but the man was brutal. Torturous, and from experience, I knew he would get much, much worse." I recalled the day Hades brought the case to our attention. It was Alecto who had first tracked him, and later Meg. The man was married by then, and infidelity was Meg's area, for he committed that crime too. They tracked him from Olympus, for the crime was reported to the mortal authorities, and we felt certain he would have been arrested for molesting the boy. He was so careless.

"He was a business owner. Well respected in the community. A member of a club called Jaycees. He was involved in political affairs. He volunteered, spearheaded fund-raising projects, supplied free food to club members and neighbors from the restaurant he owned." I paused, catching my breath. My fury was bubbling. "But the signs were there. He had drinking parties in his basement for the teenage boys who worked for him." I looked at Archer. "People really should be more mindful of who their children associate with."

Archer said, "I couldn't agree more."

I continued. "We were anticipating the man's imprisonment, thrilled that he would likely be stopped before he hurt another child. Of course he denied it, and folks rallied around him. No one wanted to believe that a man of such a high caliber was capable of such a vicious act." I gazed out the window at the lights. "Humans never want to believe that evil can hide in plain sight. They want to believe the bogeyman wears a mask. They want to believe they can trust their neighbors, their teachers, their family members with their most precious commodities—their children." I paused, thinking of my niece and nephew. How soft their skin was, how trusting their little eyes were, the way they always smelled of sugar and moonlight.

"So what happened?" Archer asked quietly.

"He was arrested, convicted, and sentenced to ten years in the penitentiary."

"And?"

"And if that sentence had held, if the man had not been a model prisoner, if the parole board had not released him just eighteen months later, thirty-three young boys and men would be alive today."

Archer's face drained of all color. "No."

"Oh yes, Archer."

He blew out a sigh and looked down. Almost to himself, he said, "No wonder you don't trust cops." He lifted his head after a moment. "So when did you step in?"

"When he graduated to murder, I was sent to track him here, in the mortal world. I used all my powers to try to get him to repent, to no avail. I followed him everywhere, hounded him, wailed at him, interrupted his dreams, fed him waking nightmares, but nothing worked. He was immune to me. A rarity in my line of work. It wasn't easy watching the police fail to connect him to murder after murder. I finally began leaving clues as best I could, both on the victims' bodies and in his home: planting receipts placing him at the scene of the crime or possessions the victims owned, even convincing witnesses that they had seen the man with his prey. When yet another victim reported an assault and the police believed the suspect's word that it was consensual, I finally snapped."

"What did you do?"

I sighed, not wanting to tell him. Not wanting to relive the memory. After a while, I said, "I confronted him one night. Threatened him. Showed him images of Tartarus in his mind, but he didn't care. He taunted me, just as he had taunted the police. Do you know he would actually invite them to dine with him while he was under surveillance?" I shook my head at the frustration of the case.

"Jesus. I bet they wanted to kill him."

I nodded. "After he was finished laughing at me, he said, 'You know, clowns can get away with murder.' That's when I strangled him with my bare hands."

Archer was staring at me, mouth agape.

"You'd be surprised how much strength is bottled up in fury," I said. "I wanted to kill him just for making me track him to Chuck E. Cheese's." I poured some water. "And for making me watch his absurd clown shows, entertaining at children's hospitals, if you can believe it."

At this, Archer perked up. "Wait a minute. Are you talking about John Wayne Gacy?"

"You know him?"

"The entire country knows who he is." He thought a moment. "But he was executed."

"That's true. After what I had done, the Fates stepped in. They decided that it was best to let the mortal law dictate his punishment. They returned his soul to his body and put me on trial for murder. My mistake could have had immeasurable consequences in the human realm. That's when the Fates changed the laws. We simply don't track humans anymore. Only gods. He was caught a year later by the local police, tried, and eventually executed."

"Seems like they would have let you slide. You probably saved lives."

I had heard that perspective from my sisters and from Hades. But the truth was, what I had done made me no better than he was. It wasn't my place to take a life. That was the Fates' job. I could have unraveled our entire system by killing a mortal. Who knows how many strings would have been cut, crossed, or knotted if Atropos hadn't cleaned up my crime? I was lucky they were watching. The tracking system for assignments hadn't been implemented then. I might never have made it home.

And what would that have meant for the mortals? Would my fury have morphed into the evil I'd spent my life fighting?

To Archer, I said, "Laws are stricter in Olympus."

We spent the rest of the afternoon going over the files and what Archer had learned in his investigation. Unfortunately, it wasn't much. We also studied the list of gods and goddesses in the area. Again, not too many. There was Rumour, whom I despised for her barbed tongue and malicious intent; Molpe, a Siren performing in a show; and Thalia, one of the Graces, who was assisting some comedian.

After we ordered some sandwiches, Archer looked at his watch. "You better get ready soon. It's almost showtime."

I groaned, ate as slowly as possible, and then got up to crawl into that ridiculous prophylactic the Shadow Bar dubbed a uniform.

The purchases from the professional shopper were still in the bag on the bed. When I opened it up, a note was resting on top of the pile of shirts, pants, shoes, and underthings.

It said, *Meet me by the Jupiter pool at 6 p.m. It's urgent.*

It was simply signed *Stacy.*

Why did that name ring familiar?

Chapter 19

He had another prison dream when he took a nap. The kind that jolted him out of bed, his clothes stuck to his sweat-stained body, his hands trembling, It wasn't the place itself that was bad—he had made many friends there, friends who shared similar interests. It was the fear of never being able to satisfy the hunger again. Trapped in the endless abyss under lockdown, he had turned to fantasy, daydreams, and writing to satiate his cravings.

It wasn't enough, but it was something.

Now that he was out, he didn't have to daydream anymore. He was free to do as he pleased.

He shuffled to the bathroom and took a leak in the dirty toilet, splashing a few drops on the floor because he wasn't awake yet. He thought maybe he should make one of his playmates clean the place. Maybe the one with the big tits. His partner would be pleased with that.

He washed his hands, shut off the bathroom light, and went to check on the women.

The one he had killed was still in the closet. He'd have to do something about that soon, before she started to smell. The other four were all tied to their respective mattresses. He had fed them, given them water and french fries left over from his lunch. He needed them to stay strong for the plan to work. It was probably time for a bathroom break. He wasn't an animal, after all. He treated his treasures with compassion.

Except that one with the foul mouth and the temper. He couldn't believe the stream of obscenities that poured from her lips. Disgraceful. He decided then that she needed some denial therapy. He hadn't fed her as he had the others. She needed weakening.

He heard something when he stepped over to her. A mumbling, a faint squeak. No, wait—that wasn't it. She was speaking. Her eyes were shut tight, her mouth still gagged, yet somehow she was speaking. No, that wasn't exactly what he was hearing.

She was chanting.

He strained to hear the words, but it sounded like gibberish to him.

"Stop that!" he yelled.

She opened both her eyes. They were swirls of light, and he could have sworn he saw an image inside them. What was that? A river? Was that a boat?

He stepped closer, and she snapped them shut.

That's it, he thought. This bitch gave him the creeps with those eyes. He couldn't kill her, because he was still short a cast member.

He decided there was only one choice. He grabbed the knife.

Chapter 20

I emerged from my bedroom wearing the skintight catsuit, black heels, and an overcoat.

Archer was downstairs, fiddling with the laptop. I explained to him that I was off to meet a woman named Stacy.

"What are you talking about?" he asked. "Who the hell is Stacy?"

I told him about the shade in the Seahorse Lounge and my encounter with the redhead.

"Hang on," Archer said. "I'm going with you."

"I think I can handle a harmless woman," I said, irritated. This hovering business was growing tiresome.

"You know nothing about this woman. What if it's a setup?"

"Archer, I'm growing tired of you questioning my judgment. I know mortals. There is nothing dangerous or even suspicious about this person. Perhaps she saw something; perhaps, because I look so much like my sister, she was reminded of Alecto. Perhaps she saw who took her."

Archer looked doubtful. It was a quarter to six. The Jupiter pool was all the way on the other side of the hotel. If I was going to be on time, I had to leave now.

"If you're so concerned, look her up on the Internet laptop. It seems to be a wealth of information."

"Do you have a last name?"

"No."

"Well, then I can't Google her, can I?"

Google her? That sounded vulgar. What did he mean by that?

He must have seen the cloud of confusion on my face. He explained, "Research. It means research. I need a last name. I can't just type in 'redheads named Stacy.'"

Oh. I hadn't considered that. We had no use for surnames in Olympus.

"Fine, you may accompany me." I said. "But stay out of sight until I've finished speaking with her."

Archer grumbled incoherently, and we left the suite.

She was standing near a row of spiky trees when I got there. The sun was just dipping beneath the horizon, staining the sky a vicious mixture of flame red, burnt orange, and magenta. The other pools I had passed on the way to meet the empath were much more populated. There were women in skimpy bikinis sunbathing, men in shorts and flip-flops drinking beer, children splashing their parents, and servants carrying trays of food and beverages to private cabanas shaded away from the sunlight. The Jupiter pool was situated in a quiet corner. It was empty of swimmers, and its wall of greenery provided privacy.

She seemed much more relaxed than when I had met her earlier. She was wearing a sundress and flat sandals, her hair was pulled back in a neat ponytail, and she wore little makeup. She fiddled with a device in her hand.

"Stacy?" I asked.

She looked up, smiled. "Hi there. Glad you could make it." She held up the gadget. "My grandmother. She didn't want me to go on this trip, so she's determined to be a pain in the ass until I check in. Just give me a minute to text her."

I nodded. What was texting? Was that like typing? Was that a pocket computer she was carrying?

The woman's fingers flew across the electronic device, which was no bigger than a deck of cards. Then she slipped it into her pocket and faced me. She glanced around the area. The nearest humans were several feet away.

"If I'm wrong, I'd just like to say I'm sorry for dragging you here."

I nodded.

"Is your name Tisiphone?" she asked.

I noticed she didn't shake my hand, which was the customary greeting among mortals. Odd, but I was grateful. If she had tried to touch me, I would not have allowed it anyway. As an empath she would be flooded with thousands of images of the mortals I had disciplined over the centuries. And no human should have to bear that.

"It is."

"Okay, then. I have a message for you." She reached into the other pocket of her dress and pulled out a cocktail napkin. She was about to read what it said, but then she stopped. "Maybe I should explain something first. Earlier, the man you saw—"

I held up my hand. "You're an empath for shades, I know."

She wrinkled her brow. "An empath for shades?"

"Ghosts. I believe you call them ghosts."

Her eyes widened a bit as she studied me, and I nearly kicked myself. *Why did I say that?* That's what all mortals called the dead.

I rushed to explain. "I'm not from around here." I hoped she would take that to mean that I was from another part of the human world. Russia, perhaps.

She raised an eyebrow. "Uh-huh. I got that."

Oh Lords, Tisiphone, hold your tongue.

"Anyway," she said, eyeing me once more, before her gaze flicked to the napkin, "the message is from Cicely Barnes. Ring a bell?"

Cicely Barnes. That was the student from Chicago. "You saw her? She escaped?"

This startled her. "Escaped? Escaped from where?"

Again, Tisi, shut your mouth. "Please, continue."

Stacy's eyes darkened. What did she know? And what had I just revealed to her?

"She came to me as a spirit...er, shade. She said your sister is safe, but not for long." Stacy met my eyes. "Time is different for ghosts. Maybe you know that."

I kept my gaze steady. Cicely was dead. Which meant her captor was losing control. Which meant all of them—Alex included—could be killed at any moment. Unless...was that the plan? A sacrifice a day until the eclipse?

If that was the case, then what was the grand finale?

"I'll take that as a yes." She looked back at the note. "She said there were three others besides your sister. And she kept saying 'he': 'he took us,' 'he tied us up.'"

"Did she say where?"

"No." She stepped forward. "Look, is there someone else I need to tell? Should I call the police?"

"I am the police," I said.

Stacy cocked her head. The look on her face told me she knew that wasn't quite accurate. She crossed her arms, a bemused smile on her face. "Really? A cop who sees spirits. That should come in handy."

"I'm not exactly a local enforcement officer. I'm more of a...justice seeker, if you will."

She looked at me for an uncomfortably long time.

"No kidding. So am I. In fact, my last name is Justice."

I smiled at her. I rather liked this mortal. "Did she say anything else?"

Stacy took a deep breath. "Here's where it gets tricky, Tisiphone. Something…geez, how do I say this?" She looked toward the sky, then to me again. "Took her."

I shot her a curious look. "What do you mean?"

"I mean, if I hadn't seen it with my own eyes, I never would have believed it." She met my eyes. "And I've seen a lot of crazy things."

"What did it look like?" Never had I heard of anything pulling a shade into the Underworld. They went willingly or not at all.

Someone plunged into the pool and splashed Stacy from head to toe. The shock of the water made her suck in her breath. She rubbed her eyes and shook out her hands. Then she pulled the handheld contraption from her pocket to examine it. It was wet. "Dammit!"

She turned to find a man with no neck, yellow hair, and brown trunks emerging from the pool. "Really, SpongeBob? Thirty-six pools in this place, and you have to cannonball right next to us?"

The man shrugged and offered her a towel.

She glared at him, grabbed the towel, and dried herself and her phone.

The man shook like a dog, and Stacy gave him a look of disgust. She tossed the towel at his head.

To me she said, "Come on, I'll show you."

She led me through the casino, which was even louder than before, and down a few hallways, until we reached what was supposed to be a replica of Cleopatra's barge, although it didn't come close to the real thing.

She pointed to a painting on the far wall.

I gasped. No, no, no. It was impossible.

I turned to her. "Are you certain?"

Stacy Justice nodded. "Only it was about ten times that size. It grabbed her and flew into the sky. Then it just vanished."

A Stymphalian was the centerpiece of the portrait. What was going on? Was there a breach in the Underworld? Was someone trying to break through the gate? Or was someone calling forth the demons of Tartarus? Feeding the monsters?

Because that would be bad. That would be hell on Earth.

I had to alert the gods. Had to arm myself.

"Are you all right?" Stacy asked.

"Yes, I'm fine." I looked at the woman. I could have kissed her. She had confirmed that I had seen that bird.

But why hadn't Archer? Having come from the Underworld, he should have been able to see it. Perhaps it had flown away before he had gotten a good look.

"Thank you, Stacy Justice. You've been most helpful. Please find me if there is anything else you remember. Or if you receive any more messages."

I didn't bother to give her the room number; obviously Cicely Barnes had given it to her. I started to rush off.

"There is one more thing," she called.

I turned.

"The woman? Cicely? She looked just like you."

"I know," I said.

She nodded, turned on her heel, and faded into a sea of gamblers, her soggy sandals squishing with each step.

Archer stepped out from behind a curve in the wall. His eyes were filled with determination and worry. I wondered if he was thinking the same thing I was thinking.

Was it me the maniac was after? Was I the grand finale? Or just the bait?

Chapter 21

"So he killed Cicely Barnes," Archer said. The anger seeped from his skin like white heat.

"It would appear that way."

"Any more messages from Hecate?"

"No." I was still thinking about all that Stacy Justice had told me: the bird stealing Cicely's soul, the other women seemingly unharmed—not yet.

I told Archer that it was time to contact the gods, that we might need help and certainly needed weapons. This wasn't something we were going to be able to fight on our own. Not with my power fading and surging randomly. We would need to go to that portal in the Forum Shops that Athena had told me about. I couldn't risk having the Graces screw up the signal.

Archer said, "I think you should keep your shift at the bar. Maybe he'll show up tonight. If there is something to the five moons of Pluto and the five women, he'll be looking for new prey."

"And I fit the profile."

Archer stopped walking, looked at me. "I don't know what you're thinking, but we're not going to use you as bait."

"Not bait. A decoy."

"What do you mean?"

"If he does show up, we'll be prepared. You can collect him."

"But what about the drugs or potions, or whatever he used to kidnap the women and make their friends forget all about them? We still don't know what we're dealing with."

"Leave that to me. As soon as the sun goes down, my power should be revived, if this gods-forsaken city has any kind of heart. I have my own magic too, you know. What I need for you to do is secure weapons. I'll need a sword to fight the bird. I'll need time to enchant it as well. And water."

"Where the hell am I going to get a sword?"

I gave him an eye roll. "This is Vegas, Archer—use your imagination."

He considered this. "Right. I prefer bullets in my weapons, so if you don't mind, I'll be getting myself a gun."

"And how will you do that?"

"I know a guy," he said.

"Delivery in twenty minutes or less?"

He smirked. "Not quite. I'll get us a couple of phones too. We need to keep in contact. They're portable now; they fit in your pocket." Archer looked at my outfit. "Well, maybe not *your* pocket."

"Humorous, Archer."

"I think your shift ends around midnight, so I'll see you back at the suite then."

A thought occurred to me. "The laptop. Is there any way to contact the gods via the laptop?"

He shook his head. "Athena made no mention of that. There was no email program that I found. But you just reminded me that I can probably access my own personal email. It's a Google account. Archer Mays at Gmail dot-com."

"I thought you said 'Google' meant 'research.'"

"I was giving you the condensed version."

"Right. So you gather the weapons, check your messages, and get us communication devices, and I'll see what I learn at the Shadow Bar. Anything else?"

I saw something flicker across Archer's face.

"No," he lied.

I grabbed him by the collar and pulled him to the corridor. "What aren't you telling me?"

He stuffed his hands into his pockets. "Thought I might try to find my body. Maybe there're some clues there."

I stepped forward. "Archer, listen to me very closely. That is not a good idea."

"Why not? I find it strange that whoever murdered me left me with my badge and took my wallet. What do you think that means?"

I thought a moment. "Perhaps it was random. A mugging. What's the last thing you remember?"

A swarm of people came rushing past us, laughing, reeking of fruit and wine.

Archer said, "Talking to Clyde about the missing women." He looked at me. "You think I was drugged too?"

"Either that or Clyde has some explaining to do."

"But he didn't seem a bit surprised to see me."

That was true. In fact, Clyde had seemed happy to see Archer the day before. Still, something about that man made my fury flame.

"Look, I'll be careful, I swear. Tommy said he heard I was buried in the desert. Couldn't hurt to take a drive out there. It's a big place, but maybe it'll spark a memory. Maybe my soul will remember what happened, if not my mind."

This was a bad idea all around. If he did find his body, he could very well go mad. It had happened to many a shade who had never made it off this plane. Or he could impede the investigation if he dug up his corpse and the authorities found it. We would need to secure him a brand-new frame. We'd have to start all over, and there wasn't time for that.

I grabbed Archer by the collar and lit the fire in my eyes. "You will not go into the desert."

His eyes glazed over instantly, as if he were entranced.

"I will not go into the desert," he repeated robotically.

I released him immediately. What had just happened? I had always known that my flame could persuade the gods to tell the truth, but it had not been able to force gods or humans to bend to my will. Was it because he had passed through the Underworld?

Or did it have something to do with my touch here, on this plane? Was my gift somehow altered after I had been away so long?

Archer seemed perfectly lucid when he said, "Okay. See you tonight."

I watched him walk away. Perhaps my power here was stronger than I thought.

As soon as I walked through the entrance of the Shadow Bar, I realized I had no idea where I was supposed to go or what I was supposed to do once I got there. The Adonis-looking bartender was behind the bar. He smiled at me and winked. He finished making a drink in a tall glass, garnished it with an orange, and set it in front of a young female who couldn't stop staring at him. He waved me over to the side of the bar.

"Hey, I heard there was a new girl starting tonight. Didn't know it was you."

"And how do you know it now? Perhaps I'm only here for a libation."

"You don't see many trench coats in Vegas except on dancers and strippers. Come on. I'll take you back."

He flipped up the bar top and came out with a set of keys. He led me around the establishment to a side door. He slipped the key inside and twisted the door handle.

There was a door to the left and a floor-to-ceiling curtain to the right. A blond girl was curling her hair in front of a full-length mirror. She had curves that rivaled Aphrodite's and six-inch platform heels on her tiny feet, although she was still shorter than I was.

"Jessica, this is..." The bartender glanced at me. "Sorry, I don't think I got your name."

"Tisiphone," I said.

"That's lovely," said Adonis. "I'm Sam. Well, I'll leave you ladies to it." He shut the door.

Jessica said, "Damn, you're tall." She was eyeing me up and down.

"Yes, I am."

"You're like a giant."

"Actually, giants are far taller. They smell much worse too."

She gave me a perplexed look, as if she had spent her last brain cell trying to get her hair in place.

She frowned. "I don't know why they would put us together. It's going to ruin the flow of the show."

"Or maybe we'll complement each other."

The look on her face indicated she didn't agree.

"So, where did you get your boobs done?" Her voice was high-pitched. Like a seagull's. "They're a little small, but they've got perk. Perk is important."

"They just showed up one day, and I've been carrying them around ever since." This had to be the most mind-numbing conversation of my existence.

Her blue eyes widened. "You mean they're real?"

What did that mean? "Of course."

She laughed. "Honey, no one keeps the original pair. I got a guy in L.A." She tousled her breasts at me. "These are number four."

What?

She thought for a moment. It appeared to be quite a strain. "Can I touch them?"

"Absolutely not." Again, *what?*

She turned to the mirror, pinned a curl in place. "Shy, huh? That won't get you far in Vegas, honey. Sam can hook you up with loose juice if you need it."

"I don't drink."

"Calories, I know, but this isn't booze. It's a special cocktail he created. It's got herbs and shit."

That got my attention.

The music started then. Jessica said, "I'll take the right, you take the left. Come on, we're late!"

She pulled me through the curtain.

Chapter 22

I wasn't a bit surprised when Jessica took the stage on the left. I shifted direction and fell into a slow rhythm, twisting my body to the music.

Sam the bartender. And "loose juice." What was that? Was it a mortal slang term I had yet to be acquainted with, or did it have something to do with the kidnappings?

I watched Jessica move to the waves of the music, trying to imitate her style, knowing I wasn't even close. What she lacked in the processing department, she more than made up for in manufacturing. She created a visual interpretation of sex itself, making love to the music—and, I imagined, also to the audience—right there on the stage.

I suspected I looked more like a newborn giraffe.

Did I really dance better when intoxicated?

After an hour and a half, we took our first break. "We get fifteen minutes. I'm going to grab a smoke. You wanna come?"

My feet were throbbing. I just wanted to sit.

"I think I'll grab something to drink. Maybe check out the audience."

"You can't do that—it's against the rules. Didn't they tell you that?"

Snake spit. How was I going to monitor the clientele if I couldn't sit in the bar?

"Yeah, Clyde's a real asshole." Jessica had her coat on.

"Breaks the illusion, he says. Come on, I'll buy you a soda."

We slipped out the door and circled around to a small bar. I ordered a Gatorade. Jessica ordered a glass of wine.

When we got our drinks, she lit her cigarette. "You know," she said, "you remind me of somebody."

Alex. Had she known Alex?

"I do? Who's that?"

"A girl I danced with last week. She was good. Didn't last." She blew a ring of smoke into the air. "Some girls can't handle it." She looked at me as she said that.

"What happened to her?" I watched her with the attention of a hawk.

She sipped her wine. "No idea. She was here one night and then gone. Only met her the one time." She puffed her cigarette. "She was a real bitch too."

I felt my fury flutter, my wings twitch.

Easy, Tisi, I thought. Alex could be a bitch. Although I didn't like for anyone but Meg or me to say so. Especially a mortal with the intelligence of a goldfish.

"I think she had a sister who danced too," Jessica said. "Clyde said she was a lot more fun."

I chose my next words very carefully. "What do you mean she was fun?"

What did you do, Meg?

"You know, she played to the crowd, got the boys riled up. That sort of thing." Jessica darted her eyes around. She lowered her voice. "Although I think those two had something going. She liked the loose juice, and girls can be a lot more fun on that shit, if you know what I mean."

That was it. Meg had ingested this juice Jessica kept talking about. That's why she had lost Alex—although I couldn't imagine her attraction to Clyde.

"And the sister? She didn't partake of the juice?"

Jessica cocked her head. "You talk funny."

I resisted the urge to yank the stool out from under her.

"No." She shook her head. "She seemed pretty straight. Kinda like you."

"So where do I get this juice?" I asked.

Jessica slid off her stool, put her cigarettes in her pocket. "I told you—Sam. The bartender who showed you to the dressing area."

Adonis? Could he really be behind all this?

We took the stage again, to a much larger crowd. I kept my eyes on Sam as much as possible, which didn't help my dance performance any.

When the crowd—men and women—actually started booing, hissing, and shouting insults and obscenities worse than any Alex had ever invented, I was a little perturbed. But when one ill-mannered man threw a beer bottle and hit Jessica smack in the eye, my fury erupted.

I don't know how it happened. Didn't even believe it was at all possible, but my wings tore through the catsuit one after the other.

The power rushed through me. Fortified my mind, my body, my blood.

That's when I flew through the screen and into the crowd.

Chapter 23

The crowd was shocked, to say the least. And then something extraordinary happened.

They burst into thunderous applause.

Patrons were clinking their glasses on the tabletops, hooting, hollering, whistling, and staring up at me in awe. I circled the room three times, grazing the ceiling, searching the crowd below for the man who had thrown the bottle.

Each wing-flap built my strength. Each lap around the room fed my magic, as the mortals cheered me on. This was how it should be, how it had once been. The humans gazing upon a goddess with respect.

I felt worshipped, and it fed my entire being right down to my core.

I fluttered my wings a few times, floating down to the ground to confront the man who had hurt Jessica. She was still standing behind the torn screen, squinting through her swollen eye.

The man was young, barely in his twenties, with a close-cropped haircut and a goatee.

I said, "Apologize."

He just stared at me. Another man came and stood next to me. He was wearing a shirt that indicated he was security for the establishment. "Let's go, buddy. You're out."

I held my hand up. "Please, wait."

To the man with the cropped hair, I said, "Apologize to the lady."

I gave him precisely one second. Then I grabbed his collar, fired up the flame in my violet eyes, and growled, "Apologize."

The man repeated the word.

"Not to me, jackass, to the lady with the swollen eye. And tip her. Handsomely."

The man turned toward Jessica, said he was sorry, and pulled a note from his wallet with the number 50 on it. He handed it to Sam, who passed it to Jessica.

She grabbed the bill.

The crowd was still raucous. They wanted another show, and I wanted to give it to them. Before I could, however, a voice whispered in my ear. "A word, please."

I turned to see Clyde standing behind me. He handed me my coat. The crowed then booed him.

I followed the manager down three hallways to a sleek black office with lights so bright they hurt my eyes.

"Please, have a seat, Tisiphone."

I folded my wings behind me and sat on a tan chair with black diamonds patterned throughout.

Clyde sat back in his chair. He was wearing an olive suit tonight. He looked like he didn't know what to say.

Finally, I said, "I'm sorry. I'll pay for the screen."

"Damn right you will. You're fired too."

"Technically, I don't actually work for you."

"You know what I mean. What the hell was that?" He stood up, circled around to my back. He came dangerously close to touching my wings.

I shot up out of the chair. "Custom-ordered, Clyde. Don't touch those."

"Were you on a wire? Are they battery powered?"

"You know, Clyde, how about you answer a question for me? What is loose juice, and why are you selling it to your patrons?"

Clyde swallowed hard and flicked his eyes away like a dog caught defecating on a rug. "I don't know what you're talking about."

"Really? Because word on the street is"—*Lords, I hope I used that right*—"that your place is crawling with it." I advanced toward Clyde, catching a hint of the catfish he had had for dinner.

Clyde offered a serpent's smile. "It's just a cocktail, Tisiphone. A Shadow Bar original. Why don't you send Archer on down, and we'll talk man-to-man?"

That was the last thing I expected him to say. So many mortals had no respect for women. It sickened me. The sacrifices, the love, the nurturing that women provided to their world, and this was the kind of treatment they received in return?

Goddesses did not put up with that nonsense.

I grabbed the back of Clyde's head and slammed it into his desk.

He screamed, which only further incited my fury. I twisted his head and bent down to meet his eyes with mine. I lit the fire.

"Tell me about the juice. Where does it come from? What's it for?"

"Okay, okay, I'll tell you," he squealed. "It's a liquid cocktail. No one knows what's in it, but it makes people happy, like Ecstasy does, but amorous too, even energetic, like they're on cocaine. We get it in a concentrated form, and people who ask for something special can get a few drops of it in their drink. Sometimes we dilute it with water and sell it as shots."

I remembered Meg saying something about drinking a blue cocktail. "What color is it?"

"Blue." That was it. Had to be.

"Who do you get it from?"

He closed his eyes. "I don't know."

I slammed his head again.

"I swear, I swear to you, I'm telling the truth."

"Look at me."

He opened his eyes.

"Who is your supplier?"

"I don't know. Sam knows a guy who knows a guy. That's all I know. I don't even have a name."

"I want you to bring Archer your stock. All of it."

"Sure. No problem." His face was smushed into the wood.

"And I want a meeting with Sam. Tomorrow morning. Contact Archer for the details."

"Sure, anything you say."

I let him go.

Clyde rubbed the back of his head. "You going to shut us down?"

Obviously, neither Archer nor I had the authority to do that. I needed Clyde to keep thinking Archer was deep under-cover. I needed him on our side. And I needed Shadow Bar to stay open in case the killer came back.

But I also needed Clyde afraid. Afraid that if he made another wrong move, he'd be imprisoned.

"For now, no. But if I hear you're still selling the juice, and if one more girl goes missing on your watch, I'll be pay-ing you another visit, Clyde."

He nodded. "I never wanted anyone to get hurt. You have to believe me."

The flame was still in my eyes, so I did believe him. Some-how, the flame of truth was finally working on humans. I extinguished it, tucked my wings as best I could, put on my coat, and turned to open the door.

Clyde may not have wanted to hurt anyone, but there was a man out there who did. And he had his hands on my sister.

If I have to tear this city apart, so help me, Hades, I will find you, Alex.

Chapter 24

I was energized and exhausted at the same time. I thought about going outside, finding a quiet place to soak up the darkness, perhaps take a flight high above the city, where I wouldn't be seen, but then I remembered what I was wearing, and that it might be a good idea to touch base with Archer and explain what had happened.

The elevator carried me back to our suite, where I found Archer sitting against the door, a duffel bag at his feet.

He yawned a greeting at me and looked at his watch. "You're early. I thought the gig was supposed to end at midnight."

"I got fired."

That woke him up. He scrambled to his feet. "What happened?"

I was about to tell him, when he interrupted me. "What's that poking out of the back of your coat?" He glanced around the hallway in a paranoid frenzy. "Are those your wings?" he hissed.

"Don't start with me. I've had quite an evening."

The man pursed his lips. He said through gritted teeth, "You have to cover them up."

"Somehow I don't think we'll find virgin tears or cloud ether within a fifty-mile radius of this gods-forsaken city."

"Tisi—"

"Relax, they'll cloak in time. They're still engaged is all. Why are you in the hallway?" Had he forgotten his key?

My moonstone ring lit up. I grazed it.

Stand by for a message.

Archer glanced over his shoulder. "I don't think I can explain it. It's more of a visual thing. You have to see it to believe it."

I checked the ring.

I've sent you a gift to assist in your mission. It should arrive shortly.

—Artemis

I gave Archer a curious glance and slipped my key card into the lock. I looked back at him.

"You first," he said.

I pushed the door open. There, taking up the entire sectional sofa, was the largest black dog I had ever seen. He had pointy ears, a long tail, and a leather-spiked collar. He was sleeping. And snoring.

"Where did it come from?" I asked.

"How the hell should I know?"

At the sound of Archer's voice, the dog woke up. He lifted his watermelon-sized head, tilted it, and blinked his amber-colored eyes.

"I don't think they allow pets in the room," Archer said.

Something about the beast's eyes were familiar.

It wasn't until he tackled me that I knew who he was.

"Cerberus, get off!"

He was nuzzling me, leaving trails of snot across my neck and chest.

Archer stepped around me and set the duffel bag on the table.

At his movement, Cerberus turned his head and growled at him.

Archer backed up. "Yeah, see, that's the thing. I don't think he likes me."

"Cerberus, be kind." I crawled out from beneath the beast.

"He's as big as a tiger. I've never seen a Great Dane that big."

"He isn't a Great Dane. He's Hades's hound, cloaked to resemble a mortal dog."

"Why is he here?" Archer asked.

Cerberus glared at Archer. The lawman took several more steps back.

"Artemis sent him. For protection, I suppose." I cocked my head and looked at Cerberus. "Maybe we've found our bird hunter."

Cerberus wagged his tale and shattered a vase.

I asked, "Has he eaten?"

"Sure, I had a midsized cow delivered about an hour ago."

I shot Archer a warning look. "Order him some food." I stretched, suddenly drained of all energy. "I'm going to bed."

"What? You're kidding, right? You're going to..." He glanced at the hound. "You're leaving me alone with him?"

I headed up the stairs. "Just feed him, Archer. He'll be your buddy for life. He adores elk."

"Elk? Where am I going to get an elk?"

I turned and smiled at him. "You're resourceful, Lawman. You'll think of something."

"Wait, you never told me what happened tonight. Don't you want to know what I did? I got you a sword and some stuff we'll need."

I waved behind my head. "Tomorrow, Archer. It'll wait until tomorrow."

The knock on my door came less than an hour later. "Tisi. Tisi, can I come in? Please?"

"Go away." I had been sleeping soundly, dreaming of flying high over the river Styx, dropping rocks on Charon's head.

The door creaked open. "Tisi, can I sleep in here tonight? Your friend crashed on my bed, and he doesn't look like he's moving anytime soon."

My eyes were still shut. "Kick him off."

"With what, a cattle prod? Tisi, please. I need a lock between him and me."

Oh, for the love of Zeus. "Fine." I pulled back the covers. "Keep your hands to yourself."

"Thank you."

A ray of light shining in from the hallway glinted off his eyes. Archer was wearing striped boxer shorts and a white T-shirt. Before he climbed into the bed, he pulled the T-shirt up and over his head. His shoulders were sculpted, his abdominal muscles defined, his back strong. He had a smooth chest, with a thick scar above his heart. I couldn't help but wonder where it had come from. Who had hurt him? Had he been a child when the wound was fresh? I watched as he turned to shut and lock the door.

He smiled at me as he climbed into bed. "Good night."

"Good night."

He rolled away from me, and something inside me wished he hadn't. There was a part of me that longed to lay my head on his chest, curl my fingers through his hair, trace the lines of his hips. I wanted him to touch me, hold me, kiss me.

I didn't know if it was the city itself, the adrenaline from the flight, or the need to feel that this mission would end well. All I knew at that moment was that I wanted us to get lost in each other.

"Archer?" I whispered.

But he didn't answer.

Chapter 25

It's amazing how a little threat goes a long way. She shut up, finally. The bitch was lucky she still had her eyes.

He drove out to the desert late that night and buried the body. It was cool; there was a west wind coming in from California. He thought about the countless times he had disposed of his playmates. Wondered how many were ever found. He wasn't the type to keep track of his victims or the families. He never took a souvenir, as some did. That was sloppy. Dangerous. The kind of rookie mistake that got you caught.

He never got caught.

Oh, he'd been in prison, true, but not for this. Not for killing. It was a trumped-up charge, if you asked him. He hadn't raped that bitch—that was bullshit. It was her job, for crying out loud. And he had paid her well. Sure, maybe he had been a bit rough, but deep down, she wanted it—he knew she wanted it. He could hear her voice in his head, telling him to hit her. Telling him she was a bad girl who needed to be punished.

Who was he to argue with her?

But he didn't have to worry about that anymore. He was much more careful now that he had his secret weapon.

The shovel was in the trunk. He'd make sure to dispose of it later, then wash the car out pretty thoroughly—something else rookies never remembered. Cleaning was key. Science had made some remarkable advances since he'd been locked up. The tiniest thread could get you pinched. A wad of gum; a fucking straw, for Christ's sake. Couldn't leave that shit lying around. After he had cleaned up the mess of her on the floor, the walls, and the sheets, he had bagged all that shit and burned it. He had bleached the place down, with the help of one of the other girls, and burned the rags too.

It was getting late, but he felt like a drink. Digging holes was hard work. He deserved some fun. He stopped over at his favorite spot, the Shadow Bar, and that's when he saw her.

He couldn't believe his luck! She was perfect. She fit the look his partner insisted on to a tee. And that flying act. Wow. That was the shit, man. That was the coolest show he'd seen in a while.

Too bad she had to die.

That was the breaks, though. You're born, you live, you die. If you're lucky enough to have a little fun along the way, then you're lucky enough.

He was prepared to nab her after her shift, but she cut out early. He had everything with him too. It would have been so easy. He spotted her again, getting on the elevator, but he missed it. So he went back to the bar and waited for her. She didn't show, but Sam gave him her name.

Tisiphone.

Sam said he didn't know when she worked next, but he did say he thought she was a friend of Clyde's. Said she had come in and auditioned on the spot. Said she liked her drink too.

Good. That would make it easier.

Chapter 26

I woke up with Archer's arm around me and something poking me in the back.

"That better be my sword, Archer."

"Huh?" he grumbled. After a moment, he shifted. "Oh. Sorry about that."

He rolled over onto his back. The sheet was draped just above his waist. The scar on his chest was a vicious red slash in the morning light. I leaned over and touched it.

"How did you get that?"

He looked down at his chest, at my hand.

I snapped my hand back. "Sorry."

He smiled lazily. "Don't be. I like it when you touch me like that. Sure beats getting sucker-punched."

I pretended to punch him. He grabbed my hand playfully, and our eyes locked. I stopped breathing for a moment, stopped thinking. The world melted away, and it was just the two of us in that great big bed. I leaned forward.

Cerberus barked, and the spell broke.

Archer sat up. He touched his scar. "That was a parting gift from my ex-wife."

I was stunned. "She stabbed you?"

"Yep." He got out of bed and put his shirt on. "Said I was always choosing my job over her. She was drunk. Things got ugly. I took her keys when she tried to drive home from the restaurant where we were having dinner. She grabbed a steak knife and ruined my best shirt. The next day, I told her I wanted a divorce."

He sounded melancholy.

"I'm sorry," I said.

"It was for the best. She was never going to stop drinking, and I was never going to stop being an agent. We were both miserable."

"And that's when you took to drink?" I asked.

He hesitated before he spoke again. "Actually, I never did that. I just said that because I didn't want to tell you that Cheryl was an alcoholic."

"Why not?" Did he still love her? Did he still think about her?

Archer sighed. "I guess it's because I protected her for so long. Took care of her for so long. It's a habit that's hard to break. Even after that person dies."

"She died?" That meant she must have been somewhere in the Underworld.

"Wrapped her car around a tree a year after our divorce was final. She told me she was trying to quit drinking the day before. Said she wanted to reconcile. I believed her. Until I got that phone call."

How awful. First she lost Archer, then her life. To not get a second chance to battle your demons, to rectify your mistakes, was the cruelest form of fate.

"It was a long time ago, Tisi. And I'm dead, remember?" Archer said when I grew quiet.

"You could find her. In the Underworld. I could help you." I didn't really want to, but if it eased his suffering, I would.

Archer stared at me for a long while. His voice was softer when he said, "I buried those ghosts a long time ago,

Tisiphone. I am not a man who looks back. I believe in starting with what's right in front of me and moving forward."

I didn't say anything. I was speechless.

He pointed at the door. "Now, there's a dog the size of a
garbage truck behind this door who wants to sink his teeth
into my ass. So are you going to escort me past Cujo so I can
take a shower and get dressed?"

I didn't know who Cujo was, but I climbed out of bed
anyway and padded over to the door.

"Hey, your wings. I can't see them anymore," Archer said.

I turned to check my reflection in the mirror.

He was right. They were cloaked again. I didn't know
how Hecate's potions worked, but I was relieved. Not only
because they were hidden, but because I knew I could call
on them if need be.

When I opened the door, Cerberus was sitting there, still
as a gargoyle, gently wagging his tail.

I patted his head and pointed to Archer. "Good guy. He's
on our side, all right, Cerberus?"

The dog swung his giant head toward my partner. He
looked doubtful, even a bit disappointed, but he slunk off
anyway.

Archer thanked me and headed for his room. I had just
opened the dresser drawer to gather clothing for the day,
when I heard. "Aw, dammit! He peed on my bed!"

I left Archer to bond with our new roommate while I
showered and dressed.

Twenty minutes later, wearing jeans, boots, and a black
tank top, I joined the two of them in the common area.

Cerberus had his head in Archer's lap. The man was gently
stroking the hound's fur as he watched the morning newscast.
A soft sigh slipped through the jowls of the beast.

I eyed Archer suspiciously and parked my hands on my hips. "That was fast."

"I gave him a beer. Three, actually. He loves the stuff."

I rolled my eyes and grabbed the room-service menu. "Did you at least let him out to do his business first?"

"He already did his business on my bed. Besides, I couldn't find a leash."

"You don't leash a hound of Hades. It's undignified. You just let him out. He'll find his way."

"I don't think they allow pets. We could get ourselves kicked out of here. Not to mention there are leash laws in Las Vegas."

I peeked over the menu at Archer. "And who would stop him?"

Archer looked at Cerberus. "Good point." The dog shifted his head to the side, indicating he wanted his left ear scratched. Archer obliged.

I picked up the telephone. "Would you like an omelet?"
"Sure. Western."

I ordered two omelets, six orders of sausage, eight orders of bacon, and two dozen scrambled eggs. Plus coffee and Gatorade.

Archer said, "I bought Gatorade."

I canceled the Gatorade and thanked the person on the other end of the phone.

Archer told me the Gatorade was in the refrigerator. I opened it and discovered the juice in every color of the rainbow. I looked at Archer.

It was so thoughtful. There weren't many in my life who were that considerate of my wants and needs.

"Thank you."

"No problem. Check the duffel bag."

I unzipped the black-and-blue bag and saw two silver, electronic-looking devices with numbers on the top of them. I pulled them out and set them on the table.

"Those are called cell phones. So we can stay connected. They're prepaid phones, so you just buy them at the store, no need to sign a contract or anything. No bells and whistles, but they'll do for our purposes."

I had no idea what he was talking about or how to use the device, but the concept appealed to me. Beneath the phones was a firearm, for Archer, I assumed, and a sword for me. I extracted the sword from the bag. It wasn't a large sword, and not nearly as heavy as I was used to, but after I enchanted it, it would conform to my hand, surge with my flesh, and become a part of me.

"Is it okay? I got it at Excalibur."

I smiled at Archer. He was wearing khaki shorts and a button-down shirt with blue waves running through it that brought out the green in his hazel eyes.

"It's perfect."

I ran my hand along the shiny blade of the sword. The hilt was a dragon's tail, the pommel its head, and the guard its wing. The dragon's head was punctuated with one purple eye.

We had two traits in common, the sword and I. Making it my own should not be a problem.

I had my sword and my wings. I was ready for battle.

"So, Sassy, you want to tell me what happened last night?" Archer asked.

I placed the sword on the table and grabbed a Gatorade just as our food arrived. Two carts full. I asked the delivery person to leave the food outside so he wouldn't see the hound.

After he left, I wheeled it in. Archer set the trays on the table while I fed Cerberus. He was a slow eater, and he took his food lying down.

As we ate, I explained to Archer about Jessica and how she had known my sisters, and about the man who threw the beer bottle and how that had ignited my fury.

Archer was slack-jawed when I finished. "You flew? Right through the screen?"

"That's not all." I sprinkled pepper on my potatoes. Archer dug into his omelet.

I took a few bites of potatoes. They were crisp on the outside and tender on the inside. I wiped my mouth with a cloth napkin before I told Archer about Clyde, Sam, and the loose juice.

Archer got up to grab a pad of paper and a pen from the desk on the far wall. He jotted down a few notes, asked a few questions, then piled a forkful of potatoes into his mouth. He sat there, chewing and stewing.

I cut into my omelet. The cheese oozed out, and I spooned it up with my toast and ate it. It was delicious.

"That son of a bitch," Archer said. "He's got women disappearing from his bar, and he's the one supplying the psycho who's taking them with the drugs?"

"It seems so. He isn't the brightest man. Perhaps he didn't make the connection." I sipped my Gatorade.

"Or maybe he's the guy."

I thought about slamming Clyde's head into his own desk and how he had begged me to stop. I didn't think he had the stomach for murder.

I took a bite of my omelet.

"What? You've got that look you get when you think you should tell me something but you don't really want to tell me."

So I did. I told him about threatening Clyde and the nice lump I had given him.

Archer smiled and shook his head.

"You're not mad?" I asked.

"Hell no. That asshole deserved it." He buttered a piece of toast. "I probably would have done the same thing." He winked at me.

At that moment, I truly felt like we were a team.

The phone rang.

Archer picked it up. "Hey, Clyde, you piece of shit, we were just talking about you."

I had almost forgotten—I had demanded a meeting with Sam this morning.

I glanced at the television set, enjoying my breakfast, as Archer spoke with Clyde. There was a mousy-haired woman standing in front of what looked like an ancient ruin. She was talking about some archeological expedition and the "find of the century." The woman motioned behind her, and the camera zoomed in on a cave surrounded by pillars and a stone doorway. The mouth of the opening was emitting steam in a steady stream.

I turned up the volume.

"Archeologists in Turkey have uncovered what they believe is the mythological Pluto's Gate, or the Gate to Hell." The woman glanced at a card in her hand. "The expedition unveiled ancient remains of a pool, a temple dedicated to the deities of the Underworld, and steps leading to the cave—which, it is important to note, still emits lethal gases."

I dropped my fork. It skipped across my plate and onto the floor.

Oh. My. Gods.

They found it.

And—worse—they opened it.

Chapter 27

Archer hung up the phone, and I heard him go upstairs. The water ran for a few minutes; then he came back down. "Sam will be waiting for us downstairs in half an hour."

I turned around to face him. Something about the way I looked made him ask, "What is it? What's wrong?"

"Remember that gate I told you about? The doorway to the Underworld?" I raised the volume on the television and pointed.

The reporter was still talking as the graphic of a scroll appeared on the screen. It was populated with a curvy text. "The Greek geographer Strabo once wrote, 'This space is full of a vapor so misty and dense that one can scarcely see the ground. Any animal that passes inside meets instant death. I threw in sparrows and they immediately breathed their last and fell.'"

The reporter paused as the graphic disappeared. "Indeed, the professor who led the expedition stated that several birds died from carbon dioxide poisoning as they flew too close to the warm opening of the underground cave. Because of these fatal gases, the team has decided to seal up the opening."

The camera cut to an image of men wearing gas masks stacking stones into the doorway.

That was good news, at least. But was it too little too late? I hoped not.

Archer swung his head to me. "That's the gate? The one you said was locked up tight from both sides? The one you said Hades himself couldn't open?"

"Yes."

"Well, that can't be good." He sighed and slid his eyes to the screen. "I guess there is no such thing as an inescapable prison."

"It appears that way."

"So what does it mean?"

What did it mean? Was there a breach in the Underworld? A betrayer among the gods? Or was it possible—and this was what I feared most—that with Alecto taken and me here in this realm, our defenses were weakened? Could a mortal have broken through our barriers from this side to call forth the demons of Tartarus?

For what purpose? Did it have to do with the upcoming eclipse? And what, if anything, had this to do with the five-moon ritual and the women?

I explained it to Archer as best I could. "That gate, that opening, leads to Avernus. It's a wide lake with underwater caves that connect to Tartarus."

"Where the bad guys go."

"Precisely. Men with souls so black, they could never be cleansed. Monsters with insatiable appetites for the flesh of gods and mortals, betrayers of the gods and our laws who could never be trusted again." I began pacing the room. "The good news is that the waters of Avernus are so tainted, so toxic, that very few who have tried to escape have ever survived the journey."

"What's the bad news?"

I looked up toward the ceiling, recalling the Stymphalian I had seen the other day. "The bad news is that the ones who can escape are the epitome of your worst nightmare."

Archer sat down, tapping his fingers on the table. "Okay, so we know the gate was opened and they are closing it as we speak. How can we know if any damage was done?"

"I will make contact with the gods through the statue in the Forum Shops. Athena said I could reach Apollo, Dionysus, and Aphrodite there." I touched the moonstone ring, recalling how Hecate had instructed me to open the clasp to send a signal to the gods. "I will alert them to the situation, and they will take an inventory of the residents of Tartarus. If anyone or anything is missing, we should know about it within minutes."

"What can I do?" Archer asked.

I flicked my eyes from the television screen to the laptop. "Is there any way you can find more video of the excavation in the Google information center? Perhaps I could study it. Perhaps I might see something."

"Sure."

I frowned, thinking of the meeting with Sam. If I could talk to him, I was certain he would reveal to me all he knew of the drug supplier. "Do you think you'll have any trouble getting the truth from Sam about the loose juice?"

Archer flashed his badge. "A pretty boy like that doesn't want to go to prison. I'll threaten him with accessory to kidnapping and murder. Shouldn't be an issue." He raised an eyebrow as if a thought had occurred to him. "I think after that I'll pay Tommy a little visit. Drugs are his specialty. If there's a new supplier in town, he'll probably know who it is."

"And once you find the supplier, we can find Cicely's killer."

"If the killer is getting the juice straight from the tap, then yes."

I grabbed the sword and slipped it through my belt loop. It was a snug fit, but it would soon be enchanted. As soon as

I was in the presence of a high god, even a representative of that god such as could be spotted all over this hotel, it would conform to my flesh.

Archer checked his weapon, then secured it in the back of his shorts. He kept his shirt loose over his waistline.

"So, what do you want to do with Black Beauty over here?" He pointed to Cerberus.

"He can come with me."

Archer looked from me to the dog to the sword. "Don't you think you'll be a bit conspicuous?"

I grabbed some currency from the safe just in case. "Like you said, Archer, this is Vegas."

"Yeah, but I still don't know if they allow dogs in here."

"That's all right. Cerberus has his own talent." I snapped my fingers, and the hellhound transformed into a stone statue instantly.

Archer lifted one eyebrow. "That ought to come in handy."

I snapped my fingers again, and the beast livened.

"You ready?" Archer asked.

"Ready."

He handed me my portable telephone. "I programmed my number and the number to the hotel into the phone. You just push this button here." He showed me how to contact him, and his phone rang. He lifted it to his ear and motioned for me to do the same. He said a few words that I could hear clearly through the speaker.

"Got it." I cut the connection and pocketed the phone.

"I'll call you when I'm done. We can meet back here."

"Agreed."

He looked at his watch. "I have a few minutes before my meeting with Sam. You go ahead. I'll look for the video."

I turned to open the door, but he grabbed both my arms and pulled me to him. His gaze was penetrating, serious. I could smell the spearmint on his breath from his toothpaste. For a moment, I thought he might kiss me, and I welcomed the idea.

"Be careful," he said.

I nodded, afraid my voice would betray my body if I spoke. He opened the door for me, and I slipped out, Cerberus at my side.

Walking down the corridor, Hades's hound at my side and a sword on my hip, I should have felt completely confident in my mission.

But I didn't.

There was a nagging voice inside my head that said, *All hell is about to break loose.*

Chapter 28

I obtained a map of the area the humans called the Forum Shops before Cerberus and I passed over the threshold. The space was massive. There were miles and miles of shops, eateries, and taverns. I couldn't help but wonder why humans needed so many treasures. Then I thought of the people living beneath the city and how they had next to nothing. It seemed immoral, unfair, unlawful, even, that some had so much while others had so little. In Olympus, the high gods had opulent palaces filled with every comfort and treasure imaginable, but their subjects wanted for nothing. Food, shelter, and clothing were provided for every soul of the Underworld, Zeus's realm, and Poseidon's sea.

Why didn't the mortal leaders provide for their people?

For the most part, people ignored us. They assumed, I imagined, that the dog and I were part of some Las Vegas experience. If a person did eye us a little too closely or a child pointed in our direction, I snapped my fingers and Cerberus stilled himself, and that solved the problem.

My first stop was at a fountain that surrounded a likeness of Poseidon. The artist hadn't come close to his height or the length of his beard, but it would do. The sculpture was all white, including the sea god's trident. I knew I couldn't reach him through this portal. It wasn't on the list Athena had provided. But it was the image that counted. I needed one of the three brothers: Hades, Zeus, or Poseidon. And while I noticed a replica of Zeus perched above the fountain on a rock waterfall, he was too far away. I needed the water surrounding the likeness of a god to enchant my dragon-head sword. Poseidon was the optimum choice.

I stilled Cerberus as I stood before the sea god. There were giant fish statues surrounding him, plus a mermaid or two and, for some unknown reason, Pegasus, who was completely out of place.

Anyone who knew the flying horse knew he hated water.

There were lots of people milling about, snapping photographs. Some were toying with their portable laptops and portable telephones. Some were tossing pennies into the fountain as an offering to the gods.

I sat down on the ledge that surrounded the sculpture, keeping watch all around me. When I felt certain no one was policing the space, I scooted back, flipped my sword behind me, gripped the handle, and dipped it into the water.

I closed my eyes and beckoned the sea god to bless my blade.

Trying not to move my lips too much, I said, "Poseidon, ruler of the seas and brother of Hades, my lord and leader of the Underworld, consecrate this sword with the power of the pantheon so that I, Tisiphone, dark daughter of the night, may do the bidding of my kingdom."

I felt the rush of the waves before I even opened my eyes. The water bubbled and heated through until my sword surged with the force of the sea and the power of darkness. Two worlds collided at once in my mind's eye—the night kingdom and the mighty sea—until the energy of the two crashed into the mortal realm. The swirling lights of Vegas flashed before me. Images of my sisters here and in the Underworld. Archer, the missing women, and finally an image so black, so dark, so cruel, it could only be a resident of Tartarus. I saw no features. Just teeth, hair, and eyes. Yellow eyes. Behind it, something even darker. A blob of blackness. Sticky and wet, like tar.

Then something bit me.

I stifled a screech and looked down. The dragon that had been fused to my sword blinked her big purple eye at me, then cooed. She lifted her head, licked the blood from my finger until the wound healed, then laid her head back down against the pommel and fell fast asleep. I watched as her body filled with the color of the Aegean Sea. She blew out small puffs of smoke as she breathed.

"I shall call you Indigo."

She fluttered her wing in approval.

It was done.

The next order of business was to head toward the talking statues to contact whichever god would come forward.

When we got there, I was grateful to see that it was out of order. There wasn't a crowd surrounding the sculpture.

Still, I made sure we weren't attracting any attention. Most mortals had their gaze focused on the elaborate shops and beautiful architecture of the space. I had to admit, I found it peaceful walking the Forum Shops. It wasn't nearly as bright or loud as the casinos or the streets of the city.

I lifted the latch on the moonstone ring and first aimed it into the eyes of Apollo. A beam of light shot right through them. I shut the ring and waited.

Nothing happened. Athena had said it might take a while, but I decided to try every other statue anyway.

After what seemed a millennium, Dionysus was the one to answer. He was my last choice, but I supposed a god was better than no god.

He fizzled into full form, and the replica vanished. He was holding a glass of red wine in his chubby hand. This did not surprise me, as he was the god of wine and revelry, but I was hoping he would be sober.

"Tisiphone, my lovely one. How's tricks?"

There was a nymph draped over his shoulders. She had her slender fingers curled into what little hair the god had left.

"Not well, Dionysus. I have news from the mortal realm. I need you to get word to Hades—"

"Have you caught a show yet? I adore Las Vegas. It was my idea, you know. Build a city in the desert, I said; fill it with wine, women, and song, I said." He hiccupped.

"I have no doubt. Dionysus, listen to me—"

"You look tense. Come, have a drink with me, dark daughter."

"Lord, I—"

"I insist." He laughed at something the nymph whispered in his ear. Then he pulled her into his lap and tickled her.

I stepped forward. "Listen to me, you drunk buffoon. This is urgent. I need you to get word to Hades at once!"

He tilted his head back and cupped his ear, swaying a bit. "What's that?" A pause. "Oh, a conga line. Be right there!"

He swayed his drowsy eyes back to me. "Lovely to speak with you, my dear. Please come have a glass of grapes soon."

Then he was gone.

"You useless, wine-soaked, gluttonous pile of hog manure!" I climbed up and kicked the statue. Which served only to injure my toe.

"Now what?" I asked Cerberus, jumping down from the still stone sculptures.

The hound simply stared at me, a trail of spittle hanging from his lip to the floor. There was a water fountain near the statues, so I led him over to it and turned it on.

145

There were always the Graces, I decided. No one else seemed to be answering my call here, although it would be much more difficult to stand there and speak with them, since they were smack in the center of the palace's lobby.

Unless... I scanned the area. It wasn't very crowded, but most who did pass were speaking on their portable telephones. Perhaps I could call on a Grace and pretend to be speaking into the device. It was worth a shot anyway. I took once last glance at Apollo and Aphrodite's likenesses.

They didn't come.

I turned to backtrack my way through the Forum Shops, Cerberus close on my heels, when I heard it.

The distinct call of evil.

It was right behind me.

Chapter 29

"Cerberus," I said quietly, "mind your mistress."

The hound looked at me with fierce eyes, his mouth set in a snarl. He nodded once.

I turned to see the Stymphalian standing there. His gold eyes were cold, hard. They centered on me.

Hungry.

I put my hand on the sword just as a ginger-haired child rushed up to the demon.

"Look, Mommy! A birdie toy."

The child reached out to feed the bird a lick from his ice-cream cone. His mother was too busy scanning the shops to pay attention.

"No!" I shouted.

The child stopped dead in his tracks and burst into tears. He dropped his ice-cream cone, and the bird didn't even blink.

It just stared at me, stuck its long, jagged tongue out, and licked its bronze beak. Then, slowly, the bird's eyes fell on the child.

I stepped forward carefully, not taking my eyes off the bird. "It's quite sharp is all. I wouldn't want him to get hurt." I slid my eyes to the mother. "I'm sure you understand."

She picked up her child, glared at me, and said as she passed, "I take it you don't have children." She rushed off in a huff.

You almost didn't either, woman, I thought.

I wasn't sure what to do. There were some shoppers and some shopkeepers wandering around the marketplace.

In other words, lots of food.

In a flash, the bird whooshed up to the ceiling, flapping its wings so gracefully, it was almost to be admired.

If you didn't know what it was capable of.

It was now or never. I unsheathed my sword, fired up my fury, and chased the bird, my wings strong, to the top of the building. We circled each other, its eyes growing and glowing with each flap of its wings. Cerberus paced down below, keeping track of both of us.

"Cerberus, the neck. The neck is the only thing that's soft."

The bird glanced down at the hound. It fired one of its sharp feathers at Cerberus. For a split second, I was worried it would pierce the dog's throat. But he caught it in his massive jaws and chomped on it. Swallowed it right down.

"Come on, Indigo, I'm counting on you." The little dragon awoke and sputtered.

The bird screeched, a piercing cry that echoed through the space.

By now, we had drawn a crowd of onlookers who thought this was a new performance debuting at the palace.

More prey.

Yet the bird seemed to want only me. I helicoptered around the space, flapping my wings, considering my options.

Who had sent it here? Or had it simply escaped and sought me out to take revenge on me for banishing it to Tartarus?

It dove down, near the statue of Dionysus, Apollo, and Aphrodite, releasing droppings on the gods' heads. They sizzled and melted the statues instantly.

Uh-oh. I had forgotten all about the poison. The bird's excrement was poisonous.

It flapped back up and shot a metal feather at me this time. I batted it away with my sword. I watched as it pierced a plaster wall.

I dove for the bird, sword ready to slice through its crane-like neck, but at the last minute it darted away and fired another feather, which tore into my thigh. I left it there, ignoring the pain, feeling only my fury.

The crowd gasped. There were so many people. Where had they all come from?

The bird must have sensed my concern, for it spotted a weak member of the herd and dove for it. A young lady on a cell phone.

It took off after her, but I was lighter, faster, and I got there first. I scooped her up, then put her back down again. I told her to run, and she did. Behind me, I heard a scream as the bird deposited another dropping, this time on a woman's hand. It looked to have burned her. I could smell the singed flesh.

I couldn't save them all. I had to end this.

"Hey, you overrated piece of scrap metal! Come after me. Or do you prefer the blood of the weaker species?"

The bird looked at me, its eyes molten lava. It hovered.

"What's wrong? Are you chicken?"

Stymphalian birds detested being called chickens.

The bird squawked and blasted me with feather after sharp feather. I managed to smack away one after another with my blade. I heard a window crash, then screams. The humans panicked. The smart ones ran.

The bird looked around the room, seeming to formulate a plan. I caught the eyes of the hound and nodded.

I knew what it was doing. If it couldn't kill me, it would kill someone, anyone.

After a few tense moments, it zeroed in on its prey.

A baby in a stroller.

The mother was pushing the stroller, just entering the area of the talking-gods statue. She hadn't spotted us yet.

The bird zipped its wings back and dive-bombed toward the baby with its spear-like beak.

I flew in front of the stroller, kicked it back, somersaulted, and pointed my sword at the Stymphalian's eyes.

"Indigo, now!"

The dragon breathed a fire so hot, so intense, it melted the bird's beak right into the floor.

The rest of it twirled and crashed, screaming as it fell. The monster fired off three more feathers as it descended, one of which hit me in the shoulder.

But before it could make a final stance, Cerberus sank his teeth into the bird's neck, killing it.

Right before our eyes, and the eyes of every human who stayed to watch the entire display, the bird melted into a heap of liquid metal.

There were cheers, applause.

"That was amazing!" said the woman whose hand I suspected had been burned. She rushed toward me.

I glanced down. It seemed to have healed instantly. But I know I had seen it burn. Smelled it, even.

In Olympus, that wouldn't have happened. She wouldn't have healed. Perhaps here the laws of the Universe worked differently.

People were applauding and congratulating us on a well-done show. Except for the shopkeeper whose window had been smashed. He was looking for the responsible party. I retracted my wings away, sheathed my sword, and called to the hellhound.

As we ran past the statues of the gods, I noticed that they were still melted. My own injuries still pained me.

Did that mean the humans would be spared devastation by a demon on this plane if a god killed it, but the gods themselves would not fare so well?

I wasn't certain. I had never battled the monsters of Tartarus in this realm. But I knew one thing for sure.

We were down one portal to get home.

Chapter 30

He was nervous today. His partner had finally showed up in town, but he hadn't come by to see the girls yet. Said there would be a surprise for him.

He hated surprises. He liked to be the one who did the surprising. Still, it could be something fun for the party. Toys, maybe? Or maybe another girl. That would sure save him a shitload of hassle.

He went to get his to-do list. The playmates had all been fed already. The place was clean. He had gotten the supplies. Looked like that was it. He put the list away.

He wondered how his partner would take it that he'd had to let one go. He would understand, he was sure. His partner knew what it was like. Knew the need. The hunger. You had to feed the beast within, or it would eat you alive.

They'd been working together a long time, and he had done most of the dirty work, after all. His partner owed him. It wasn't easy finding these girls, getting them alone. Not to mention what he had to do to the friends.

Good thing he had his secret weapon.

He ducked his head into the room to see how everyone was doing. Two of the girls were playing cards. They seemed to enjoy the fact that they could still lead a regular life. Of course, he had to chain them, but you could still play gin rummy with the cuffs on. One thing they had to admit: he treated them well.

Except the troublemaker. He hadn't carved her eyes out yet, but he was still thinking about it. The strangest thing was, even the lack of food didn't seem to break her. Nothing did.

Until he had opened the blinds.

She had whipped her head away from that Vegas sun so fast, you'd think it had burned her skin clear off.

So he left them open. Nobody was gonna see her anyway. Not where they were.

And it worked. Before he had done that, he could have sworn the bitch was getting stronger.

How was that possible? How could a girl get stronger when you denied her food, water, and exercise?

She had head-butted him the other day, the fucking whore. He had hauled off and cracked her a good one for that, but she had just looked at him with those creepy eyes like twinkle lights. Damn, did he regret the day he'd picked her up.

She'd had a sister when he found her. But she didn't fit the profile. His partner insisted on a type, for some goddamn reason.

What difference did it make? That's what he wanted to know. Broads were broads. They all bled. They all had holes between their legs that needed fillin'.

But his partner had insisted. And now he was one short, goddammit. But there was time. They had a few days before the plan went down.

He went into the kitchen to fix himself a ham sandwich. His cell phone rang.

His partner was here.

It was time.

Chapter 31

I hurried back to the room to tend to my wounds, while Cerberus went outside to take care of business. My left wing was a bit sore, and I couldn't understand why. Was it because I hadn't been flying much? Was it muscle pain?

Archer was in the room when we arrived. I was surprised to see him, certain the meeting with Sam would have taken longer.

He glanced up from the laptop when I shut the door. He was wearing a smile until he looked at me.

He stood up. "What happened to you?" He approached me, leading me gently to the sofa by my arm. "Come sit down."

I did, right after I pulled Indigo from my belt loop. She was still steaming from the blaze but no longer hot. She was resting peacefully, curled around the hilt of my sword.

Archer looked at the sword. It was apparent that he wanted to ask about our new roommate, but he seemed to decide that question could wait. He reached into the refrigerator and grabbed a red Gatorade. He handed it to me, and I drank the entire bottle in three large gulps.

I felt a little better after that, but my wing was still sore, not to mention my shoulder and my thigh where the metal feathers of the Stymphalian had ripped into my flesh.

Archer's face was contorted into a strange combination of worry and anger. "What happened? Who did this?"

I told him about the bird, the battle, the portal, and the sword as quickly as my lips could move.

He ran a hand through his thick waves. "Jesus Christ, Tisi. You could have been killed."

"But I wasn't."

He knelt down, studied my injuries, contemplating the best way to extract the weapons. Then he looked up at me, a cloud of darkness in his eyes.

"Could that happen? Could you be killed here? I mean, I know you're a goddess and that technically you're immortal, but—" He stopped when he saw the look on my face. "Shit."

"It's not likely when we have our full power and I have been gaining strength." Not to mention using it up as fast as it came. "But yes, Archer. I can be killed in this world."

He scratched his head, turned it away from me for just a moment. When he faced me again after a while, he wore a mask of determination.

"Then let's find your sister and get the hell out of Dodge."

I grinned.

"Why are you smiling?"

"Because I know that one. Hickok uses it all the time."

Archer shook his head, but I saw a smile. He stood up and grabbed my hand. "Come with me, my goddess. Let's get you patched up."

I placed my hand in his. The moment I did, I felt an electric jolt that tingled my skin all the way to my wings. They fluttered.

Archer slid a sideways glance at them. "Oh, hell, it got your wing."

"What?" *Oh no, not my wing! Not my source of power!*

Archer gently lifted a few feathers. "It's not bad. Just looks like a few feathers were clipped."

"A few!" I tried to twist my neck around, but I couldn't see the wound.

"Is that bad?"

"It's not good." I explained that my wings were my source of strength. Even one lost feather weakened me, and without the Fates here to repair it, I was that much less powerful.

"Let's get you into the bathroom, and you can check it in the mirror."

We climbed the stairs together, and Archer led me into the bath. He gathered some towels and wet one down. Then he paused, assessing my wounds. "I'll be right back."

I studied my wings in the mirror. The tank top was bunched up in the middle between them. At home, I had clothing specially fashioned to fit around my wings. If they made such garments here, I was not aware of it. Perhaps I should wear halter tops for the remainder of our mission.

There was just a trickle of blood on the shirt. All my feathers seemed to be there, yet one was lying at an odd angle.

Broken, but not gone. It could be taped. That would help it heal.

Archer came back with two small bottles.

"What's that?" I asked.

"Vodka. We need to disinfect the wound. Those things are metal. You don't know where that bird has been." He unscrewed the cap of one of the bottles.

"No way. I don't want that stuff anywhere near me." I backed up slowly, put my palm up to shield my face.

Archer looked at the bottles, then at me. "You don't drink it, Tisi. I'm going to pour it on you."

I shook my head. "Uh-uh."

"It has to be done."

"No. When I return, Hecate will give me a cleansing potion."

"They could get infected long before that."

I looked at the feather sticking out of my shoulder. It was dull, with specks of white smeared across it. "Looks perfectly clean to me."

Archer smirked. "You're being ridiculous."

I gritted my teeth at him. "I said no."

Archer shifted his stance. "Do you really want to be the goddess who conquered the great Stymphalian only to lose an arm from an infection left by its freaking feather?"

I rolled my eyes. It sounded stupid when he put it that way. "Fine."

He came toward me. "Okay. I'm going to pull the blade out of your shoulder first. Then I'll pour the vodka on it, then cover it with the towel."

"Okay."

He grabbed a washcloth and wrapped it around his hand, then put it on the blade. "Count of three. Ready?"

"Ready."

"One, two, three." Archer pulled the blade out, and it stung like a piranha bite.

"Ow!" I slapped him upside the head.

"Hey! What was that for?"

"Sorry. Instinct. It's what I usually do when someone causes me pain." The wound was throbbing. It wasn't too deep. I didn't think it would need sewing up.

Archer grabbed a vodka bottle. "This might sting." He backed up. "Do not hit me."

I nodded.

"You're going to hit me, aren't you?"

"I might."

"Tell you what—squeeze my hand if it hurts."

"All right."

He gave me his left hand to hold. I held my breath as he poised the bottle.

"Don't look," he said.

I turned my head, he poured the vodka, and I squeezed his hand as hard as I could.

The vodka burned my flesh. "Ow, ow, ow!"

"Yow! Tisi, let go, let go!"

I did.

Archer was white. He shook out his hand and looked at it. "Jesus, I think you broke my finger."

He wiggled his fingers. They didn't appear broken. He grabbed the wet towel with his other hand and told me to hold it against the cut.

After he shook his hand out for a few moments, he said, "One down, one to go." He grabbed another towel, wet it, and reached for the vodka.

I looked at my bloody leg. "Let's just leave that one in there."

Archer cocked his head. "You know, for a Fury, you're acting like a total wuss."

"I don't know what that means, but I'm sure I don't like it." I shot him a hard stare.

"It means stop being a baby and take it like a goddess."

I glared at him. "How dare you call me a baby? I'll have you know I've punished more men than you could ever hope to meet. I've battled demons the likes of which would have you soiling your pants. I've chased monsters that would give you night terrors for all eternity, and I've banned souls to Tartarus so diseased that just one encounter would send you screaming into the night."

Archer just stood there, smirking. "And yet you're afraid of vodka."

Oh, the man could exasperate me! "Just get on with it."

He looked at my jeans. The feather was embedded high in my thigh. Nearly to my hip.

"Pull your pants down."

"I will not."

"Tisi, pull your goddamn pants down so we can get this over with and get on with the business of stopping bad guys."

"Oh, all right!"

I unzipped my jeans and carefully slid them down, lifting them up and over the bird feather.

They fell to the floor, and I stepped out of them. Archer slid his eyes down my legs, pausing briefly on my lacy black panties, and back up again.

I put my hands on my hips. "Just what do you think you're doing?"

He shrugged. "What can I say? I'm a leg man. And I've never seen a pair that went on for quite so many miles."

That tingling sensation filled me again. How could one person be so irritating yet so charming at the same time?

"I don't know if I want to slap you or kiss you," I said.

Archer froze in place. His face took on a color of surprise. "You want to kiss me?"

Damn. Did I say that out loud?

"No. It's the vodka talking."

"You didn't drink any vodka."

I waved my arm. "Doesn't matter. It seeped into my blood through osmosis."

He didn't say anything more, just wore a cocky smile as he held the towel and the bottle and knelt down near my thigh. His face was practically at the level of my panties, and I could not control the pulsating going on beneath them.

I hoped he didn't see it. Or hear it.

He pulled out the feather without warning, cleansed the wound, and held the towel to it. I yelped softly, but this time it didn't hurt nearly as badly. My body was electrified, heated through and through. I glanced down at Archer. He looked up at me, still kneeling, his face still dangerously close to the most sensitive part of me.

Not only was this city draining my power, it was robbing me of good judgment. *Do not get involved with a mortal, Tisi. It can only lead to trouble.*

At least, that's what my head was saying.

My body, apparently, had not received the memo. My nipples hardened as Archer pressed the towel to my wound. He held it there, looking up at me as I gazed down at him. He was so frustratingly sexy. So tender and caring. I had never known a man or god like him.

His breathing grew a bit heavy, his eyes a bit darker, and I couldn't stop staring into them. My lips parted slightly.

Archer kept his eyes focused on mine, his hand still holding the towel to my wound. He grazed his other hand across the outside of my panties, and my heart pounded in my chest. I groaned softly. He cupped my backside, still holding my gaze. When I didn't object, he kissed my inner thigh, one and then the other. He moved to my outer thighs, still holding the towel to my injury. He hesitated, glancing at me again, and I closed my eyes, tilted my head back. Slowly, he kissed his way up the curvature of my body, leaving no crevice untouched. His lips traced my hips, stomach, ribs, until he finally (finally!) reached my breasts.

His hand was still pressed against my thigh, so close to my panties, I felt certain he could hear my body hum.

Without saying a word, Archer curled his other hand through my hair and pressed his lips to mine.

A thousand tiny explosions erupted all over my body as I felt the firm sweetness of his mouth, his lips, his tongue. I didn't want him stop, didn't want him to pull away; I just wanted to feel his body pressed to mine, his skin on my skin. I wanted to feel him inside and out. He could have taken me right there, right on the counter, in the shower, on the marble floor, even, and I wouldn't have protested.

I dropped the towel I was holding to my shoulder, and my arms found their way to his shirt and ripped it open. He moaned softly as I traced the muscles of his chest, his stomach, his hips. I wrapped my good leg around his waist, and I felt the cold barrel of his gun there, but I didn't care. He dropped the towel he was pressing against my thigh and lifted my other leg, careful not to touch the cut. I expanded my wings and cupped them around us like a cocoon. He groaned, louder this time, and pushed me against the wall, kissing and sucking my neck, my breasts, my shoulders, every inch of me that he could reach.

I wanted him. I was more than ready for him to fill me, to feel him inside me. I needed to put out the fire that had been building ever since we'd met.

And just when I thought we were going to, there was a knock at the door.

Chapter 32

Archer whispered, "Damn."

"What?"

"I forgot. Sam had to postpone our little meeting. That's probably him."

"Damn."

He smiled at me and set me down, his chest heaving. He put his hands flat against the wall on either side of my head and said, "I'm not done with you. Not by a long shot."

"Well maybe this was a one-time-only offer."

"Oh, no, I don't think so, Sassy."

Another knock.

Archer sighed. "Better go answer the door."

I nodded at him. He kissed me one last time, sighed, and left the room.

Frustrated, I folded my wings away and took a quick, cold shower. Rummaging around in the bathroom, I found some bandages and patched up my cuts, making a mental note to ask Archer to tape my feather later.

There was a pair of shorts and a baggy T-shirt in the wardrobe, so I threw those on and joined the men in the common room. I had forgotten all about Indigo until I saw her. I picked her up and tucked her behind the sofa, out of Sam's line of view.

The men were sitting at the large table, a notebook between them. There was also a large jar filled with blue liquid.

"Is this all of it?" Archer asked.

"Yes, yes, sir," said Sam.

Archer was wearing his cop face. I had first noticed it when he was talking to Jeremy in the tunnel. He wore it well, and Sam must have thought so too, judging from the nervous way he kept licking his lips.

I pulled up a chair to join them.

Sam smiled weakly at me. "Hi."

"Hello."

Archer was examining the liquid. "And you don't know what's in it?"

"No. It's some huge secret. The guy I get it from, Greg, he never told me."

"Does Greg have a last name?" Archer grabbed a pen.

"I don't know his last name or where he lives, but I can give you his number."

Archer handed Sam the pen, and he scribbled on the pad of paper.

Archer went over to the laptop and turned on the large screen. He pulled up the photographs of the missing women, including Alecto.

Sam flinched.

"You remember these women we talked about, Sam? Remember what I asked you?"

"You asked me if I had served them."

"And what did you say?" Archer's voice was sharp.

"I said I couldn't remember." Sam licked his lips.

I enjoyed watching him squirm.

"You want to revise that statement?"

"N-no, sir. I never saw them."

"What about her?" Archer pointed to Alecto.

Sam looked at the photograph of Alex standing by the three-Graces statue.

Sam knew he couldn't deny it. Alex had danced at the Shadow Bar.

"I think she danced once or twice."

Archer nodded. "Better." He pointed to the photograph of Cicely Barnes. "What about her?"

"No. Never saw her before."

Archer slammed his palm into the table. Even I jumped. I wondered if that was an act for Sam's benefit, sexual frustration, or a combination of the two.

"You expect me to believe that?"

"It's the truth. Look, the juice is strong stuff, man. Some people can't handle it. Maybe she overdosed or something."

Archer put both hands on the desk and looked down. He had a new expression on his face when he stood back up. I wasn't familiar with it. He looked at me. "You know, I never thought of that. Maybe they all overdosed. Maybe they just ran away."

"Yeah, maybe," Sam said, warming up to the idea.

Archer positioned his body in front of Sam's. He crouched down. "Yeah, that could explain everything." In a fit of rage that I didn't see coming, Archer grabbed Sam by the shirt and lifted him out of the chair with one hand. "Except she was murdered last night!" He threw Sam back into the chair.

Sam's cheeks lost all color.

"That's right, you son of a bitch. Her body was found in a Dumpster; she was cut up into little tiny pieces."

That couldn't be true. Archer would have mentioned it to me if the police had found her body, but the tactic worked.

Sam shook his head. "I didn't sign up for this, man. No one was supposed to get hurt."

I leaned forward at this. "What do you mean, no one was supposed to get hurt?"

I glanced at Archer. He pulled a chair over. "You better talk to me, Sam. Because right now you're the only suspect I've got. You know what they do to pretty boys like you in prison?"

"Okay, okay, there is no Greg. I'll tell you everything I know."

Sam started to sweat. Archer grabbed the notepad and the pen.

"A few months ago, when I first started, a guy came into the bar. Said he was looking for some girls. He had a side business, he said."

Archer asked, "What kind of business?"

"Escort service. He said he had a high-end client that paid very well for long-term dates. His job was to find the girls, and if they were interested, he would set up a meeting to introduce them to his client. Said it was a sweet deal for everyone. The client was some super-rich dude. He'd pay for their schooling, clothes, even let them live in his mansion if they wanted." Sam looked at me. "Who wouldn't want that, right?"

I resisted the urge to kick him in the head.

"Uh, anyway." Sam turned back to Archer. "He offered me a finder's fee. A thousand bucks for each girl. Cash. He even paid cash for the drinks. The guy had a real specific type. Black hair, tall, thin. I called him whenever a girl like that would come into the bar. That's when he gave me the loose juice. Said it loosened them up to the idea."

"But you served it to other guests. Even Jessica," I said.

Sam looked at me. "Jessica has an iron liver. Nothing affects that girl." Then he turned to Archer. "The other guests—that was never my idea. When Clyde saw the jar behind the bar, I told him it was a cocktail for a specific customer. It was his idea to spread it around to people who asked for something special. We set a limit, though. One per guest per night."

"And the guy? How much would you give him?" Archer asked.

"As much as he wanted."

Archer sat back and shook his head.

Sam said, "I didn't think it would hurt anyone, I swear."

"So when I came to you, told you the girls went missing, why did you lie to me?"

Sam shrugged. "People come to Vegas to get lost all the time. I thought the rich dude was like a Hugh Hefner or something. Thought he was building a *Playboy* mansion. I thought...I thought the girls wanted to disappear."

"I should kill you just for being stupid," Archer said.

Sam put his head down, then lifted it up. "You don't think they're all dead, do you?"

"For your sake, you better hope not."

Sam swallowed hard.

"What's this man's real name?" I asked.

"I don't know, I swear to God. All I have is his number. He wouldn't tell me his name."

"I take it that's not the number you just wrote down."

Sam shook his head. "That's my ex-girlfriend's number."

"Charming," I said.

"What does he look like?" asked Archer.

"My height. Average build. Shaves his head bald but wears a hat a lot. Light skin."

Archer frowned. "Any distinguishing features? Tattoos? Birthmarks?"

Sam thought a moment. "The only thing I noticed was his eyebrow. He has one eyebrow—the left, I think—that's slashed through with a scar. Almost like he has three of them."

Archer jotted something down. "Call him."

Sam looked from me to the lawman. "Now?"

"Right now," said Archer.

Sam pulled out a portable phone. He stopped. "There's one more thing."

"What?" asked Archer.

Sam wiped a trail of sweat from his brow. "He came in last night." He looked at me. "He asked about you. You're his type."

"What did you tell him?" I asked.

"Just your name. I didn't say you were a cop or anything."

A thought occurred to me. "Sam, did you slip me that loose juice when you served me martinis?"

"No way. You acted like you were on it, though."

I looked at Archer. Clyde? Had he put it in my cocktail? Or was it just vodka that affected me so poorly?

Archer said, "Call him. Tell him you got a girl for his client. Tell him to come to the bar tonight."

Sam picked up the phone.

Chapter 33

After Sam left, Archer sat back in his chair, deep in thought.

"What are you thinking?" I asked him.

"I'm thinking we're finally getting somewhere. I'm thinking that whoever took the girls might have murdered me."

I met his gaze.

"Think about it," he said. "If he was there at the Shadow Bar, maybe he heard something, maybe my questions spooked him."

I considered that. "Then that means you can't be there tonight. I have to do it alone."

Archer shook his head. "No—no way."

"Archer, I can handle a mere mortal," I said. "Besides, I've got backup." I reached for Indigo, and she woke up. She batted her long lashes at Archer and cooed.

Archer leaped from his chair. "What the?" He looked at me. "I knew it looked different, but I didn't know it was... *alive.*"

I waved my finger at him. "Never underestimate a goddess."

Archer stared at Indigo. She yawned and stretched her wings.

"Speaking of goddesses, did you make contact before the portal was toasted? Did you tell anyone about the gate?"

"Yes and no." I told him about that wine-soaked moron, Dionysus. "I'll try again with the Graces statue."

Cerberus scratched at the door then. I let him in. He ran up to take a nap on Archer's bed.

Archer said, "I was able to manipulate a video of that archeological expedition." He walked over to the large screen and touched a few images. Up popped a video of the ancient ruins I had seen earlier at the site of Hades's gate.

"Please turn off the sound if you are able," I said.

Archer hit another button, and the video played. Then he manipulated his fingers and the screen zoomed in on the entrance of the gate I had seen earlier on the newscast.

He said, "Do you see that? Right there. What is that?" He paused the video and pointed to something in the lower-right-hand corner. Something just outside the entrance.

Something with yellow eyes.

"Son of a snake charmer," I whispered. "It's Lamia."

So that's what the vision meant. When I consecrated the sword, those were the yellow eyes I had seen.

So then what was the inky blackness? The tar-like blob?

"Lamia?"

I grabbed a Gatorade—purple this time—and started pacing, thinking, and playing with the cap from my drink. This was bad. This was horrible, in fact. How in Hades's name could they possibly have let her escape?

Archer was waiting for an explanation.

I took a deep breath. "Lamia is one of the worst monsters I, or anyone, has ever known. But she didn't start out that way, as I've said before. It is a process to become a demon. She was once a regal queen, quite beautiful, an enchantress who caught the eye of Zeus. They had a brief affair, and when Hera found out, she was furious. She said it was the last time he would make a fool of her. Said either he could break things off with Lamia or she would leave him and take half the kingdom for herself." I took a swig of the drink. "Zeus begged Hera's forgiveness. Despite his roving eye, he really does love her. He vowed fidelity forever from that moment forward. When he told Lamia that it was over, she cried, she wailed, she begged him to choose her over Hera, all to no avail. Then one night, steeped in a depression so deep she couldn't crawl her way out of it, she drowned her five children. That heinous act blackened her soul, devoured the beautiful woman she was, and transformed the once-regal queen into a twisted creature with the torso of a serpent and the upper body of a woman. The monster took over, and she went on a rampage, feeding on the blood of the young, until I banished her to the bowels of the Underworld."

Archer had the look of a man who had just folded pocket aces. "And now she's here, in this world."

I glanced at the screen. "It appears so."

"Can she—it, whatever—be killed?"

"Now that she's left her only sanction, yes. Let's just hope she doesn't feed in the meantime. She isn't large in stature, but her tongue has the power to lift a bull and her tail can flatten a stone wall with one whack."

"You said before that you weren't sure if something was trying to get out through the gate or if someone wanted to banish something into the Underworld through the gate. What do you think now?"

I looked at the image of Lamia. All I could see were those piss-colored eyes, but I knew there was a ragged mop of hair above them and fangs below them. I knew that her thick torso had slid out through the poisonous vapors unharmed, as only cockroaches and snakes could do. I stared at the screen, remembering the day I had imprisoned her. The day I had warned the gods that if she ever got out, she would kill relentlessly, ruthlessly, and without remorse. The Fates had given me carte blanche to track her to the ends of the earth if need be. "Do not hesitate to destroy her," Atropos had said.

Lamia had been bound, strictly. She had no tasks in Tartarus, as others had. She was sentenced only to listen to the cries of her drowning children over and over again. She was given no leverage. No mercy.

Which meant she was hungry.

And it meant one other thing. "Someone summoned her here. Someone who knows who she is. And someone aided her escape."

Archer said, "Sounds like a good time to call in the cavalry."

"I couldn't agree more."

Archer reached for the notepad. He tapped the pen. "You said she had five children?"

"Yes," I said, catching his meaning. "Oh. You don't suppose..."

"I don't believe in coincidences. Do you?"

I shook my head. "Five women. Five moons. Five months. It has to tie together, but what is it? What could it be?"

"I don't know. I can do some research here while you try to contact headquarters. Maybe I could find more on the spell Hecate warned us about."

I agreed to that arrangement and ran upstairs to change into a halter top. When I came back down, I grabbed some tape from the desk. Archer splinted my broken feather for me, and I locked my wings away, the cloaking spell functional again. I grabbed a granola bar.

Archer asked, "She's never escaped before? Are you sure about that?"

I slipped Indigo through my belt loop. "Yes. Why?"

He shrugged. "I just wondered. She feeds on the young, you said. If she was able to escape now and then, it would explain a lot of mysteries to me." He looked at me. "Horrors, really."

I met his eyes. "I told you, Archer. Evil exists within us. Don't seek answers elsewhere. Look no further than gods and men."

I called to Cerberus, and after he met me in the hallway, I shut the door behind us.

My words echoed in my head as I walked down the hallway. *Gods and men.*

Was there a god working with a mortal? Was that how Lamia had escaped?

I was about to find out.

Chapter 34

His partner was not pleased. Despite all he had done, all he had sacrificed for their plan, his partner wanted only to point out that now they were one girl short.

"The party can't go on without the last girl," said his partner.

He explained about the call from Sam, explained that he needed just a little bit more time, that tonight there would be a new girl waiting for them at the Shadow Bar.

This seemed to appease his partner. He showed his partner the girls he did have, showed him everything he had already set in motion.

His partner smiled.

Redemption! he thought.

They could work together forever. They made a great team. He knew he was worthy. He was in the presence of a mastermind—better than all of them combined. His partner made Jeffrey Dahmer look like a choirboy, and he wanted to work with *him*. He was over the moon.

Soon, it would all fall into place. Soon, he would make his mark on the world. He would become a legend. He would become immortal.

He was fixing a snack for them. A couple of beers, a plate of cheese and crackers. He worried—just for a moment—that the girl might not show tonight. What would he do then? Would his partner leave him? Abandon the whole plan?

He put the thought right out of his mind. Of course not. Loyalty still meant something to some folks. He was certain of it.

He wasn't sure what the surprise was yet, but he felt a bit better about it. He decided that some surprises could be a good thing. Life should include those unexpected moments. That was what made it so much fun.

Except when he turned around—when he saw his partner standing there with that look on his face, something hiding behind him—he thought maybe surprises weren't so good after all.

One of the girls screamed.

The plate of cheese and crackers crashed to the floor.

His partner raised his hand, pointed at the center of his forehead. "I had hopes for you. For us. I thought you would serve me well, but, alas, you have failed me."

He couldn't even scream as his partner peeled the skin right off his body.

Chapter 35

I stood before the statue of the three Graces in the center of the lobby at Caesars Palace. Cerberus was stone-still next to me, and little Indigo was sleeping. Her tail flicked every so often as if she were dreaming.

I opened the moonstone ring and beamed a ray of light into the eyes of the Grace closest to me. Slowly, I made my way around the statues, signaling to all three of them. Then I pulled out my portable telephone, stuck it to my ear, and waited for someone to arrive.

After a while, I heard the voice of Thalia. "Tisiphone, lovely to see you." Her voice was all bubbles and sunshine.

Odd—the statue hadn't moved, hadn't transformed at all, as the replica of Dionysus had.

"Thalia, thank Hades. Listen, I have an urgent message for the lords."

"Why are you talking to the statue, Tisi?"

I paused, looked at the phone in my hand. Had she somehow come through the electronic device? I studied it a moment. Someone tapped my shoulder, and I spun around.

"Hi, Tisi."

Thalia was standing behind me. She was a slight goddess with tightly wound dark hair, a Cupid's-bow mouth, and wide, bright eyes. She was wearing a polka-dotted halter dress and red heels.

I looked from her to the sculpture and back again.

She giggled a joyous carnival ride laugh. "When we're here, the signal comes direct. I don't need to transmit through the statue."

"I see."

"Are you on holiday?" she asked.

"I'm afraid I have business here." I scanned the lobby. "Perhaps we should find a more private location to talk."

Thalia's smile melted away. "Of course."

She led us to a quiet cove with very little traffic. We sat down on a silk bench. Cerberus lay down at our feet, his enormous head resting on his lion-sized paws.

"What is your mission?" Thalia asked.

I explained about the missing women, the dead girl, and Alecto's disappearance.

Her hand fluttered to her mouth. "Oh, Tisiphone, I'm so sorry." Her gaze fell to the floor. "I don't know what I'd do if I lost one of my sisters."

"I assure you I intend to bring Alex home unharmed." My voice was more stern than I had planned it to be.

Thalia said, "Of course. I meant no disrespect."

I put my hand up. "Please, say no more. I'm just edgy."

I rubbed my hands on my thighs. Thalia waited patiently for me to continue. I was grateful she wasn't trying to make light of the situation by cracking jokes, as was her gift.

"First, I need to know if you have easy access to return to Olympus."

Thalia looked even more concerned. "Of course. Except for the high gods, those of us with replicas here have the ability to slip in and out at will, as long as the travel is approved by the Fates."

"Well, that might be a problem, since I have no way to contact them."

"My work here is with a comedian on a six-month tour. I'm permitted to travel freely once per month, round-trip."

"And have you used up your stipend this month?"

"No."

Excellent! "All right. I need you to listen very carefully."

The petite Grace inched forward. I explained about the gate, how the humans had likely closed it by now but a few residents of Tartarus had already escaped. "I killed a Stymphalian just this morning. I'm afraid it destroyed one of the portals during the attack."

Thalia's eyes widened at this news. "So, then, the Graces statue is the only one left?"

"Unless you know of another one."

"That's the only one I've ever used." She picked at a perfectly manicured nail. "It's not as strong as the other portal was, I'm afraid. Graces do not have the power of the higher gods."

That was what I was afraid of. Athena had warned me about the city and how its energy sucked the power from the portals. She had cautioned that I had but a short window to find Alecto and return the three of us—Archer, and Alex, and me—home. Alecto's trip was on a tight schedule, and under the laws of the Fates, the punishment for breaking that schedule was cutting the tether to Olympus, which meant she could not return. No excuses. Athena had also warned that the new moon would deplete the energy it would take to bring the three of us home.

We were running out of time.

Thalia said, "The bird. You think it escaped through the gate?"

"I believe so. That isn't all." I explained Hecate's theory about the five moons of Pluto ritual and told her about the solar eclipse that was coming, and how perhaps this whole thing centered on that. I told her about Lamia too.

She gasped. "How is that possible?"

"Perhaps a mortal called to her, and when the gate opened, she was able to slither out."

"But the gods, Charon, how could they not have known? How could they not have stopped her?"

I hesitated. Should I tell her my thoughts? That perhaps a god was betraying Olympus? That a mortal might be working with a god? I decided right now she was my best chance of reaching them, so I had to.

Thalia absorbed this bit of information. "Do you suppose there's a hecatomb coming?"

A hecatomb was a large-scale sacrifice to the gods that mortals believed would appease them. We had worked very hard to kill the practice, and it had died out ages ago.

"Doubtful. That belief was squelched. Besides, it was thought that one needed at least a hundred animals or humans to perform the ritual."

"All right, Tisiphone. I will make contact with Hermes to warn Hades. I'll get back to you as soon as possible, but first I think it best to warn the others. Molpe the Siren and Rumour are both here as well."

At the mention of Rumour's name, my face instinctively set into a scowl.

Thalia whispered, "I don't care for her either, but it must be done. Besides, she is related to you, after all. You'll need more Underworld forces when battling Underworld demons."

"She's part demon herself, thanks to her dark heart." Rumour reveled in telling tales, even if they were untrue.

As long as they stirred up trouble, she flapped her tongue to anyone who would lend an ear. She was a hateful shrew whom I despised.

"Even so," Thalia said.

"Fine."

Thalia stood up. "Come. Molpe is performing at Treasure Island. If we hurry, we may be able to catch her before her show. Then we can find your cousin."

Cerberus stirred. A low growl rumbled deep in his throat. He was staring at something.

I followed his gaze to a painting of Hades. Cerberus inched closer, practically crawling to his god.

I trailed him.

"What is it?" Thalia asked.

"I'm not sure."

Cerberus was snarling, spittle pouring from his snapping jaws.

I looked at the painting, trying to see what the beast could see.

Hades was perched on his throne, listening to the concerns of the dead. He held his staff in his left hand, and the silver threads embedded in his black velvet robe glinted in the moonlight that shined through the window.

It was a remarkable likeness. Closer to the real thing than any I had seen in the entire palace, right down to his coffee-toned skin.

I saw no reason for the hound's reaction, so I lit the flame of truth in my sight.

Through that filter, I was able to detect that the dark lord was not wearing his crown.

Behind him glowed a pair of yellow eyes.

Chapter 36

I spoke with Archer on the portable telephone and told him where I was going. He told me that he had tried to trace the number Sam had given him for the suspect, but that it was a disposable phone, so there was no address linked to it. He told me that he was planning to pay a visit to Tommy in an attempt to gain more information about the man who was snatching the women and the loose juice, and perhaps to learn more about his own murder.

The sun seemed even brighter today, despite its being early evening. I ate my granola bar as Thalia chatted on about her visit, her mission with the comedian, and her success in inspiring him. I supposed that upon having heard about my suspicion that Lamia was planning to overthrow Hades, she had become a bit nervous.

I couldn't blame her.

Cerberus stopped to drink from a fountain. When a man tried to shoo him away, the hound told him in no uncertain terms that he would do as he pleased. I realized he was likely hungry, so we popped into an eatery and ordered six hamburgers for him. He gobbled them up on a bench near the Strip, as the mortals called it, and we headed off toward Treasure Island.

I heard the Siren's song before we arrived.

Thalia said, "I fear we're too late. The performance lasts twenty minutes, so it shouldn't be long before we can speak with Molpe."

Around the corner was a large crowd gathered in front of two massive pirate ships surrounded by water. I couldn't smell the salty air of the sea, so it must have been fresh water. The vessel on the left was covered in thick ropes that crisscrossed each other, with a staircase that spiraled up the center, leading to a lookout. I noticed two long planks protruding from the ship, one on the top level, one near the ship's deck. The ship on the left had red sails with black *X*'s in the center of them. It wasn't lit up as brightly as the other vessel. There were cannons poking out from the sides of that ship.

A female voice called out over a speaker.

"Gather round, ye seafarers, and come enjoy the song. The beauty of the Sirens is as fair as the day is long. Stay a spell and watch our show, as the Sirens dance and delight. For a pirate's ship is about to collide with the Sirens' cove tonight."

Soft music began to play, and someone whom I could not see broke into a haunting melody. It was pure auditory beauty.

Women clad in not much more than skimpy shorts and bras danced seductively onto the ship that was lit. A spotlight shone on a man in a pirate costume standing in the center of the spiral staircase.

"Where am I?" he shouted.

There was laughter, long and mocking.

"You don't know?" said the voice that had been singing.

The dancing girls stopped, pointed, and giggled at the man. A few pirouetted around the ship's deck, waving their arms in invitation.

"Tell him, sisters!"

The music changed to a fast beat, and the dancers broke out into a high-energy song. They danced around the man, luring him to join them, but he shook his head. He held fast to the rail of the staircase.

"Well, now, that's not very polite," said the female I still could not see. "If you dare to enter a Sirens' cove, then you must play with us. Isn't that right, ladies?"

The dancers broke into another routine, climbing the ropes, reaching out to the man, tugging at his clothes.

"I am a pirate under the command of Captain Blake Falcon. I demand you release me."

"Oh, well, if you demand it," said the sultry voice.

A curtain dropped from the highest lookout point. There stood Molpe, wearing a shiny silver costume, her golden hair sailing behind her, her hands on her hips. "But first, a little fun."

She broke into another song, dancing her way down the staircase until she met the pirate. She gyrated her hips around him, and the two of them moved back and forth to the music.

When the music stopped, the pirate shook his head as if coming out of a spell. He ran down several steps, then looked up. She crooked her finger at him, and he made his way back up one step.

"Come on, lover boy," she cooed.

He ran all the way back down, and the Siren made her way down to the second lookout.

The music began again. I was looking forward to hearing Molpe sing. Her voice was hypnotic.

When she didn't, I was surprised.

And so, apparently, was the rest of her crew. The dancers scrambled to keep the show going, but it seemed as if Molpe had forgotten her role.

She stood there, dazed.

Then she climbed up the stairs and out onto the highest plank.

Thalia said, "Something's wrong."

I lit the fire in my eyes and stared at Molpe. She was straining to hear something, I could tell, but without being able to hear her speak, I had no idea what had her distracted.

She tilted her chin down toward the waters.

The actors were growing ever more concerned. I saw one signal to a security guard, who spoke into an electronic device.

The flame still vibrant in my sight, I scanned the waters for a clue. That's when I saw it.

"Thalia, it's a lymnade. There." I pointed to the water demon. Its talent was mimicking the cries of loved ones, sending those who followed the call to their deaths.

Molpe stepped to the end of the plank and dove.

Chapter 37

I didn't hesitate. My wings erupted behind me. I leaped onto the thick ropes that kept the crowd at bay, rocketed off them, and flew to snatch Molpe just before she reached the jaws of the eager demon. It spat at us, shooting a stream of steaming water into the air and spraying the crowd with it. Most people gasped, some clapped, some snapped photographs.

"I've got you, Siren," I said to Molpe. "Do what you do best—let's make it a good performance."

Molpe blinked her eyes once or twice, nodded, then opened her mouth to share her gift. As she sang, I flew around the ship a time or two, then deposited her on the highest lookout. She continued singing, and the dancers picked up the cue, not sure what to make of the incident or of me but knowing the show must continue.

I kept flying, searching for the demon again. It was just a moment before I saw its ugly, scaly green head and black eyes pop out of the water. Its jaws were moving, and I noticed a man, obviously bespelled, drifting dangerously close to the edge of the dock, a camera loose at his side.

I squeezed Indigo and shot down toward the water demon, and she set its head ablaze. It screeched in pain, succumbing to the dragon's power. Its jaws stopped moving after a few fruitless snaps. Then it oozed into a heaping pile of seaweed, slipping deep beneath the surface of the water.

How many more demons had escaped when the humans had opened the gate? Was someone—some god—purposely sending them through?

How would I ever focus on finding my sister if my task was being foiled by one of my own?

The crowd burst into whistles, catcalls, and applause. I caught Thalia's eyes and tilted my head toward the Venetian hotel across the way, and the Grace nodded. I hovered for a moment, looked at Molpe—who winked, signaling she had caught that—and disappeared behind the building. I landed near a Dumpster of trash, tucked my wings away, and waited for Molpe, Thalia, and Cerberus to join me.

As I paced, my fury built. This whole thing was a kaleidoscope of sewage, and I was standing in the middle of it. I was growing tired of dealing with demons. It was as if this entire thing had been planned—the kidnappings, my sister, the escape.

But by whom?

And for what purpose? Lamia couldn't possibly have orchestrated all of this. Her mind was too diseased for such an elaborate plot. She had to have had help. Or perhaps someone had wanted to partner with her, and in exchange, her reward would be assistance in overthrowing Hades.

I didn't have all the pieces of the puzzle, and that infuriated me. I wasn't used to these types of cases. I was used to knowing the facts before I chased suspects. I was used to having more open access to the gods. One thing I knew for certain: when this was all over, I was going to urge Athena to work on better communication methods. Perhaps the Google that Archer always mentioned. Or that electronic-mail system he had told me about.

Thalia, Molpe, and Cerberus showed up then.

Molpe clasped my hand in hers. "Thank you, dark one. I am indebted to you."

"Nonsense. It is my job to protect and serve."

Thalia shuffled nervously. "Tisi, look who's here."

She stepped aside, and Rumour emerged from behind her.

Oh, lords, give me the patience not to stab her with my sword.

Rumour was fairer skinned than most gods of the Underworld. She had perfectly straight teeth, a perfectly cut bob, and a perfectly foul sense of fun.

"There's my favorite cousin." She stepped forward to hug me, reeking of rose petals. I put my hand up.

"No," I said.

Rumour smirked. "Still don't like to be touched, is that it?"

"I don't like to be burned, Cousin."

Aside from the falsehoods she spread all around Olympus, the pain she caused, the disruption, Rumour had testified against me at my trial. Said there was a cover-up, that I didn't even have the right man. She had made a mess of things that took ages for the Fates to sift through.

Rumour stuck her lower lip into a pout. "Aw, still sore about that stupid trial? You really should learn to let go of grudges, Tisiphone."

I advanced on her, ready to grab her throat, but Thalia stepped between us.

"Tisi, remember why we are here."

I closed my eyes, called on the meditation that Athena had taught me, and calmed my fury.

"We need to go someplace to talk," I said.

"How about your place?" Rumour asked. "I've been dying for a look at the high gods' suite." She smiled wickedly. "Plus, I hear you're keeping a delicious mortal in there that you don't want to share with the rest of the class."

I really wished someone would cut her tongue out. It was my understanding that the room Archer and I shared was reserved for high gods and those who served them. Lesser deities, such as the Muses and the three standing before me, were accommodated elsewhere.

But I wanted Rumour nowhere near Archer. Besides, we had a meeting in a short while with the man who was targeting the women. I felt it wasn't safe for any of them to be in his presence.

"That's not an option." I glared at Rumour so she knew I meant business.

Thalia said, "There's a small café around the corner. It usually isn't too crowded at this hour."

We followed Thalia to the café, where there were a few tables spread outside. A tired-looking waitress took our order, and Cerberus curled around my feet.

Thalia and I took turns explaining to Rumour and Molpe what was happening. The kidnappings, Alecto, Lamia, the gate, all of it. Somewhere in the middle of our story, the waitress (I learned they didn't like to be called servants) brought our coffee.

Rumour snorted when we were finished. "Come now, Tisi. Lamia is no match for Hades. And as for your sister, well"—she looked me straight in the eye—"you know Alecto has probably just gone rogue. Probably got sick of bedding all the gods of the Underworld, so she wanted to try her hand at the mortals. Maybe she wanted her tether to break."

I reached over and slapped her across the face.

Molpe lurched back and Thalia jumped. "Tisi!" said the Grace.

But I wasn't listening. I kicked a chair out of the way and advanced on Rumour.

She rubbed her cheek. "You will pay for that, Cousin, I promise you."

I narrowed my eyes at her. I could feel a vein throb in my head, and my wings were vibrating. "Have you no shame? No compassion? No loyalty to your own people?"

"And what have my people ever done for me, huh, Tisiphone?" She flicked her eyes to Thalia, then Molpe. "I have not the gift of music, of comedy, of poetry." She returned her gaze to me. "I have not the duty of discipline. Of setting the course of history right where the humans have failed. The Fates never saw fit to bestow upon me any such talent save for my tongue, and that is what I use."

I took a deep breath and moved closer. Her defiant chin was inches from mine. I could smell the coffee she had ordered on her lips.

"It is up to the individual to develop talent. With talent come gifts; with gifts comes power. It is earned. It is a privilege and a responsibility. If your power never came, you have only yourself to blame. Not the kingdoms."

I flipped some currency on the table and called to Cerberus. The dog stood.

I tossed my telephone to Thalia. "Input your contact number in there. Do the same for Molpe." She did and programmed my information into her telephone.

"Contact me at once when you return from Olympus. And for the love of Zeus, tell Athena we need better communications. Email, perhaps. Archer has one for Google." I relayed the address to her.

Thalia nodded.

I looked at Molpe. "I think you should go with her. You'll need to rebuild your power, and the best place to do that is home."

Rumour said, "You really should learn to curb your fury, Tisiphone. It could get you in a lot of trouble." She tapped her lip. "Oh, wait, that's right. It already has."

I wanted to slap her again, but after the flight, the water demon, and the anger pumping through my blood, I could feel my strength fading. And I needed every ounce of it tonight.

"And you'd better pray that whatever leaked from the Underworld doesn't come after you. A demon, a dark deity, or perhaps a soul you crossed? Someone whose afterlife you may have ruined with your lies?"

Rumour didn't blink, but I could tell that last part shook her up.

I leaned to whisper in her ear. "Because if that were to happen, Cousin, I won't be there to save you."

With that, I picked up my portable telephone, and the hound and I left.

There was no time for Rumour's nonsense.

I had a meeting with the man who had stolen my sister.

Chapter 38

It was almost dark when I got back to the suite.

Archer asked, "How'd it go?"

He was sitting at the laptop, drinking a soda, looking even sexier than when I had left him.

I told him about the portrait of Hades, my thoughts on an upheaval, the water demon, and that maggot Rumour.

"Sounds like you had an interesting afternoon." He came over to me and rubbed my shoulders.

I dropped my head, enjoying the calming feel of his fingers walking along my neck, my shoulders, my back. I wished I could crawl into bed with him to finish what we had begun earlier that day, but there was no time for that.

I had a job to do.

"Were you able to meet with Tommy?" I asked.

"No. He wasn't home. But I did find out something interesting."

He drifted away from where I stood and punched a few buttons on the laptop. "I was thinking about what you said. About Hecate's warning about the eclipse, and the five-moon spell. I did a cross-reference check in the FBI database for criminals in the area who are into...what did you call it? Dark arts?" He shifted to look at me. I nodded. He turned back to the screen and tapped a few pictures.

A man's image sizzled into view. He was standing before a lined sign, holding a card in front of him. A mug shot, I recognized. His eyes were so dark, they seemed to have no color at all, and his head was covered with stubble. He looked young, not unlike some of the waiters and bartenders I had seen across the city. He could have been anyone. He could have been someone's next-door neighbor, a musician, a deliveryman.

Except he had three eyebrows.

"Meet Jason Helm, registered sex offender and devil worshipper." He hit a button, and another machine on the desk spit out the image.

Humans and their absurd religions. Now I had heard everything. Worshipping the evil that lived inside you had to be the ultimate display of narcissism.

I locked eyes with Archer. "You think he's the one who stole Alecto? Who killed Cicely Barnes?"

Archer said, "I think he's the guy. He's been heavy into the occult for years, and I don't mean witchcraft. I mean scary stuff. Got a few raps when he was younger for sacrificing animals, desecrating churches, that kind of thing."

I wrapped my arms around Archer and kissed him. He pulled me into his lap. "Good work, Lawman."

His hands began roving, and I let them for a few moments. "Don't we have work to do?"

Archer sighed. "Yep. We do. One other thing." His voice took on a foreboding tone.

"What is that?"

He scratched his head. "Remember when I said the eclipse was four days away yesterday?"

"Yes."

"Well, I double-checked that. It isn't. It's tomorrow."

I straightened my spine. "What?"

"I'm sorry. It was bad information. That's the trouble with the Internet."

"Are you certain?"

He nodded. "I checked about ten different sites. Tomorrow. Five fifty-five our time."

That number again. Five. Which reminded me. "Have you heard anything about another woman gone missing?"

"No. I checked the news a few times." He squeezed my hand. "Seems he's waiting for you."

"Well, let's not keep him waiting."

Archer looked at his watch. "I have an address, but we have only a few minutes until you're supposed to meet with him. What do you think we should do? Let him come to us? Or should we go to him?"

I thought about that a moment. If we let him come to us, then the women and my sister would be safe, at least for the time being. If we stormed his home, there was no telling what would happen. He could have it booby-trapped. He could try to shoot his way out, harming the girls in the process. No. It was probably safer for him to come to us. If something went wrong here, we could always track him to his home. Unless...

"We could split up. I could bait him, keep him talking, pretend like I'm interested in his propositions while you go rescue the victims."

Archer frowned. "I don't know. I don't like that idea much." He tapped his fingers on the chair. "Maybe we should disguise you. We know what he looks like now. Maybe that would give you the upper hand. You'll likely see him before he spots you."

"Unless there is something here in the suite, we don't have time to shop for a disguise."

Archer frowned. I knelt down before him and grabbed his hands. "He is a mortal. This is what I was born to do. Trust me. I will not fail. My sister's life depends on it."

Archer reluctantly agreed to split up. He tried to supply me with a firearm, but I declined. He did, however, tuck a pair of plastic restraints in my hand. I quickly changed into a fresh pair of jeans, thigh high boots, and a silk halter top. I hid Indigo inside the right boot, making sure there was enough room for her to breathe.

I decided it was best to leave Cerberus in the room, although I left the door slightly ajar in case he needed to relieve himself.

Archer asked, "Are you sure that's a good idea? What if someone breaks in?"

"Then Hades help him," I said.

Archer looked at the large black dog. "Good point."

We traveled down on separate elevators. I took the one that would get me closest to Shadow Bar, while Archer ducked around to the elevator that was closest to the palace entrance.

Sam was tending bar when I arrived. I grabbed a small table in a corner, ordering nothing to drink, and waited for the suspect to arrive. His image was ingrained in my brain. As soon as I spotted him, I would sweet-talk him down a quiet corridor, restrain him, possibly knock him out, and shove him in the closet, then call Archer. He would know how best to approach the local authorities with the information.

And then we could all go home.

It was only a matter of time.

Chapter 39

"Sssssoooo," Lamia hissed. "Is it feeding time?" She slithered over to him.

He didn't know which was worse, that disgusting voice or the slimy trail she left behind her when she moved. He turned to look at the snake woman. "Not yet."

Four girls. He needed one more before tomorrow for the plan to work. Luckily, that moron he had been working through had given him a tip on just the girl. She'd be at the Shadow Bar tonight.

Lamia's tongue darted in and out of her mouth, assessing the girls who were tied up. They were terrified, that was obvious. All but one. That one seemed calm. Too calm. Even with the gag and blindfold. He didn't like it, but he also didn't have time to worry about it. In his experience, people dealt with dangerous situations in a host of different ways. Take the moron who had summoned him here. A serial-killer junkie. Guy aspired to be Jeffrey Dahmer or Ted Bundy. What a joke. He'd killed more than those amateurs combined. But the funniest part was that the asshole actually thought he was dealing with Satan. Kept calling him the Dark One the last few times they spoke. Which completely annoyed him. He hated the dark. He loved color, lights, laughter. That's why he had chosen this particular moron in this particular city to channel in the first place all those months ago. It wasn't too hard. Even where he had been, it seemed, anyone could be bought if you greased the right hand with the right bribe. The escape, though—that part was trickier. That's why he had needed the snake woman.

Lamia licked the toe of one of the girls, and she yelped.

"Knock it off," he growled. The snake woman could be a real pain in the ass. He couldn't wait to get rid of her. Send her back where she came from. She had come in handy during the escape, but he didn't really need her anymore. He'd kill her if he thought the bitch would die, but he wasn't so sure of that.

She spat at him and slithered down the hallway.

He checked the skin in the cracked mirror. What a shit-hole this place was. Where had Jason found this dump? He adjusted Jason's face for a better fit. It was a little tight, but it would have to do. He couldn't very well wear his own. People might recognize him. Besides, the contact Jason was working through would be expecting to see his face. He doubted he could waltz in with his own image and ask for the girl. That might rouse suspicion, and he didn't need that. Not now. Not when he was so close to getting what he wanted. What he'd dreamed about day in and day out for all those years.

It was almost showtime.

He grabbed the juice, the formula that he himself had delivered to Jason through the Ouija board. It was Lamia's recipe. Then he left.

Chapter 40

After half an hour, I called Archer. When he didn't answer, I left him a message telling him I was still waiting at the Shadow Bar.

I debated ordering a Gatorade but decided against it. I didn't want to give anyone the chance to poison my drink.

I sat there, watching the girls dance behind the new screen, watching the crowd happily chatting, and wondered for the millionth time where my sister was, why I couldn't feel her, and if she was hurt. Sam stopped by my table, set a drink down, and said he didn't know what had happened to the man who was supposed to meet me. "He said he was coming by at eight o'clock sharp," the bartender said.

There was no reason not to believe him. His ass was on the line, after all. Archer had made that very clear.

When another hour snailed along with no word from Archer or Thalia (why hadn't she returned yet?), I got up and wandered through the casino.

I stayed close to the Shadow Bar, feigning interest in various slot machines. Gladiator's Gate, Wizard's Ward, the Enchantress —where did they come up with all the themes? I watched as slack-jawed elderly women pressed button after brightly lit button, occasionally reaching for the long arm of the machine, hoping to fall into fortune, pictures of cherries and diamonds reflecting in their glasses. Potbellied men wandered around with stacks of chips, assessing which table would bear the highest windfall. There were young men and women, dressed to the nines in suit jackets and glittery cocktail dresses, headed out for the night. I watched as a cheerful blonde tossed her head back and laughed at something her friend—or perhaps sister—had whispered in her ear, and it reminded me of Alecto and Meg.

I so wished I had traveled with them. I so wished the three of us were closer. We had been once. Before the trial, before I had killed a man. I hoped we could be again.

I kept a watchful eye on the door to the Shadow Bar for a bit longer, hoping Jason Helm would walk through it at any moment.

I had no such luck.

Indigo gurgled beneath my boot, so I decided to take us both outside for some fresh night air. It seemed my date was a no-show.

I walked the streets of the city, drinking in the blackness of the night sky, while adjusting my eyes to the lights of the buildings. I passed groups of people deciding where to dine, where to play games, which show to see.

I looked up at the sky, yearning for the moon and its energy, but there was none. Which served only as a reminder that the eclipse was coming tomorrow, the new moon along with it, and Hades only knew what else.

Was it to be some sort of sacrifice? Was that the purpose of stealing the women? I didn't know for certain. What I did know was that with the new moon, there would come a drain of power for Alex, and, I suspected—although Athena hadn't mentioned it—for me.

For I was on a short pass too. And time was running out.

I lifted Indigo from my boot and secured the sword in my belt loop. Two drunken men approached me to tell me

I was hot and asked me if I wanted to get a drink. I thanked them and said I was quite cool, actually, and they stumbled off into a casino called the Flamingo, a gaudy-looking building draped in far too much pink for my liking. I stopped to watch some showgirls, as Archer called them, posing for pictures with tourists. I resisted the urge to tell the one with the long black hair that she might be in danger. Instead, I lingered near her, watching the people who passed, looking for any signs of ill intent among them.

When the women moved on, so did I. Indigo fluttered her purple eye at me, and it occurred to me that she might need to feed. Dragons rarely drank water, because it doused their fire. They obtained most of their sustenance, including hydration, from insects. We wandered down a low-traffic side street that was fairly empty. When I was certain we wouldn't attract attention, I released her from the sword to catch her meal.

I watched her small blue body fly up into the air, circle the space, and dive-bomb for prey after prey in rapid succession. She was quick, nimble, and I couldn't help but admire her skill as a huntress. Artemis would be proud.

Something caught her attention, and her ears perked. She looked over her shoulder at me and twitched her nose.

That's when I felt it too.

Eyes on me. Heat. Hatred. Hunger.

Chapter 41

He passed a group of young men on his way inside Caesars Palace. They were thin, handsome, unlined.

Fresh.

He breathed in the scent of them. Just out of the shower, one of the boys had a spicy aroma. Clove, perhaps? Or allspice.

He preferred the spicy scent to that of musk.

No time for that now, however. Fun time could wait until later. Right now he had business to attend to.

He made his way through the casinos, past wrinkled men with scowling faces. The faces of his father. He shuddered. He noted the women in leather costumes dealing out games of blackjack, wishing that he could get into costume. It was something that was near and dear to his heart: entertaining. He hadn't put on a performance in a long time. But that would have to wait too.

He found the Shadow Bar, with its slinky women traipsing behind the sheer screens, but just as he was about to enter, something told him to stop. Wait. Identify the prey. Study it. Get to know its habits, its movements.

Its desires.

Women were mostly easy to capture. They rarely carried weapons, rarely paid attention to their surroundings or even their instincts. He shook his head. So foolish. He wondered how many had died because they hadn't listened to their inner warning bells. Danger! Danger, Will Robinson!

He chuckled at his joke.

There was a potted fern and a tall ashtray off to the side of the entrance. He camouflaged himself there. He scanned the room just beyond. It was a small space with a long bar, a young male bartender behind it. He was handsome, chiseled. Could that be the infamous Sam Jason had told him about? He was pouring drinks for a flirtatious crowd of giggling girls. He wore a bright smile, wide and welcoming, like they all did at that age. He liked them younger, but this age was nice too. They carried just enough sin under their belts to get a taste for it, but not so much that it soured them.

Yes, he just might come back for Sam.

He craned his neck a bit. Saw no one who fit the profile of what he wanted. What he needed.

He decided to try the other entrance.

He melted back into the crowd, then took a wide turn around a smaller bar and circled back around to the second entrance.

That's when he saw her. Sitting at a sleek round table alone. Her head was tilted toward a cellular phone. Oh, how he hated those things! They could often foil a perfect plan. Jason had wanted to get him a cell phone, but he wanted nothing to do with them. The board worked just fine for his purposes of communicating.

She lifted up her head, long hair spilling all around her shoulders, and his mouth fell open.

Those eyes. He would never forget those violet eyes.

It was her. Her!

He couldn't believe his luck and felt a twinge of guilt for

having killed Jason. He should have rewarded the man for finding what would soon be his trophy.

His vengeance.

He had waited so long for this, and he thought—just for a moment—that he could abandon the plan altogether. After all, he didn't care one bit about the ritual. As far as he was concerned, it was designed to pull him free but also to entice *her* away from the comforts of home. He hadn't realized she would come before they set the plan in motion. What had brought her here? What had been so urgent that she would come out of hiding?

Then again, did it really matter? She was here now. That was the important thing.

And he certainly didn't care one bit about what Lamia was after. He just wanted *her*. Wanted to make her pay for what she had done. He would have gotten away with everything if she hadn't messed it all up. He could have gone on for years.

No matter. After tomorrow, he would go on forever.

Oh, he couldn't wait to get his hands on her. Couldn't wait to stifle that wail, gouge those eyes out, and tear those wings apart. He got hard just thinking about all the nasty things he would do to her. He almost came right there.

She turned her head for a moment, and he ducked behind the wall. He grabbed a newspaper that someone had tossed in a nearby trash can and hurried out through the lobby doors. It would have to wait until tomorrow. He wasn't prepared for her yet. He didn't have all his tools with him.

Then he stopped and went back inside the lobby.

He stared at the statue for a moment. He had heard rumors, but he wasn't certain.

Was that the way?

Better safe than sorry, he decided.

He walked back outside, down a dirty side street, and found a hobo. He paid the man handsomely with a wallet he had discovered at Jason's place.

He couldn't wait to see the look on her face.

Chapter 42

I locked eyes with Indigo. "Go get Cerberus," I whispered.

The tiny dragon whipped around and flew off into the night.

Slowly, I turned around, hand on my sword.

Lamia's yellow eyes were glowering at me. "Tisssssssissss-phone. We meet again."

"Lamia. Shouldn't you be tied to a rock in Tartarus?"

The monster slithered toward me, her thick serpent's tail slapping the ground as she moved. "I was growing tired of the dark. Don't you ever grow tired of it?" She spoke in long, trailing notes, dragging out the vowels of every word as if they had tails attached to them.

I stayed my ground. Lamia bared her teeth at me.

"Actually, I prefer the dark. Tends to keep the rats in their holes."

Come on, Cerberus. Come on.

She advanced on me again, swerving her body as if to cover every inch of the sidewalk with her tail. She thumped it against a metal trash can, crushing it.

This time, I took one step back.

All I had was my sword and my wings. Lamia should be weak, having not fed in so long, but I had no idea what she had been up to since she had traveled to this realm. Perhaps she had used all her power just to escape. Or to make the journey here from the gate.

I pulled the sword from my belt loop, making quite a show of it.

She cocked her head to the side, her greasy hair shifting in messy clumps. "My, what a pretty toy you have there."

She snapped her teeth and licked her entire head with her whiplike tongue.

"That's disgusting, Lamia. Now cut the theatrics and surrender to me. You know I have to bring you in." I tried to inject an air of confidence into my voice, but, truth be told, she was one of the worst demons I had ever battled, and that was on my own turf. Here, I wasn't sure what to expect.

She gave me a disdainful look, flipped her head back, and cackled like a hyena. "I think not, Fury. I have planssssss."

She seemed certain of herself. Was she stronger? Had she fed?

"I know all about your plans, and they won't work. You will never wear my lord's crown." I gripped the sword tighter as she slithered even closer.

Something caught her eye, and she shifted her head. A mouse scuttled out from the building we were standing next to. She unleashed her tongue, snatched the mouse, and swallowed it whole.

I grimaced. The monster made me sick just looking at her. Her scales weren't shiny, like a true snake's, but flaky, dull, and dripping with a mucus so foul smelling, it invoked a gag reflex in anyone who stood less than ten feet downwind from her.

She flicked her eyes to me. "My, my, aren't we the loyal one, Tisssssssiphone."

I hated the way she said my name. I darted my eyes around, looking for a place to leap. I could fly straight from the ground, but it expended more energy. If I had a catapult, I could get airborne quicker and fly higher straightaway.

Lamia scraped her gnarled fingernails along a wall. "You know, I could use a goddess like you when I take the throne. My little plan will be complete tomorrow, the planet Pluto well appeased by the sacrifices I will offer it. Wouldn't you like to be there by my side when I force Hades to his knees?"

"You will never take the throne. You had a crown once, remember? You failed to keep it."

She flicked her tongue at me and glowered. She hated to be reminded of her lost regal status.

"Don't be so sure. You have no idea what I am capable of, Fury."

She moved forward once again, and I moved backward. I noticed some steps behind me that led to a fire escape. If I could just get to those steps.

"I know exactly what you are capable of. Why do you think I locked you up in the first place?"

"Yesssssss, you did, didn't you? Perhaps I'll do the same to you when Hades's crown is on my head, hmmm?"

She seemed more powerful than I had thought she would be. All those years of being locked up in Tartarus should have drained her. Had she fed? Was that it? Had she stolen a child? Or was it something else? Whom was she working with?

Then the most terrifying thought entered my mind. What if I was wrong? What if she couldn't be killed here? I knew her weakest spot to be her midsection, where her snakeskin met her once-immortal skin. If she were sliced in two at just the right angle, she could be killed in my world.

But here, on this plane, did it have to be so specific?

There was only one way to find out.

"Why would you lock me up, Lamia? I didn't kill my children."

She screamed the cry of a thousand tortured souls. "*Liessssss!*"

I shuffled back, jumped onto the stairs, and leaped.

I flew to the top of the building, but before I could land, Lamia wrapped her tongue around my ankles, binding me.

She slammed my body into the side of the building, and I felt my forehead tear open.

I folded my wings so they wouldn't break. Then I bucked my feet up, whipped my sword around, and severed her tongue.

She screamed as I fell to the ground.

I scrambled to my feet, sword at the ready, and lunged at her midsection. She managed to slap me away with her massive tail, but I cut off a chunk of it. Then she grew her tongue back, thicker than before, and lashed my hand, forcing me to drop the blade. She grew her tail back too and smacked it into my back, knocking me to the cement.

I reached for the sword. Just as my fingertips met it, she batted it away, and I heard it clank against something. I couldn't see it.

I was defenseless. I had no choice but to retreat.

My wings expanded to their full girth, and I leaped.

But Lamia was faster. She whipped her tongue around my left wing—the damaged one—so tight that I could barely flap the other one.

Not my wing!

She left me dangling there in the air, nearly out of breath. I could hear her hissing, could feel her hunger.

By Hades! She was going to eat me.

"Lamia, put me down!"

"I think not, Fury. I feel like a snack."

She coiled me toward her.

Chapter 43

I heard Lamia scream before I smelled the smoke, but she held fast to my wing anyway. Her tongue squeezed tighter, and I felt my lungs constrict. My bodily forces—my breath, my organs, my blood—were all connected to my wing bone, and I feared she would suffocate the life from me. I was hovering just in front of her snapping jaws. I could smell the fear of the children she had killed, the rot of her own soul.

Indigo fluttered around her, searching for another good spot to set her on fire without harming me. She blew a flame at the demon's hair, but the slime covering it only doused it out. Indigo sputtered in frustration, diving this way and that, snapping her dragon jaws. She got close enough to bite Lamia. The monster cried out once more and snatched the little dragon from the air with her clawed hand, clamping Indigo's mouth shut.

The dragon grunted and kicked, enraged.

I reached out, trying to punch and kick the demon with all my might, but every time I did, it only inspired Lamia to squeeze harder.

Cerberus roared from somewhere. Judging from Lamia's scream and the way her body bucked and twitched, I guessed the hound had sunk his teeth into her torso. He likely held her there too, for she steadied a moment. I didn't hear another bark or snarl. I suspected Cerberus was deciding which was the best strategy—continue to maul her or hold her steady.

"Tisiphone!"

I lifted my head to see Archer standing there, a twisted look of dismay and concern on his face. He was holding his gun, aiming it at Lamia's head.

"The middle! Shoot her in the middle," I said.

He fired off six rounds, one after the other.

Blood like black oil spurted fountain-style out of the serpent beast. She wailed and bounced me on the ground a few times, her tongue still wrapped around me. She was frothing at the mouth, her bile dripping on my head every time her tongue slackened. Finally, I felt her loosen her grip around my wing. I wiggled around to punch her again and again, before she finally released Indigo and me.

I unfurled her tongue from around me, watching as her piss-colored eyes lost their hue. Her tongue slackened, and she opened her mouth to say something.

But nothing came out.

She was still breathing as I untangled the tongue from my wing. I flapped it a few times to make sure it was still functional. It seemed to be working properly, although severely weakened, and I with it. I would need to find a source of power soon.

I scanned the dark street, searching for my sword to end her, but I couldn't find it.

"My sword, Archer. Help me find my sword."

The lawman was still a bit stunned, but he tried not to show it. We searched the area, all four of us, until Archer finally spotted the glint of the blade in a sewage drain. It took some doing, but we managed to free the sword from the space between the grates, and Indigo stationed herself at the grip.

When I turned to slay the monster, she was gone. All except the portion of her tongue I had severed in the beginning of the attack.

I sent Cerberus off to scout the area, but he came up with nothing.

Archer put his hands on my shoulder. "You okay?"

I nodded. "I think so," I said, a bit short of breath.

"Let's get you home, Sassy."

On the way back to the palace, I asked Archer how he had found me.

"It's not every day you see a blue dragon riding a black horse down the Strip. That caught my attention. I followed them."

I smiled. Archer had grabbed some paper towels from a nearby restaurant, and I was dabbing the cut on my head. I had already wiped the muck of Lamia from my hair and face.

"You've got a pretty good-sized lump there." Archer gingerly lifted my hair away from my face. "You sure you don't want to visit a hospital? You might have a concussion."

"No. I'm fine. I just need a pain reliever."

"I don't know what you use back home, but I think we can find some aspirin at the hotel."

"That would be wonderful."

As we walked, Archer explained that the address listed for Jason Helm turned out to be a dead end. "Sex offenders are supposed to update the information in our database when they move, but that doesn't always happen."

"Don't the authorities track them?"

"They should. Hey, watch your step." He guided me around a broken beer bottle. "But the parole officers are usually overworked and underpaid. Things slip through the cracks. Don't worry, though—I asked around, and according to one of the neighbors, he moved to the same apartment complex Tommy used to live in. I plan to visit him first thing in the morning. Flash Helm's picture. Maybe Tommy does know the son of a bitch after all."

Cerberus was keeping pace at my side while Indigo was sleeping soundly on my sword. Every so often, she would kick her tiny feet, mew, and blow out puffs of smoke as if she were dreaming.

We stopped to get Cerberus two slabs of ribs, three baked potatoes, and an order of green beans. He ate everything on a bench near the Bellagio hotel.

"I can't believe he didn't show." Archer poured extra barbecue sauce on his pork sandwich. "I'll kill Sam if he tipped him off."

I sipped my Gatorade. I didn't have much of an appetite after losing Lamia. "I don't think that's the case. Perhaps Jason Helm misunderstood the message. Perhaps he thought the meeting was tomorrow."

Tomorrow. I had until 5:55 tomorrow to find Alecto. After that, I had no idea what was going to happen, but my instincts told me it would spell disaster for all of us.

"Maybe," Archer said, although he seemed doubtful of that explanation.

Cerberus finished his meal and went off into some bushes. Archer picked up the empty food containers and tossed them in a nearby garbage can. I watched as he handed a dirty man with torn clothes some currency.

Something twittered in my chest, and another electric jolt ran through my body.

I was losing my heart to this man—I could feel it. I sighed and tilted my head back to look at the inky sky. I cracked my neck and stretched my legs, yearning to take flight, but my wings were retracted and resting from the battle.

So many battles. My energy was draining, I could tell, and I feared that if my power faded any more, I would be of no use to anyone. There were ways for me to refuel, however, and I just might have to indulge in them if I was going to save my sister.

Archer said, "What's so funny?"

"Nothing. Why?"

"You're grinning."

"Oh. Just thinking. How do you feel about Texas Hold'em?"

"I like it."

"Wanna play?"

"Now? You want to play poker now?"

"When I use my brain, it energizes my body."

Archer bent to put his hands on my thighs. He had a mischievous look on his face. "And what about when you use your body?"

I leaned my head toward his. "That works too."

He wrinkled his nose and smiled.

"What?"

"You stink."

I pulled my hair forward and sniffed. He was right. "Lamia. She smells worse than the giants. I guess I'll shower first."

We took the side street off the Strip to enter Caesars Palace. We received a few odd stares as we descended the escalator. I must have looked a wreck.

Cerberus trotted back to the room while we inquired about a Texas Hold'em table. One was beginning in two hours.

I said, "Archer, before we go up, I'd like to visit the Graces statue. I have yet to hear from Thalia, so I thought I'd try to connect with her."

"Sure. Why don't you try calling her on the phone first?"

I did. No answer.

When we got to the lobby, instantly I realized exactly why neither Thalia nor Molpe had made contact.

There were policemen in the lobby, questioning a few people. Staff were milling about, trying to calm customers, and the maid service was sweeping the floor all around the statue.

All of the eyes of each Grace were knocked out. There was a hammer lying on the ground where the vandal must have dropped it.

The portal had been destroyed.

Thalia couldn't return.

And neither could we.

Just beyond the café to the right stood Rumour. She was staring right at me.

Chapter 44

I lurched forward. "I'll kill her!"

Archer grabbed my elbows and forced me to look at him. "Whoa, Tisi, Tisi, calm down. There's cops crawling the place. Let's not get you arrested. Who are you talking about?"

"Rumour," I spat, my eyes locked on her. "She did this. She did this out of sheer spite because she has no gifts." I raised my voice. "I see you. Come over here!"

"Tisi, shhh," Archer said. A few uniformed heads swung our way.

I looked at him. "You don't know her like I do."

Archer said, "I'm sure it wasn't her. I'm sure it's just a punk kid."

"You have that badge. Can't you find out who did this?" I asked.

Archer frowned. "I can, but what if they know I'm dead? I know one of the guys."

He turned his back to the officers.

"What's the worst that could happen? You tell them you're a ghost."

Archer rolled his eyes, pulling me farther away from the statue. "Oh, that should go over well."

I glared at him and lit the flame in my eyes.

Archer grumbled and said, "Fine. But stay right here. And don't give me that look."

I extinguished the fire and thanked him. After he left, Rumour sauntered over to me, her curved hips sashaying as she walked. "Tisiphone, my hero."

"Give me one good reason I shouldn't kill you right now." I glanced at the statue.

She pursed her lips and put her hands to her hips. "What? You think I did this? Are you crazy?"

I was getting there. I hated this case—hated this damned city—but I said nothing to my cousin.

She blew out a sigh and flicked her gaze to Archer for a moment. "All right, look. Your words got to me, okay? Everything you said made me a tad nervous, so I thought I'd go home. At least until things settled down."

"Coward."

"Oh, very cute. Easy for you to say. You've got Cujo, Dirty Harry, and Puff the Magic Dragon to defend you. Plus your powers. What have I got?"

She stared at me for a minute.

Finally I had to ask. "Who is Dirty Harry?"

Rumour rolled her eyes. "Lords, Tisi, you really need to get out more."

"Well, did you at least see who did this?"

"No. I arrived after it happened."

We stood there in silence for a moment. Then she asked, "Can I stay with you?"

I laughed. "Now who's crazy?"

"What if he comes after me?" She sounded genuinely worried. Not that I cared.

"I don't think he will. He seems to be collecting women who are dark haired, tall, thin."

Rumour knitted her brow. "You mean those who look like you?"

"Yes."

"So *you* inspired him."

"What?" She really was trying my patience. I thought about shoving her head into the reflecting pool but decided that might drain even more of my power.

"Think about it. What you told us before. Pluto's moons, which are really Hades's moons, the dark daughters. He is probably trying to summon a Fury, if not all three."

I considered this, then shook it out of my mind. "No. The moons, the ritual—I suspect that is all part of Lamia's plan to overthrow Hades. The women—that is a mortal's plan."

"And who is to stop a mortal from taking Hades's throne? What better way to do that than for the Furies to rise up and revolt?"

Had Jason Helm known when he abducted Alecto that she was a Fury? But then what of the portal? How would he have known about that? Lamia, perhaps?

"I suppose it's possible. We know a mortal took the women, but we've suspected he was working with a god. Perhaps it wasn't a god; perhaps it was only Lamia."

Rumour tapped her lip and thought for a moment. "Or Charon."

I snapped my gaze to her. Of course! Charon. That greedy, club-footed weasel would sell his own mother for coin.

"Did I help?" Rumour's eyes sparkled with excitement.

"Actually, Cousin, you did."

"Then may I stay with you?"

"No. But I would recommend you secure accommodations within the hotel."

Rumour breathed a little easier.

Archer stepped up then. "Hello," he said to Rumour.

He raised an eyebrow at me.

"It's okay. What did you learn?"

"It was a homeless man. Said someone paid him to do it. They're still questioning him."

"Did he say who?"

"He didn't know. But I flashed the picture of Jason Helm."

"And?"

Archer nodded, and a smile spread across his face. "We're getting closer, Sassy."

I matched his grin. "Yes, we are."

Rumour shifted her eyes from Archer to me. "For Hades's sakes, Tisi, a mortal?"

I shot her a glare.

"Whatever rows your boat," she said. She stuck out her hand. "Rumour."

Archer shook it. "My pleasure."

"So what now?" Rumour asked me.

I looked at Archer.

He said, "They've got some boys out looking for Helm. Told me I could question him when they found him. I tipped them off about the possible new address."

"Well, then I guess now it's shower time." I started off toward the elevator, but Rumour grabbed my arm.

"Tisi, wait. Maybe I can help."

"How?" I didn't trust her one bit. Just because she had a mildly plausible theory didn't mean she was any less sneaky.

Her tone was serious. "If this ritual is strong—if the eclipse will somehow change you, control your actions, your will—then you need to learn how to do something that only I can teach you."

I smirked. *This should be amusing.* "And what is that, Cousin?"

"Lie."

Rumour was convinced that the best offense was a good defense. She thought that if whatever ritual the abductor was planning was strong enough to crack the gate and pull Lamia through, then it might be strong enough to bespell me, weaken me, or somehow suck me into its vortex.

What was it Lamia had said? She wanted me to be by her side when she took over Hades's throne? What had led her to believe that was even possible?

Perhaps Rumour was right. As good a poker player as I was, I wasn't the best bluffer in the Underworld. Intimidator, yes, bluffer, no. I decided that she had a point. That maybe I would have to put aside my righteousness and "play along," as she put it.

"If they think you're on their side, you'll have a better chance of defeating them," she had said.

I wasn't in the habit of pretending to be someone I was not. I was proud of my role as a Fury. Proud of all the sinners I had forced to repent. But maybe, just maybe, this was stronger than my will.

We had agreed to meet back in the casino in an hour. Right now, Archer and I were in the suite. Cerberus was sprawled across the sectional sofa, allowing no room for anyone else. Indigo was sleeping on a chair, still wrapped around the sword, and Archer was fiddling with the laptop.

I went upstairs to take a shower.

My hair was freshly rinsed of the muck of Lamia when I heard the door creak open. My wings ruffled.

Archer said, "Brought you some towels and a couple of aspirin for your head."

He set a stack of fluffy white towels down on the marble counter, and two white tablets on top of them. I could see through the glass that he was about to step from the room. He stole a quick peek in the mirror at my silhouette through the glass, then turned away.

There was one other way to replenish my power, and I couldn't think of a better man to assist me with the task.

"Archer," I called. "Would you please wash my wings?"

He stopped and turned toward the shower door slowly.

"Um, sure, if you want me to."

I poked my head out. "Oh, I want you to, Lawman."

It didn't take long for him to shrug out of his clothes. He grabbed a washcloth and joined me under the steamy water.

I danced my eyes up and down his body for a moment, enjoying the cut of him—the sculpted bone of his hips, his muscular legs, and, more importantly, what was between them. It was more than ample.

"I know. I'm not a god," he said sheepishly.

"No, you're not. You're better."

He flashed a cocky grin. "Good to know."

I turned, and he gently soaped up my feathers, stroking them with his hands, caressing them with the washcloth. He asked if the pressure was okay, if he was hurting anything, and I assured him his touch was perfect. When he was done soaping up both of my wings right down to the last feather, he explored farther down my body, washing my back, my buttocks and thighs, all the way to my ankles. Achingly slow, he crawled his way back up to my neck, kissing it in a gentle figure-eight pattern. I could feel him hardening, could feel his hands becoming more adventurous, more daring, as he wove them up and down my thighs, my hips, and around to my stomach.

In a hoarse voice, he said, "All clean on this side. Time to do the front."

The essence of me was throbbing, pulsating with heat. I was slick, through and through. I turned, pleased to see that Archer's eyes had transformed into dark depths of desire. His hair was wet from the water, his skin deliciously moist, with beads of soap bubbles painted across his chest.

My nipples hardened instantly when he brushed the warm washcloth across my breasts. I leaned my head back, enjoying the sensation of his hands on my body, and stretched my arms overhead in an open invitation.

"Don't worry about a thing. I've got this," he said, his voice rich, sensual.

I smiled. The water rained down on top of us as I gripped the edge of the shower door with both hands, resisting the urge to take charge, to lead the way, to be in control. Instead, I allowed the gratifying touch of his hands, his mouth, his tongue, to shimmy up and down my body, delving into its caverns.

He lingered between my thighs longer than I had anticipated, his hands on my hips, his mouth doing things I didn't even think were possible. He pulled me closer to him, squeezing my backside while his tongue plunged inside me and back out again, until he finally succumbed to my squirming and satisfied the most delicate fold of my body.

I cried out, gripping the shower door harder, riding wave after wave of pleasure until my force cracked the glass.

Archer kissed his way back up to my neck, glazing his hands along my sides, until he reached my face.

"I'm not done with you," I said.

He raised his eyebrows. "Oh?"

I pushed him against the back wall of the shower and wrapped one leg around him, sliding him inside me. He moaned, softly at first, then louder the harder I thrust. We moved in sync, in tandem, and just when the rhythm was perfectly poised for me to explode again, he lifted me up, twirled me around, and pushed me against the wall.

He changed motion, slowing the beat down, and it felt so achingly good that I came again and bit him on the shoulder. He cried out, but it didn't seem to hurt him; it seemed to excite him. He pumped harder, digging his hands into my waist as I wrapped my arms around his back, pulling him tighter to me. We moved together even faster, our bodies slippery against each other, soapy and wet and fitting each other perfectly.

He brought me to ecstasy once more, and I let him know with an audible gasp before he burst into me, filling me, fortifying me, satisfying me like I had never been satisfied.

Chapter 45

He decided not to stick around for the show. As much as he relished the idea of watching her face turn to horror when she realized she was never going home, he worried that perhaps the hobo would give the cops a description, and since he was wearing Jason's skin, he couldn't have that.

He went back to the dump where Jason lived to prepare the girls for their roles. Lamia was likely growing impatient, and he didn't want to risk her killing any of them before it was time. The last one—the one he really needed—would be captured tonight. He knew where to find her now.

The streets were buzzing. He watched a gaggle of girls cross the street, laughing and chatting about what fun they were having, the boys they would meet, and where to go next. They were dressed like hookers. It disturbed him.

This city never slept. There was always something to do, every hour of every day, and he enjoyed that. He enjoyed that the crowds were faceless, nameless, and completely oblivious to the dangers that lurked around every corner. Unaware that in a split second, their lives could be wiped out. Gone. Extinguished.

A shame how many people took life, freedom, for granted.

He walked for half an hour. He would have grabbed a cab but thought it best not to show his new face to too many people. He was kicking himself that he hadn't worn a hat.

Rookie mistake. He had been too eager to get the girl to think about it.

He crossed the street to a dimly lit corner where a group of young people was huddled around a burning trash can, drinking and smoking weed. That's how he had lured many a victim. Kids loved getting high. Loved getting loaded. All he had to do was buy them beer or pot, and it was easy as pie.

The apartment wasn't far from here. It had been a long walk, but the fresh air did him good. Cleared his head. The plan was in motion. He was prepared. Lamia was prepared. All he needed now was *her*.

"Hey, Jason! Where you been, man?"

A stringy-looking kid who walked like a duck approached him.

"Busy," he said, and kept walking.

"Yo, wait up."

He walked faster—he couldn't risk being seen.

"Jason, man, I said wait. I have to tell you something." The kid caught up to him. He was midtwenties, but he had the facial lines of someone much older.

"The cops came by looking for you."

He stopped. Turned.

"For what?"

"I don't know, man. They wouldn't tell me."

He looked the boy straight in the eye and growled. "Did you tell them where I live?"

The boy backed away, shaking his head. "No, man. I said I didn't know you, but they knocked on a few doors. Don't know if anyone else told them."

They knew Jason's identity. This complicated things. Had Jason been stupid enough to use his real address? Or had they tracked him here on a tip?

"What's up with you? Haven't seen you around lately."

"Busy," he snapped.

The boy raised his hands, backed away again. "All right, man, chill. Jesus. I was just trying to help."

He watched as the boy went back to join his friends. They all took turns glancing at him.

He left. Perhaps he would have to begin sooner than he had planned. And perhaps he would need another disguise.

Chapter 46

I dressed in a halter top, jeans, and boots. My power felt like it was at full throttle, as Archer would say. I slipped the moonstone ring back on my finger and checked it for messages.

Still no word from home. Why hadn't they contacted me? How would we return?

More disturbing than that was that I still didn't know where Alecto was and didn't know how to warn the gods about Charon's possible involvement in the escape, nor was I certain that Thalia had been able to deliver the message of Lamia's plans to replace Hades as ruler of the Underworld.

You'd think with all these modern conveniences that Athena would have designed a better way to keep in contact by now.

"Archer?" I said when I descended the stairs.

"Hey, Sassy." He was sipping a red Gatorade and tossed me an orange one. His hair was still damp from the shower.

"Would you please check your laptop computer for a message from Athena?"

"I can try, but I've already checked my email. There's nothing there."

He pulled out a blue plastic package from the icebox and handed it to me. "For the lump on your head."

I put the cold bag to my forehead while Archer tapped a few keys and waited for the screen to come alive. He poked around a bit, seemingly checking files. After a few minutes, he shook his head.

"Nothing here, Tisi. I'm sorry." He looked at his watch. "We better get going if you want to play poker."

I felt guilty about doing anything besides looking for my sister and the women. I felt like a failure. I felt helpless. There were no leads as to where Jason Helm lived, I had no idea what Lamia was doing or if she was still alive, and there was no portal to make contact with the gods. Or to get home.

My fury flushed through me, and before I could calm it, I punched a hole in the wall.

Archer said, "Hey, stop that before you break your hand."

He came over to me. "Listen. It's not just us looking for this guy anymore; it's the boys in blue now. I'm going to knock on a few doors, see if I can't get some answers about where Jason moved to, and then I'm going to visit Tommy. Now that I have a face to flash him, he's bound to know something."

"I'm going with you."

"No," Archer said. "You stay here, play poker with Rumour, learn whatever she needs to teach you, and try to keep an eye on the Shadow Bar. Maybe he'll show up."

I hadn't thought of that. I nodded. "Okay, I'll speak to Sam."

He kissed me on the cheek. "Don't worry. We'll get this guy, we'll get your sister back, and we can all go home."

His confidence was inspiring. "You seem so certain."

"Hey, why shouldn't I be? I've got a hellhound sleeping on the couch, a dragon snug in a chair, and a goddess standing right in front of me. I couldn't be more confident if Rambo was in the room."

"Who is—"

Archer held his hand up. "Not now. I gotta go before Tommy hits the sack." He opened the door. "But when we get back to your world, I plan on watching a lot of movies with you." He winked. "In bed."

I smiled at him, my heart tugging a bit, as the door closed behind him.

"That's not possible, Archer," I whispered.

For the first time in my life, a tear rolled down my cheek.

The lump had subsided some, so I refroze the cold pack. I decided to leave Indigo and Cerberus in the room to rest, leaving the door ajar. They'd both had a long day, and since I was only going to play poker until Archer returned, I thought it best to give them time to refuel. Tomorrow would be a big day, after all.

Rumour was tapping her foot impatiently when I arrived. "It's about time." She narrowed her eyes at me. "Did you have sex?"

"Yes."

"Wrong answer. You just failed lesson number one."

Oh.

"Where's the mortal?"

"He left to do some investigating."

She made a buzzer sound. "Wrong again."

Dammit. "Stop that."

Rumour darted her eyes around. In a hushed tone, she said, "The proper response is: He works as an acrobat in a nightly show. That's why the sex is so good."

I sighed. What had I gotten myself into? "Perhaps this was a mistake."

"Lighten up, Tisiphone. I'm only having a laugh." She grabbed my arm. "Come on, let's hit the poker table. You'll learn the true benefit of lying."

She dragged me through a sea of cigarette smoke and gamblers to the Texas Hold'em table. It wasn't far from the Shadow Bar.

"I'll be right there. I just need to check on something," I said.

I popped my head into the bar. Sam was there. I asked him if anyone had been in looking for me, hoping he got my meaning. He told me no, and that he'd been there all evening.

It was close to midnight when we handed our currency over to the dealer. He passed our chips to us, wished us luck, and put a sign on the table that read Next Game in Fifteen Minutes.

Someone tapped my shoulder. I turned to see Stacy Justice standing behind me. She was wearing dry shorts, running shoes, and a tank top. She pulled out the chair next to me and sat down.

The dealer said, "Fifty-dollar buy-in, miss."

Stacy looked at him. "I'm not playing. I just need to speak with her." She pointed to me.

The dealer shook his head. "Sorry, I need to leave the seats open for players.

Rumour walked over and whispered something in the man's ear. The dealer's eyes widened. He looked at Stacy, then at me.

"Five minutes," he said.

Stacy thanked the dealer. I looked at Rumour, who was gleefully stacking her chips. How had she done that?

Stacy leaned in to me. "I have a message for you from Bill."

"Hickok?" Odd. Once a shade was rested, Hades rarely allowed them to travel ethereally. I supposed perhaps they knew the portals had been destroyed.

She blew out a sigh, ran her fingers through her hair. "That would explain a few things, so, yes, let's go with Hickok." She pulled out a piece of paper. "He says to tell you all hell broke loose, but they're handling it. They're on lockdown now, no gods in or out, but the head honchos are trying to find a way to bring you home."

"Lockdown." I shot a glance to Rumour. She raised an eyebrow.

Stacy continued, "He said—and I quote—'the funny filly told them everything, and the big guy is well guarded.' I'm taking a stab in the dark that you know what that means."

The funny filly must be Thalia, the big guy, Hades.

"Did he mention the name Charon?"

Something flickered in Stacy's eyes, like a key twisting in a lock. She gave me the oddest look for a moment. Then she shook her head. "He said don't worry. Keep checking your messages for instructions." She glanced back at her note. "Oh, he also said it looks like everyone is accounted for."

Everyone is accounted for. He must have meant the shades. The mortals. That was good news. A mortal soul escaped from Tartarus could well become a demon.

"He also said 'be aware' or 'beware' of dead man's hand. I'm not sure which."

I smiled at that. Our little joke.

Stacy stood up. "I hope I helped."

"You did. Thank you, Stacy Justice."

She nodded and rushed off toward the man I had seen her with earlier.

The table had filled up by then, so Rumour and I didn't discuss anything that Bill had said. It would have to wait until later.

After an hour and a half, I was up in winnings, but Rumour was on fire. Either she was incredibly lucky or she was bluffing her ass off. It was fascinating to watch. She treated every player at the table like her personal pawn. She sucked on a straw for one young man wearing a sports jersey, smiled innocently at the elderly gentleman smoking a cigar, stared down the woman drinking a beer, and relayed a face of stone to me whenever I was up against her. It was as if she could read all of her opponents' personal fears, confidences, and insecurities at once. Not only that, but whenever a hand finished, she would tell these elaborate tales about where she was from (New York), what she did for a living (casting director), and how many children she had (three: Bobby, Joe, and Sarah). None of this, of course, was true.

This was not just watching a good poker player learning her opponent's tells. (A tell in poker is an unconscious tic that leaks information from one player to another.) This was a shark feeding on a feeble, lesser species and showing no mercy.

This was her art form. Lying, it seemed, was Rumour's gift.

Fifteen minutes later, it was down to the two of us. I was short-stacked. She had a mound of chips.

The dealer passed out the cards. I was holding a pair of tens.

Rumour bet twice the blind. I called. The dealer flopped the cards: 6-8-9, off suit. I had an inside straight draw, needing only a seven. Rumour was the first to act, which put me at an advantage. Depending on the size of her bet, I could venture a guess as to whether she had flopped a straight or not. She could be holding a 7-10 or a 5-7. Or she could be holding a pair of deuces. There was no way to know.

"All in," she said, straight-faced.

The dealer ushered in her chips.

I lit the fire in my eyes, just to unnerve her. She sat back and glanced away, and I was certain she was bluffing.

"I call."

The dealer scooped my chips toward him.

We both flipped our cards over. When I saw what she was holding, I looked at Rumour, shocked.

She had flopped a straight. Her cards were 7-10.

The turn came, a jack, which gave her an even higher straight. The river was another six.

I sat there staring at her with my mouth open. The dealer congratulated her, and she tipped him.

"Don't look so shocked, Tisi. I don't always bluff."

I was so certain she had.

"You don't even know how to play poker," I grumbled.

"Oh, please, what's to know? I can count, can't I? If the cards are in order, then that means I win." She stacked her chips into a tray.

"What? No, that's not at all how it works." My fury twinged. How could I have lost to this ninny? How?

We left the table and headed for the cashier's window to exchange Rumour's winnings for currency.

"By the way, what did you tell the dealer to make him allow Stacy to sit down?" I asked while she was counting the paper bills.

She folded up her winnings and put them in her pocket. "I told him she was off her medication and that you were her doctor. That you were keeping an eye on her until she came down from a manic state, and that if he didn't want a scene, he should just let her speak with you a moment."

"That's reprehensible," I said.

"It worked."

I couldn't argue with that, so I didn't bother trying. We discussed what Stacy had told me, what Hickok had told her.

Rumour chewed her lip. "So, they are coming for us?"

"Of course they are." I gave her my portable telephone so that she could input her number into it. She did the same with her phone for my number.

"Do you think they'll make it in time? Before the eclipse? Before whatever is going to happen happens?"

"Yes. I have faith in our gods."

Rumour sighed. "Okay. Keep me posted. I'm going to get some rest." She told me her room number, and I gave her mine. She started off, and I spun around toward the Shadow Bar.

"Tisi," my cousin called.

I turned back.

"Just remember what I said, okay? Whatever it is, bluff. If you believe it, he will too."

I nodded. Rumour spun around to head toward the elevator.

Chapter 47

A cruiser was parked in the pothole-ridden lot of the complex. Normally he would be polite to the cops, ask them inside for a drink, invite them to dinner. He was smarter than they were, and he loved to screw with them. Loved the game of outwitting them. But he couldn't risk that now. There was too much at stake.

He saw the cops pounding on doors, although he doubted they would think to go to the basement apartment. It wasn't even legal to rent; it was supposed to be a storage area. Jason had assured him he was living there off the books. He doubted the manager would risk his tax-free income over a busted-up statue.

Still, he didn't like the fact that they knew his borrowed identity and possibly even what his face looked like.

Best to get the disguise now. Best to hurry things along.

He turned on his heel and walked toward town. This time he did hail a cab, asking the driver to deposit him on the Strip.

It didn't take long to find what he was looking for, and he still had the money from the wallet he had found in Jason's apartment. He tossed the ID card in a trash can just outside the shop. He selected his purchases quickly, careful not to look the clerk in the eye, paid for them, and left.

He took his shopping bags and slipped into a bathroom at the nearest casino. He dressed with care, then shoved Jason's clothes into one of the empty bags. After that, he pulled out the makeup kit and carefully applied the thick paint to Jason's face until he was satisfied with the outcome. He adjusted the wig, took one last look in the mirror, and left the place, tossing the rest of the bag of Jason's clothes, along with the empty bags in the garbage.

He felt confident and comfortable as he walked the Strip. He even posed for a few pictures—free of charge, of course, just like the old days.

Children rushed up to hug him, and he thought it was criminal that they were out so late and not in bed, dreaming of good things to come. He obliged the little ones, of course, while cursing their parents under his breath.

He continued on, toward his destination.

Caesars Palace was abuzz with activity. He was happy to see the statue of the three broads roped off. He marched right up to the concierge desk and asked for an envelope and a piece of paper. He helped himself to a pen.

He wasn't worried about being spotted by the cops or anyone in his new disguise. It was perfect. He blended into the crowd easily, just another performer walking around Las Vegas.

He saw her approaching a poker table. She was with another woman. One of *them*? He wasn't sure. She didn't look familiar. She was thin, with blond hair cut in a sharp line. They sat down and handed the dealer some money. He found a slot machine that provided the perfect camouflage while still allowing him to watch her. He put some bills into the machine and played for about an hour. Then, when it looked like her table was winding down, he wrote a note, licked the envelope, and sealed it.

He wove his way over to the Shadow Bar and delivered the note.

If he could play with the cops, he could certainly play with her.

Chapter 48

The Shadow Bar was vibrant by the time I made my way over there. The music was pumping, the dancers writhing behind the screens, as hues of blue, pink, and green flashed across the stage. Sam and another bartender were busy pouring drinks, flirting with patrons, and putting on a flamboyant show of tossing bottles back and forth to each other.

I had to admit, it was entertaining.

I finally managed to catch Sam's eye after ten minutes.

"Hi, Sam. Any news for me?"

"Actually, yes." He turned to reach beneath the cash machine. He pulled out a long white envelope. It was addressed to me. The envelope was sealed.

"Is this from our friend?" I asked.

Sam scratched his head. "I don't think so."

I cocked an eyebrow at him. "What do you mean, you don't think so? Was it him or not?"

"I didn't take the note. Bret did." He pointed to the other bartender, who was busy pouring drinks.

I guessed I would find out soon enough.

Sam wandered over to say something to Bret, and I spun around to leave, tapping the note against my hand. The handwriting was scratchy, my name spelled out in block letters.

A moment later, Sam chased me into the casino. "Tisi!"

I turned.

"Bret said the guy was dressed like a clown."

Chapter 49

He couldn't help himself—he had to watch. From a safe distance, of course. He wasn't a complete lunatic. He circled around the far side of the bar, down Cleopatra's Way, and back over to the area where people placed bets on horses and sporting events. Jason had given him the layout of the place, and he knew it like the back of his hand. He waited for her to duck into the bar, knew she couldn't resist checking to see if he would show up. As soon as she slipped inside, he positioned himself near the escalator that led to the Strip.

When the show began, it was like slow motion.

Her leaving with the envelope in her hand. The bartender rushing after her a moment later. The look of stunned realization on her face when he told her who had delivered the letter.

And then those beautiful eyes filled with fury when she scanned the casino floor, darting this way and that, looking for him.

Until finally she lifted up her head and spotted him.

He couldn't help but chuckle.

Chapter 50

"Gacy!" I shouted.

He was on the escalator that carried people up to the Strip, and I was yards away, but my fury pumped through my legs and I ran faster than I ever had before, shoving the letter into my back pocket. I had to dodge cocktail waitresses, drunken patrons, gamblers carrying around notebooks, and the occasional chair-confined human. I knew my wings could get me to him faster, but I doubted the width of the escalator could accommodate them. He was just reaching the top when I made it there.

I took the moving stairs two at a time, but he had a head start on me and was faster than he had been as a mortal.

He was still in my sight when I reached the moving pathway. I ran, pumping my legs as hard as I could. He ran too, knocking people down along the way.

I heard shouts of "Hey!" and "Watch it!" and "Stop him!"

That last one was me.

He made it out of the tunnel before I did. The crowd was thick, as if the city was just waking up. I looked left, then right. I saw a rainbow-colored wig like the one he was wearing bobbing along in the sea of humans and took off after it, launching my wings.

Except they didn't open.

Oh no. No! Had I used too much power already today? Why weren't they functioning?

I ran faster, dodging this way and that, careening left and right, narrowly missing a trash can, a chair-bound human, and a furry human in a cat costume.

Minutes later, I spotted him again. I took a running leap and tackled him to the pavement. People gasped all around me, jumping out of the way.

"I've got you now, you son of a demon's spawn!"

I flipped him over, clutching his shirt in my hands, my fury engorged, my eyes still illuminated. I stared at his big red nose, daring him to say something that would make me want to end him.

But he didn't say anything. He just lay there shivering, his blue eyes filled with fright.

Blue eyes.

Mortals who had been to Tartarus never had anything but black eyes after they entered. It was their mark. Even if he had somehow changed his appearance, these eyes were filled with light, with hope, and love.

"Please don't hurt me," said the man. His voice trembled.

I let go.

Someone pulled me off the man as people stared at me with disgust.

It was Archer. "Hey, I told you there was no practice tonight," he said to me, a strained smile on his face.

He extended his hand to the tearful man and said, "Sorry, pal. She had you mistaken for me."

I scanned the crowd. Was Gacy still here? If he was, I couldn't spot him.

The man accepted Archer's assistance and scrambled to his feet.

"My deepest apologies. Is there anything I can do?" I said.

The man inched away, straightening out his costume. "I'm fine. Simple mistake." His voice was still shaky.

I stepped forward. "I feel terrible. May I offer you some currency?"

"No, no, I'll just be going." He turned and ran.

After a few frustrating moments of not seeing Gacy anywhere and feeling like a complete jackass, I heard Archer say, "I'm not crazy about clowns either, but maybe it's best we don't tackle them just for looking creepy."

I pulled him off to the side. "You don't understand. It's him. It's been him this whole time." I kicked a garbage can and it toppled over, spilling out half-eaten food, some foul-smelling clothes, beer bottles, and plastic cups.

Heat was rising off my body in steamy waves.

"Who?" Archer asked.

I said through gritted teeth, "Gacy."

Archer looked behind him as if the serial killer would be standing right there at the mention of his name. He swung his head back to me. "John Wayne Gacy?" he whispered.

"Yes."

"Are you sure?"

I flamed my eyes.

Archer raised his hands. "Okay, okay. You need to calm down."

"Don't tell me to calm down. I put that heartless snail sludge away years ago. And now he's back!" I was angry. I wanted to tear something apart.

My wings fluttered then. They were working. Why hadn't they worked moments ago? The thought of Gacy? Had he somehow paralyzed my flight?

Archer said, "You really need to work on your use of profanity. It may help ease your temper."

I glared at him and pivoted. I had to find him. I had a trail and I couldn't lose it. But which way?

There was a clanking sound behind me. Archer had picked up the trash can. I knelt down to assist him.

We tossed bottles and paper bags back into the bin. Archer reached for the clothes, then jumped back, wrinkling his nose. "Oh, that's nasty-smelling." He put his arm in front of his nose and mouth.

He was right. The clothes smelled foul. I leaned in to sniff.

"Ick. What are you doing?" He gagged.

I knew that odor. "Lamia. He's the one working with Lamia. These were his clothes before he changed. He must have found the costume nearby." I sifted through the trash with a pencil someone had tossed in the can. There was a bag with the name Costume Central printed on it. I stood up, saw the name of the store just two doors down.

"Archer, he purchased the clown suit right there." I pointed to the small building. The shop windows held three caped costumes, and one black-and-white, giant, furry animal costume. "Should we talk to the clerk? Maybe she'd remember something that could help."

Archer wasn't listening to me. He picked something up off the cement. Some small card. "That son of a bitch has my wallet." He frowned.

"Archer," I hissed.

"Huh? I'm sorry."

I tossed the remaining trash in the can. "Well, let's go talk to the clerk."

Archer said, "I have a better idea. Let's go get Helm and Gacy."

"How?"

"I got his address." Archer smiled, waving a little piece of paper in front of me.

"Let's go get the son of a bitch."

"That's my goddess."

Chapter 51

As a partner and an assistant, Lamia proved to be useless. Besides stinking up the joint, she had gotten herself injured and was moving quite slowly. She was asleep now, so at least he didn't have to listen to that god-awful voice. As if it weren't bad enough that he had to arrange practically everything himself, from dressing up the girls to their transport, since Lamia had no legs, he also had to put up with her constant bitching about being hungry. Her only redeeming quality was her penchant for potions. He decided he would have to kill her soon.

Once the girls had all been dosed, it was easy to get them dressed in their custom costumes. He bound them together two by two, deciding it best to feed them on the way.

The calm one was still wearing her mask, and he was growing tired of her lack of emotion, lack of tears.

He removed it, and she looked at him with dead eyes for a moment.

Then she blinked, and her eyes sparkled as if they contained a thousand tiny stars. One of those stars shot at him, landing on his cheek. It melted his makeup and singed his skin.

He yelled in anguish, quickly put the blindfold on, and then backhanded her with both hands.

The girl tied to her whimpered.

"Well, well, well, I do believe I am in the presence of a Fury," he said. He patted his cheek where she had burned him. "Funny, though, you don't seem as strong as your sister."

At the mention of the word "sister," the Fury's forehead twitched. Just a smidge. Just a hair. In fact, to the untrained eye, it looked like she hadn't moved a single nerve ending at all. But he was well versed in his Furies. Though he had met only the one. The one whose name he could not speak, for it had been taken from him after his trial. He could never utter her name—no matter how hard he concentrated, how hard he focused, his tongue was simply no longer equipped to form the name. He couldn't even think it or write it, unless he wrote it backward, which was what he had done on the envelope.

Such a strange restriction. He had wondered over the years—over those many years he had been locked up, chained to rocks, forced to attend redemption seminars—what that meant. Was there some sort of power in her name? Would that have allowed him to control her? Or was it simply because she was the only one who had served in Tartarus to guard the blackest of souls?

The other two, he knew, had never been assigned such a daunting task. Was that because they were weaker? Or because they lacked the guts to kill as she had?

"So, who do I have before me?"

Silence, though she was no longer gagged.

"Alecto? Megaera? Come on, fess up."

She didn't flinch.

"I suppose it doesn't matter. I now have two Furies for the price of one."

Her brow twitched.

"Oh, didn't you hear? Your sister has come for you, but I'm afraid she's been captured as well." He whispered in her ear, "There's no one to save you."

She head-butted him, sending his wig flying. He thought about slicing her throat right there, but that would ruin everything. Now that he had the sister, he had bait, leverage.

Which meant even more pain and suffering for her.

He wondered if perhaps that other—the blonde—was worth anything to *her*.

Only one way to find out.

He smiled as he slipped out of the apartment and locked the door.

Chapter 52

Archer explained in the taxi that Tommy had indeed known Jason Helm; they had lived in the same complex, gotten drunk together, done drugs together, before Tommy had tried to get sober. When he had, he had noticed that Jason seemed to be unstable. Tommy had pulled away from the friendship even before he lost his apartment. Helm, Tommy had told Archer, was becoming increasingly unhinged.

"He was obsessed with black magic, Satan, and serial killers," Archer said.

That explained Gacy and, in turn, Lamia's draw to him. He had probably called to the monsters many times. Perhaps at first they had arrived as voices. Then maybe visions. Ouija boards were known to be a conduit to all kinds of souls, even the darkest ones. I suspected that when the gate cracked open, the monsters Tommy was worshipping had become stronger, which allowed them to escape in full form.

Most likely with Charon's assistance.

We arrived at the apartment complex within minutes. Archer tipped the driver.

"He said we can access it through a back door. The place is in the basement."

I took a deep breath. *Let this be it. Let no one else be harmed.*

We crept around the back of the building. It was dark, no streetlights anywhere to be found, and the moon was still hidden.

There was a ramp on the far side of a rusty green Dumpster. Archer pointed, as if to say, *This way.*

I followed him, wishing I had brought my sword. Archer had his weapon, but if Lamia was here, only a blade would do the trick. At least, that was what I suspected after she had seemingly taken several bullets to the abdomen and slithered away.

Then a terrifying thought occurred to me. How could I kill Gacy? Did it work the same as with Archer? If his body were injured—his reanimated body—would it rot and fall off piece by piece? Or was he now immortal? I hated all of these unknowns.

Down the ramp was a small steel door with a metal lock. Archer pulled out some sort of tool and used it to crack the lock open. It worked. The door creaked open, scraping the cement ramp.

Archer motioned for me to follow him, and I did.

We hugged a wall, ducking down because the ceilings were low. He took out a small flashlight and shone it into the hallway.

Behind me, something screeched.

We both spun around, Archer with his gun pointed at the noise, and me lighting my fury. Archer shone the flashlight down the hall on two beady eyes.

A rat.

I shook my head, and Archer blew out a sigh. We continued down the dark hallway and turned right at the end of it.

There were two doors. One on the right, one on the left. Archer pointed to the one on the right. I nodded.

The door wasn't steel like the outer door. It had a simple lock.

Oddly trusting for a criminal.

Archer put his ear to the door. He looked down at the ground, looking for a light, a sign of life, anything.

There was a soft glow coming from beneath the door.

Archer held up his fingers. He mouthed, *One, two, three.*

He turned and kicked the door open, gun drawn, and I flipped on the light and engaged my fury. I was strong now, prepared for battle with my bare hands if need be.

A rotten, putrid smell engulfed us, and we both gagged.

The room held five rickety bed frames with five soiled mattresses. Five sets of handcuffs were bolted to the ceiling. There was a tiny closet to the left and a dinky kitchen to the right. Next to one of the mattresses, on the far wall, was a window. Beneath it lay a pulpy, bloody, crusted body.

The skin had been removed.

"What the hell?" Archer walked over to the body. He leaned over it. "What did this? Lamia?" He couldn't stop staring at the corpse.

"No. Gacy. He must be wearing Jason Helm's skin. I've seen this before."

Archer leaned in for a closer look. He shuddered. Then he kicked the corpse.

"Archer."

He looked at me. "What? This dirtbag killed me."

"That's not what I meant. Look."

I trained my eyes to the space just above the window.

Two words.

You're late.

They were written in blood.

I realized then that I hadn't yet read the note Gacy had dropped off.

I tore into the envelope.

So you like to play poker, eh? And I thought I knew everything about you. That should liven up the festivities tomorrow. So here's how it's gonna be. Meet me in the desert, five thirty sharp. The coordinates are below. Every minute you're late, I'll chop a finger off one of the girls, starting with your sister.

PS: I see you brought a friend. Is it true that blondes have more fun?

"Oh my gods."

"What?" Archer asked.

"He's going after Rumour."

Chapter 53

I ran outside, Archer close on my heels, and attempted to phone Rumour. No answer, but I left a message warning her.

"I'll get a cab," he said.

"Not fast enough," I said.

I bear-hugged Archer, pumped my wings, and flew us to Caesars Palace.

I was able to land in a quiet lot at the back of the building reserved for delivery trucks. We hustled through the entrance and over to the elevator. I didn't see Gacy anywhere in sight. I told Archer to get Cerberus and Indigo and gave him Rumour's suite number. He tossed me his firearm.

The elevator spit me out on a floor two rows up from ours. I followed the signs to the room where my cousin had told me she was staying.

The door was wide open.

The room looked like it hadn't even been occupied. The bed was made; there were no dishes on the table, no personal items in the bathroom, no towels hanging over the shower door.

Did I have the wrong room?

Archer came up behind me then, out of breath. "Here."

He handed me my sword. I walked farther into the room, parted a curtain with the tip of my blade. Nothing.

I pivoted to Archer. "I'm pretty certain this is the room number she gave me."

Archer swung his head to the closet and back to me. I nodded, gripping the sword with both hands.

He flung the door open, and out toppled a suitcase. The bag was covered in a cabbage-rose pattern, so it was definitely Rumour's. Roses were her favorite.

I bent down to unzip it. Inside was another note.

It said simply, *Tick-tock.*

"Agh!"

I threw the suitcase across the room, ripped up the note, and stormed out. How could I have allowed this to happen? Two goddesses were now in the clutches of a madman. Two. I should have insisted Rumour return with Thalia and Molpe. Should have demanded it. How could I have been so stupid? Now Zeus had his Thalia back and Poseidon his Molpe, but my lord was missing two of his charges.

Damn you, Gacy! Damn you to the fiery pits of Tartarus!

I couldn't believe this. Couldn't believe I had to battle this mortal yet again. Except now he wasn't mortal. He was a monster. And I had no idea if he had powers or not. Perhaps he had only weapons.

I prayed that was so.

I rushed into our room, slammed the door behind me, and put my sword on the table. I took the stairs two at a time, peeled off my clothes, and crawled into bed. It was four o'clock in the morning when my head finally hit the pillow, but I was so full of adrenaline, I feared I would never sleep.

There was a knock at the door.

Who would be knocking on my door at this hour?

I flung on a robe and tiptoed out into the hallway, listening.

"Um, Tisi, can you let us in? I left my key in the room."

I opened the door, and Archer and Cerberus entered. "Sorry," I grumbled.

Archer didn't say anything. He just pulled me into him and kissed the top of my head. I was grateful for that. It melted some of the tension away.

We climbed the stairs hand in hand and buried our bodies under the covers.

I awoke to the nuzzle of a gigantic hound's head. Cerberus was poking me with his nose, sniffing my neck and hands, searching for signs of life.

I petted him to let him know I was awake, and he trotted from the room. I flung my legs over the side of the bed, and sat there a moment, willing the fog from my brain. The drapes were closed, so the room was still quite dark. I glanced at the clock.

It was 4:00 p.m.

That woke me up. I shot out of bed and dressed hurriedly in jean shorts and the last halter top I could find. My wings were resting beneath their enchantment, but I really should have brought my own clothes to better fit them. I slathered on some sunscreen and darted downstairs.

Archer had a tray of food and a purple Gatorade waiting for me. He was wearing a T-shirt, jeans, and boots.

"Good, you're up. I was just about to wake you."

"Let's go." I grabbed my boots and sat down to put them on.

"We have a few minutes. You need to eat something." He grabbed the plate of food covered by the silver tray and popped it into a small box. He punched in some numbers on the box, and it lit up. I could see the cheeseburger and potatoes spinning around.

"There's much to do, Archer. I can eat on the way." I zipped up my boots.

The box chimed, and Archer removed the plate of food. He put ketchup and mustard on the sandwich and set it in front of me. I was tucking Indigo into my right boot.

"I already rented a car with GPS, plugged in the coordinates, stocked it with food and drinks for the women, and secured more ammo."

He sat down across from me and took a long pull on a water bottle. I shoved a few fried potatoes into my mouth. As soon as I swallowed them down, I realized I was famished. I had hardly eaten at all the day before.

"How long will it take to travel to where we need to be?"

I bit into my burger. It was juicy, and seasoned with just the right amount of salt and pepper.

"Forty minutes." Archer reached for a fried potato.

I took another bite of my burger and grabbed a napkin to wipe the mustard from my mouth.

Archer reached behind him for a bag. He pulled out three guns, two knives, and some orange sticks—flares, he called them.

"Have you ever shot a gun?"

I shook my head and shoveled more potatoes into my mouth.

"Well, you're about to. There's a place I used to go in the desert to shoot. Just so happens it's on the way."

I shook my head, chewing on the last of the cheeseburger. I hated guns. Hated the carnage they caused, the destruction they could wreak in the blink of an eye.

I swallowed my food. "No guns."

Archer leaned close to me. His face had more color in it today than it had when we had first arrived in Las Vegas. He smelled like lime and basil.

"Don't argue with me. We have no idea what we're up against. I want you to be prepared."

"I have my sword and I have Cerberus." I shot him a contentious look. "I do not need a firearm."

Archer stood and pushed his chair in. "This is not up for debate. Now get your shit together, get your ass in the car, and stop giving me attitude."

I stood up and kicked the chair out of the way. "Just who do you think you are? No one has ever spoken to me like that in my life!"

Archer met my glare with his own. He stepped forward. "Is that so? Well, maybe somebody should have. Would have saved me the trouble."

I reached up to slap him, but he caught my hand. He smirked at the look of surprise I must have been wearing. "You can bite me in the shower, babe, but that's my limit."

I wanted to scrape that smug look off his face. "I hope you enjoyed it, because that's the last time that will ever happen." I gave him my own smirk.

He stepped closer. He was less than an inch from my face, still holding my wrist. He lingered there for a long while. My heart beat faster when he leaned in to kiss me, and my eyes closed involuntarily.

Only he didn't kiss me. He whispered in my ear, "Don't make promises you can't keep."

He dropped my hand, grabbed the duffel bag, and walked out the door.

Chapter 54

The blonde was easy. She didn't put up much of a struggle after he threatened to slice her throat.

The drive out to the desert was one of the longest of his life. Lamia stunk up the entire car, but he still needed her, he decided. He didn't tell her about the other Fury. Best to keep that to himself. He guessed that she, like he, had seen only *her*. Not her sisters. He wondered why that was. Why they used only the one to deal with people like him. He wondered if the sisters weren't as good at their job, or if they just didn't have the skills to take down someone as smart as he was, or as twisted as the snake woman. He wondered what would happen in the desert. Would the other sister show up?

Because that would be delicious.

Lamia was lazing around in the sand, complaining about the sun and the heat, not helping him set up, as usual. The bitch was useless. More trouble than she was worth, and he wanted to strangle her with her own tongue.

Right now, the girls were all in place, all doing what they were told. He had blindfolded all of them, dressed them in matching, loose-fitting black dresses. Not to be cruel, because that wasn't his style, but if he wanted to play with her, he had to make sure she couldn't identify any of the game pieces.

Always stack the deck in your favor.

He smiled at his cleverness. He had even bought a black wig for the blonde to wear.

He lined them all up, spaced them out just enough that she couldn't compare them side by side. It was perfect.

The sun was beating down on the sand, and he was drinking water to keep hydrated. He made sure they all had enough water before they took their places. He couldn't have anyone passing out from dehydration.

It wouldn't be long now. The eclipse was coming. Soon he would have his sweet revenge and Lamia would get her kingdom. Not that he gave a shit about that. It was this world he wanted, this world he had come back for. And when he took the Fury's life—the life that had taken his once—her immortality, Charon had told him, would leap into his soul.

He could go on killing forever.

He smiled at the thought, adjusted his wig, and went to get the cards.

Chapter 55

We drove in silence for a while. I was still angry, but I was trying to curb my fury. I suspected I would need it.

Finally Archer said, "We're here."

He exited the car, grabbed the bag, and swung around to my side. He opened the door. "Are you coming?"

I didn't answer him.

Archer sighed. "Look, Tisi, we've got a job to do. You can be mad at me later, but right now I need you focused."

I looked at him. "I don't like guns."

"I know, and I'm sorry I yelled at you. I just want you to be safe. I want us all to walk away from this unharmed."

I got out of the car. "But don't you see? Your bullets didn't kill Lamia. My sword will."

"That's true, but they did stop her."

He was right about that. He had been right about a lot of things. Perhaps I was being too stubborn. We truly didn't know what we were dealing with. A soul had never escaped from Tartarus. Were there more of them than just Gacy? Would they be walking into an ambush?

Perhaps, when you've been dealt a wild card, it's best to approach it with an equally wild plan of attack. "Okay. Tell me what to do."

We had traveled deep into the desert. There were no buildings around, no lights except the sun. Aside from the mountains off in the distance and a few cacti, we were alone.

Archer led me to an area between two boulders. He explained how to load the weapon, how to hold it, where to position my eye to aim a shot, and the stance that he used.

He went first, calling each shot before he fired. A cactus leaf, a red rock several yards away, and an abandoned soda can someone had carelessly left behind.

He was right on target.

"Your turn."

The weapon was heavier than it looked. I stood the way Archer had and aimed for the same soda can. The shot was loud, and my fingers tingled a bit from the impact, but it wasn't as awkward as I'd thought it would be. It was quite exhilarating, in fact—although I completely missed the can.

"Try closing your right eye," Archer suggested.

I did and came much closer to the can. I fired a few more rounds, hitting the soda can twice, before my ring glowed.

"There's a message from the gods." Finally!

Archer liberated the gun from my hand, and I tapped the moonstone.

Stand by for a message.

Archer reloaded the guns while I waited to hear from Olympus. It felt like it was at least a hundred degrees today, and my skin was already damp with perspiration.

A moment later, the message came.

The Norse god Thor has agreed to assist Zeus with your retrieval. At 5:55 an eclipse will blanket Las Vegas. You will have exactly five minutes to be in position. The gods will open the sky and pull you through the human realm and into ours. If your mission is not complete, you are to abandon it. I repeat, abandon mission and get to the location. The energy that will

be expended for this rescue could rock both worlds, severing all portals across the globe. Any god left behind will become mortal, banished to the human realm forever. Godspeed, and good luck.
—Athena

The message was followed by the coordinates.

I relayed the information to Archer. He frowned. "That's close to where we're headed, but not as close as I would like."

Athena hadn't mentioned what would happen to Archer if we missed the window. Would he become mortal too? Or would he simply cease to be?

Archer looked at his watch. "We better go."

When we got back to the car, Cerberus was missing.

I scanned the desert, called to him, and Archer whistled. He didn't respond.

Perhaps his time here was done. Perhaps Artemis had called him home.

"I don't understand it. Where could he have gone?" I asked.

"I don't know, but he can take care of himself, right? I mean, he got here all by himself."

"Not quite. Artemis sent him. Animals can travel more freely between realms, it's true. They often act as spirit guides for humans, and when they receive the call, they must go." I shielded my eyes from the sun and did another search. "I just think it's strange that he would leave when he was specifically sent to assist us."

"What do you want to do?" Archer asked.

I called to the hound one last time. He didn't come.

It was getting late.

"We have no choice. We have to go."

We secured the various weapons Archer had purchased to our bodies and drove the rest of the bumpy way into the desert. I asked Archer about the orange sticks, and he said they were "just in case."

I told Indigo to ready herself for battle. She snorted a puff of smoke at me and blinked.

The car bumped along the desert sand to the coordinates Gacy had given us.

Archer rolled to a stop. He turned the car off, turned to me, and squeezed my hand. "You ready?"

I looked at him. "Let's end this."

We got out of the car and walked toward the sun.

Lamia was leaning against a rock, looking as if she had been trampled by a pack of wild boars.

Past her were five women, all of them very close in height, all of them with black hair, all of them dressed alike in roomy, gauzy black dresses. They were facing away from us and seemed to be blindfolded, judging from the trailing ties that hung from the backs of their heads. Their hands were bound.

What was his plan?

Lamia hissed. "Soooooo, Fury, we meet again." Her tongue was lolling from her mouth. It wasn't taut like it had been, but stretched out and torn in places. Her eyes were paler, her skin scaly and dry. The mucus gone. Her midsection where Archer had shot her bubbled and gurgled, still filled with holes.

"Lamia, you look like a deflated elephant scrotum. You should see someone about that," I said.

She tried to snap her tongue at me, but it just waved and fell.

"Ssssooooon," she said tiredly.

"Whatever you say."

I studied the women. They were ten feet away. Which was Alecto? Which was Rumour? More importantly, did Alecto have any power at all? Or had the sun and her captivity stripped it?

Gacy popped out from behind a rock, and I couldn't help thinking how appropriate that was.

"You're on time. Good. For now, at least." He chuckled. He was wearing that damn clown suit.

"All right, Gacy, I'm here. Tell me what you want, and I'll see what I can do about it so that no one gets hurt. So what is it? A warmer rock in Tartarus? A view of the fire pit?"

"Right down to business, eh? I see you're even wearing your uniform."

My wings had been exposed since we had left the shooting range.

Archer moved beside me, and Gacy flicked his eyes to him. "Uh-uh-uh." He wagged a finger. "Don't even think about it." He pulled out a knife and put it to one of the women's throat. She gasped.

I knew then she was not Alecto.

"Drop your weapons or she dies."

Archer pulled a gun from the back of his shorts and dropped it.

"Now the other one," Gacy said.

Archer swallowed hard. He bent down, lifted his pant leg, and removed a second gun. He dropped it on the ground.

"And I suspect there might be one more," Gacy said.

Archer shook his head. "Nope. That's it."

Gacy looked at me, his black eyes gleaming. "Who is this joker? I thought you worked alone."

When I didn't respond, he said, "No matter—I'll show him who I am." He pressed the knife into the woman's neck, and she cried out. A trickle of blood dripped down her dress. My fury flared, but I fought to steady my wings. I didn't want them activated. Not yet. Not until I knew where all this was leading.

"Okay!" Archer said, and removed a third gun from his boot.

"Now kick them over here," Gacy said, and Archer complied.

The voice of the woman he had cut did not belong to Rumour either. It belonged to one of the mortals.

Gacy looked at me. "Your turn, Fury."

I removed the gun Archer had given me from my boot. The lawman winced.

Gacy locked his eyes on me. "A gun, Goddess? Really? Didn't anyone ever tell you not to bring a gun to a knife fight?" He laughed. "That is so beneath you."

His gaze was still on me, and I fanned the fire in my eyes. If I could get close to him, perhaps I could impose my will, as I had on the man in the bar, Clyde, and Archer.

Gacy squinted. "You don't actually think that will work on me, do you? You should know better than that."

He was probably right. His soul was too twisted to bend.

"Kick the weapon over to me."

I did.

"Now lift your hands and turn around."

I did, keeping my wings steady.

"You too," he said to Archer.

He complied.

"Lift up your shirt."

He did and pivoted.

Gacy ordered Lamia to empty the ammunition from the weapons. She crept over to him. It took her some time, but she did it. She seemed to be exhausted. She didn't return to her rock but hovered right where she was, near Gacy.

She was weak—that was obvious. I knew she wouldn't be a problem. If I could separate Gacy from the girls, then I could kill him.

But how? And with what?

Something was niggling at the back of my brain. A lesson I had learned long ago from Hades about the souls of Tartarus. Something that I had never had to retain, because no soul had ever escaped, but that I could sure use right now.

What was it?

"Now the sword."

Indigo. I had to keep her safe. He couldn't know about her. Lamia knew, but she was losing consciousness.

I slowly slipped my hand into my thigh-high boot and quietly snapped my finger, hoping she had picked up the trick from Cerberus. It worked. Indigo stilled. I pulled out the sword.

"Go put it in the car." He cocked his head.

I had to turn my back on him to walk to the car. He was smarter than I thought. He knew if he asked me to kick it, I might just sail it into his skull.

So that was one option down the drain.

I considered reanimating Indigo, but I knew Gacy would be watching me closely and I didn't want to risk anyone's life. I placed her in the backseat, tucking her in Archer's bag, leaving room for her head to stick out.

When I returned, I said, "All right, Gacy, we're unarmed. Now tell me what you want."

He tilted his head, and that goofy, painted-on smile shifted. "Don't you know? Why, you, of course."

This was getting irritating. "Fine. You have me. Now release your captors and allow them safe passage."

He acted as if he were considering it. "Hmm." He shook his head. "No, no, I don't think so. I think we'll have a bit of fun first."

He pulled out a deck of cards.

What in the world?

"I think we'll play a little poker first." He tossed me the deck, and I caught it. "As you can see, it's never been opened, so you can't accuse me of cheating."

I tossed it back. He let it hit the sand. "I'm not playing poker with you. Enough is enough. Let them go, and battle me as you intended."

Archer was stone silent. I knew he was itching to do something, but that knife at the woman's neck was giving him pause. We were several feet away.

"Tell you what: I'll make it interesting for you. We'll play best out of three. If you win, you get to choose who lives and who dies."

Lamia stirred at this. She hissed at Gacy, slapping him with her tongue. "No, mortal. That was not the arrangement. We need all five for Pluto's moon rite."

Gacy kept his blade to the woman's throat and his stare on me. "I don't give a shit about that anymore. I have the Fury right in front of me."

Lamia lunged at Gacy. He whipped a machete out from behind him and sliced her in two.

She didn't make another sound, but the odor was almost unbearable. I didn't bat an eye, just kept staring at Gacy as if nothing had happened. Lamia evaporated into the sand in a whirl of gargling screams and bubbling innards.

One monster down, one to go.

"And if you win?" I asked.

He stared at me with those coal-colored eyes. "They all die. And I get your soul—and with it, immortality in this world."

So that was his plan. He wanted to stay here. To keep killing.

But could he do that? Could he gain immortality by stealing my soul? I thought it was protected. That the reason my name was stricken from my mortal enemies' vocabularies was so they couldn't rob any of my power, including my immortality.

Only the Fates, and perhaps Charon, would know for certain if it was possible. And given all that I had seen in the last few days, it seemed anything was possible.

"Shall we begin?"

I thought of what Rumour had said. *Play along. If you believe it, so will he.*

Ordinarily, I wouldn't make a deal with evil, whether I intended to keep it or not. Wouldn't give in to their sick games on any level. I would attack, I would battle, I would fight for justice.

But this was no ordinary circumstance. Sometimes when the chips are stacked against you, it's best to bluff.

"I'm in."

Chapter 56

Gacy pulled out a pair of metal handcuffs. He tossed them to Archer. "Put these on."

Archer did as instructed.

Gacy looked at the spot where Lamia had disintegrated. The machete was still in his hand, dripping with her black blood.

"I guess she can't deal, so it'll have to be you, Stretch."

"You want me to shuffle and deal cards with my hands cuffed?"

Gacy turned his stone-cold eyes on Archer. "Is that a problem?"

Archer set his mouth into a firm line. His jaw was tense, but he didn't say anything.

"Good," said Gacy. "Now, what shall we play?" He counted the females out loud. "One, two, three, four, five. Not enough for Texas Hold'em. I guess it'll have to be Five-Card Draw or Five-Card Stud."

Archer removed the jokers and shuffled the cards.

Best two out of three. I had better odds with Five-Card Draw because I could discard up to three cards and redraw. With Stud, each player received only five cards. No discards. No draws. I almost opted for the former, but then Gacy explained to Archer where he was supposed to deal the cards.

Each of the women had a pocket in the front and a pocket in the back of her dress, crudely sewn. Gacy wanted Archer to put a card in every pocket.

I asked, "If I were to choose Five-Card Draw, are there any house rules?"

Gacy smiled sinisterly. "My, but you are a worthy opponent, aren't you?" He held up the machete. "The rule is, I get to kill any discards."

He licked the blade of the machete, and I nearly vomited.

Alex, give me a signal. You must have some fight in you, even if your wings don't work, I thought.

A cloud passed overhead then, and I looked up.

Only it wasn't a cloud, it was the new moon approaching the sun.

Gacy was staring at me when I lowered my head. "Tick. Tock."

I swallowed a lump. How was I going to do this? Archer was handcuffed, Indigo was stilled, and Cerberus was nowhere in sight.

I did have an ace up my sleeve—or, rather, my wing—but I wanted to wait for the right moment to use it. My eyes were stinging from the dry heat and the desert sun. I blinked a few times, to moisturize them.

And that's when I remembered exactly how to annihilate an escaped mortal from Tartarus.

"Let's make it even more interesting, Gacy. One hand, Five-Card Stud. Winner takes all."

Archer made a funny sound and shot me a look like *Are you nuts?* as he dealt the cards.

Gacy rocked back on his big, red, flappy shoes. "I do like your style, Fury. Agreed."

The eclipse was coming, which meant there was not a minute to spare. We needed to be at the exact spot where the gods would pick us up, all of us, by 6:00 p.m. I was leaving no one behind.

Gacy stepped forward to the first female and ordered me to do the same. I did.

He picked up the first card, eyes on me, still holding the smaller knife. He positioned the machete to curve toward the neck of the woman.

I picked up my card. Ace.

Gacy tucked the card back in the pocket, and I did the same. He moved to the next girl and put the machete at her throat. He picked up the card, and I did the same. Eight. Ace-8.

"I want to see both hands, Fury."

I tucked the card back into the pocket of the dress and showed him my hands.

He moved to the next female, the machete poised, and I moved in tandem.

My card was a five.

That number again.

But this time, something clicked.

I kept my eyes trained on Gacy, because he was watching me closely.

But there were other senses I could use that were undetectable.

He slid over to the next female, and I mimicked his movements.

The next card was also an eight. Ace-8-5-8.

We moved on to the last female.

The card I took out of that pocket was an ace.

Gacy leaned between the gap of the last two women and cackled. "You feeling lucky, Fury?"

I held my muscles steady, my face blank. "I think I may have you beat."

Two pair. Aces and eights.

Be aware of dead man's hand.

That's what Hickok meant.

"Shall we look again before we place our bets?" Gacy asked, wiggling his painted eyebrows.

Right then and there, I decided to rally for a law to ban all clowns from Olympus.

I said, "If you insist." It would give me a chance to be absolutely sure.

We went through backward this time, checking the cards. Gacy's eyes were still trained on me, and mine on him over the females' shoulders.

The sky was blackening; the eclipse was almost here.

When I got to the middle card, the five, the scent was unmistakable. Night-blooming jasmine.

Off in the distance, there was a deafening clap of thunder and the low growl of a giant hound.

The noise, or maybe the growl, broke Gacy's concentration. His eyes flicked away, and he slackened the blade in his hand for a split second.

But that was all I needed.

I wailed, and Alecto shot straight up into the air, kicked Gacy in the head, and knocked him off balance. He dropped the smaller blade and swung the machete at her feet, roaring. But she was already in flight.

He advanced on me then, swinging, and I ducked, just as Cerberus sank his teeth into Gacy's leg.

The clown swung the blade at the hound, grazing his right ear.

I didn't give him a second chance. "Gacy!"

He twisted his face toward me and charged, even with the dog still attached to his leg.

He swung the machete with both hands, but he was off balance and missed.

I didn't. I yanked the knives from my wings with both hands and plunged them into his eyes.

The effect was instant. Gacy's face froze into a painted grimace as his soul poured from his eyes in liquidy black smoke over the Las Vegas desert.

Just as the moon eclipsed the sun, the clown suit evaporated into dust.

We had five minutes to catch our ride.

Chapter 57

Archer got busy cutting the ties from the women and removing their blindfolds. He spent some time calming them down and assuring them that they were out of harm's way. I watched for a moment as he ushered them to the car, lifting the bag containing Indigo out of the backseat.

I gathered Rumour and Alex.

"We need to hurry," I said. I explained about the plan for Thor and Zeus to crack the sky and carry us home. "But we must be at the coordinates specified."

Alex and Rumour shrugged out of their dresses and kicked them aside.

"Let's go," I said.

Then I heard a car start up.

I spun around to see Archer trotting back to us, Indigo and the canvas bag in his hand. "I thought you might need your sword."

I clutched my hands to my head. "No!"

He stopped short. "What?"

Then he heard the tires squeal. Archer turned to meet the dust with his face as the car made a doughnut formation and sped off toward the horizon.

I tried to run after the car, thought about flying after it, but my power was draining. I didn't know how much I needed to get home.

"We need to get to our coordinates, Archer!" I yelled.

"Shit! I told them to wait! They said they wanted the air conditioner on!" He dropped the bag and chased the car, but it was too late.

They were gone.

Alex walked over to him and punched him in the gut.

Archer doubled over. "Ow! Jesus Christ, why are you two so violent?"

Rumour said, "Because they're shape-shifters. They were actually raised by wolves. Tisi is the pack leader."

Archer looked at me, stunned.

I rolled my eyes. "That is not true. Knock it off, Rumour."

She grinned wickedly.

Alex said, "We can take his car." She pointed to the other car in the desert.

"The stink-mobile? No freaking way," said Rumour.

"I'm really sorry, ladies," Archer said.

"Shut up, mortal," Alex said.

"Yeah, shut up," said Rumour.

"*All* of you shut up! I need to think," I said.

The moon was slowly sliding away from the sun.

Archer was unzipping his bag. He glanced at his watch. "Three minutes."

I looked at the moonstone ring. This was supposed to be a tracking device. Athena had given it to me as such, before Hecate had enchanted it to receive messages. Maybe, just maybe, they would come to us.

"Everyone gather round. Alex, I'll need you to lock hands with me and expand your wings, and I'll do the same. Rumour and Archer can stand in the center."

"Don't order me around," my sister said.

"Just do it, Alex, or I'll leave you here to mortalize."

She rolled her eyes.

I turned to Hades's hound just as a violent bolt of lightning cracked the sky, followed by thunder that shook the ground. Thor and Zeus were close. I could feel it.

"Cerberus. Can you find your way home? Or do you want to come with us?"

The hound backed up a bit and sat down.

"Very well."

Archer stood up, holding the three orange sticks. He handed me Indigo, I snapped, and the small dragon opened her eyes.

"We're going home," I told her. She blinked and cooed.

Archer said. "These may work. They flame up and shoot into the sky. Lost travelers use them all the time here."

I nodded. "Great. Fire them off."

I watched as Archer sent the flares off into the darkened desert sky, feeling just a little sad. Would I ever see him again? There were laws in place to prevent the gods from mingling too often with mortals. I broke them harmlessly at times. But playing poker wasn't considered a serious offense. Interworld dating was. It had caused us nothing but trouble in the past, so the Fates had decided it was best to outlaw it altogether.

Archer jogged back to me. He smiled and embraced me. "You did it, Sassy."

"We did it, Lawman." I kissed him. Alex cleared her throat and glared at me. "Can you give us the game play, Coach?"

I sighed. She could be so rude. "All right, everyone. At the next lightning bolt, we all lock hands and focus on home."

Archer and Rumour stood centered.

My sister and I expanded our wings and clasped hands around them.

The light of the sun was nearly at full force.

I heard Thor's thunder boom first. I scanned the sky.
Rumour pointed. "There!"

I opened the ring and fired it at Zeus's lightning bolt.

The beam from my ring curled around the electric bolt, forming a connection from the ground to the sky.

The sky tore open, and the hands of the gods reached down and collected us.

Chapter 58

I hadn't seen Archer in two weeks, but today was the day, and I was giddy as a woodland nymph. Today was the hearing on our case. The Fates had been studying everything that had transpired, and they were to rule on Charon's involvement in Lamia's and Gacy's escape, how Archer and I had handled the mission, and my proposal for better communication between the realms.

I was brushing my hair when I noticed Megaera behind me.

"Meg. What are you doing here?"

She eyed me suspiciously. "The question is, what are *you* doing?"

I was about to apply lipstick. I stopped and narrowed my eyes at her through the mirror. "I don't know what you mean."

I grabbed a blouse that was hanging from the shower rack.

"I think you do," Meg said, a twang in her tone.

Alex popped in then. "I think she's in love with him." She crossed her arms.

I glared at her as I buttoned my shirt.

"Are you wearing perfume, Tisi?" Alex asked, sniffing the air.

I brushed her aside to get to my sink where the lotion sat. I dabbed it on my hands and elbows.

"And lipstick," Meg said in a little girl's voice.

Alex puckered her lips in the mirror. "Oh, Archer, kiss me like you mean it." She pretended to swoon.

"I saved your ass, and this is the thanks I get?" I said to my little sister.

Alex rolled her eyes. "Please. If it wasn't for me reserving my strength and building my power by channeling home, we would all be dead."

I felt my fury flutter, but I wouldn't let them get to me. Not today of all days.

"And if it wasn't for the two of you pretending to be mortals with the minds of lost sheep, none of us would have been in that mess to begin with," I said.

"Hey, I didn't get abducted," Meg said.

"No, but you were foolish enough to drink that juice," I said to my older sister. "And really, Meg? Clyde?"

Steam whistled from Megaera's ears. "I told you—that was a rumor you-know-who started."

I sighed. "This bathroom is not big enough for the three of us." I turned and walked out, leaving my sisters in the dark.

They followed me out.

"Don't be so serious, Tisiphone. We're only teasing you because we're happy for you," Meg said.

"That's right. It's about time you got some action. It'll dry up if you don't use it," Alex said.

I gave her a disgusted look. "You are vulgar."

I grabbed my sword and slipped it into a proper sheath. Indigo was out feeding.

"It's true," she said.

"That's what I heard," said Meg.

I opened the door and stepped out. Then I turned to my sisters. "Do not embarrass me. I mean it." I shot them each a stern look.

Alex stuck her tongue out at me, and Meg crossed her eyes.

I threw up my hands. "You act like children. The both of you."

My sisters snickered, and the three of us headed off into the dark night toward the courtroom of the Fates.

It took about an hour for the Fates to relay their verdicts. I learned that the escape was made possible through a combination of events: the black soul of Jason Helm and his ever-increasing knowledge of and faith in the dark arts, the unearthing of the gate via the humans, and, of course, the greedy, greased palm of Charon. It was the perfect storm.

The ferryman was found guilty of bribery, treason, and murder, since his actions had led to the deaths of Cicely Barnes, and Jason Helm, despicable as he was. His punishment for his crimes was banishment to a locked box in Tartarus.

I couldn't have been more thrilled.

Athena was given a chance to speak to my proposal. She informed the court that she was working on an interworld communication system. "Much like the mortals' Internet."

A technology I would welcome.

At last, Atropos called on Archer and me to approach the bench.

"Tisiphone, I am pleased with your performance, although I must say the life Gacy took might have been prevented with more diligence on your part."

My wings fluttered, but I bowed out of respect anyway. "Yes, Your Highness. It shan't happen again."

Archer stiffened beside me. He was about to say something to defend me, so I pinched him to keep his mouth shut.

He did.

"Archer Mays," said Clotho, the middle sister.

Archer stood with his hands clasped behind his back. "Yes."

"You have served the gods well. I must say, I was impressed with your part in this mission."

"Thank you. But Tisiphone did most of the work."

Clotho smiled. She looked to her sisters. "Modest too. We don't see much of that around here, do we, Sisters?"

I heard Hades cough behind me.

The other two Fates nodded.

"How did you feel about working with a Fury?" Lachesis asked.

Archer cleared his throat. "It was my pleasure."

"Hmm." Lachesis nodded.

The three Fates huddled together, their heads bobbing.

Archer and I exchanged a look. I shrugged. I didn't know what was going on. Then again, I never did when it came to the court.

After a few moments, the three old goddesses sat upright.

"Archer Mays," Clotho said, "I hereby deem you a demigod." She cracked the gavel on the bench.

"Excuse me?" Archer asked.

She ignored him. "Tisiphone, see to it that he fills out the proper paperwork."

I nodded.

"Paperwork?" asked Archer.

"He'll need training, of course, and a formal introduction to the gods," said Atropos.

Clotho said, "And a gift. What is it that he's good at, Tisiphone?"

One thing sprang to mind, but I didn't think it would make a good answer.

"A gift?" Archer asked.

"Well, you must be good at something," Lachesis said. "What do you think you should be the god *of?* You understand, I'm sure."

Atropos counted off on her fingers. "There are the gods of music, poetry, war, hunt, wisdom, technology... The list goes on."

I looked at Archer with a raised brow.

He was completely dumbstruck.

"Perhaps, Your Highness, we can first assure that his gift does not interfere with that of another god," I said. "I'm sure the new demigod wouldn't want to impose on anyone's duties."

The three Fates considered this.

Clothos said, "Quite right. No rush, I suppose. You can just fill it in on the paperwork."

With that, court was dismissed.

I waited for the Fates to file out. Then I grabbed Archer's hand and said, "Come on" before they changed their minds.

Outside, beneath the full moon of the Underworld, I kissed the newest god of the pantheon.

Archer put his hands around my waist. "What just happened?"

"What just happened is that we don't have to be separated anymore."

"Well." He kissed me back. "I like the sound of that."

"Me too." I snuggled closer in his arms and buried my cheek in his chest, drinking in the scent of the clover soap he used.

"Hey, Tisi," he whispered.

I looked at him. "Yes?"

"I'm really glad I died."

I smiled. "Me too, Lawman."

For the first time in as long as I could remember, I was happy. I had given my heart to another, and it felt good. It felt like it was meant to be, like it had always been Tisi and Archer.

Meg and Alex came out then, making smacking noises with their lips.

I broke away from my partner's embrace.

"Oh, Archer, I love you," Meg said to Alex in a singsong voice.

Alex turned to her and said in a similar tone, "Oh, Tisi, I love you too."

Then they pretended to hug and kiss each other.

I tried, I really did, but the stress had been piling up for too long, and I couldn't keep my fury at bay.

"That's it." I flew at both of them, tackling them to the ground simultaneously, and we rolled around, trying to strangle each other.

"Hey, stop that! Tisi, break it up." Archer danced around us, not sure whom to pull off of whom.

Meg cut a right cross to my shoulder while Alex kicked me in the stomach. I grabbed my younger sister's leg and flipped her on her back. She howled like a baby. I laughed. Then Meg body-slammed me into the ground, knocking the wind from my lungs. I grabbed her waist, and we tumbled into the sandaled feet of our dark lord.

I heard Archer ask, "Are they always like this?"

Meg slapped the back of my head, and I elbowed her ribs. Alex took a flying leap and piled on top of us.

Hades lit a cigar and put his arm around him. "Son, you have no idea. Come on, I'll buy you a drink. You like to play poker?"

THE END

Author's Note

This book is for anyone who has ever battled a demon. For anyone who has ever stared evil in the face and dared to fight back. For anyone who has refused to be a victim—and for those who were, who never had a voice, you do now.

While writers often invent villains, I chose to use a real-life monster in this story. What you read here regarding the details of John Wayne Gacy's crimes, convictions, and pastimes is true. When the idea popped into my head (or, rather, the name, as I was writing one dark scene), I shunned it. I didn't want him anywhere near this story, but the further away I pushed it, the more stubborn the muse grew. Something was telling me that Tisiphone had to battle this murderer—this once-living evil—and since the story knows best, she did.

Perhaps it was because the crimes and Gacy's eventual arrest occurred close to my childhood home. Perhaps it was to enact a kind of literary justice for the victims, some of whom were never identified. Or perhaps it was to better understand Tisiphone's views on humans and our justice system.

Whatever the reason, I hope this book encourages you to take back your power, no matter what you've battled.

There's another historical figure in this story, James Butler Hickok. Wild Bill led an interesting, full life. This is from Wikipedia:

Born and raised on a farm in rural Illinois, Hickok went west at age 18 as a fugitive from justice, first working as a stagecoach driver, before he became a lawman in the frontier territories of Kansas and Nebraska. He fought for the Union Army during the American Civil War, and gained publicity after the war as a scout, marksman, actor, and professional gambler. Between his law-enforcement duties and gambling, which easily overlapped, Hickok was involved in several notable shootouts. He was shot and killed while playing poker in the Nuttal & Mann's Saloon in Deadwood, Dakota Territory (now South Dakota).

Hickok was holding two pair when he was shot, all black aces and eights, known today as "dead man's hand."

One other component of this mythological tale that happens to be true came to me when I was nearly halfway through writing the book. I was researching the moons of the planet Pluto, Hades's ruling planet, when I came across an article titled "Pluto's Gate to Hell Uncovered in Turkey." A Google search will lead you to articles about it and videos of the discovery, as well as to a visual interpretation of what the site may have looked like in ancient times.

Finally, fans of the Stacy Justice series might have noticed the appearances of that heroine in Tisiphone's world. What can I say? I thought the woman needed a vacation. For readers unfamiliar with that paranormal-mystery series, I invite you to visit my website at www.barbraannino.com to learn more or head to Amazon to read a sample. If you would like to be notified about upcoming releases of any series or title, feel free to email me at authorbarbraannino@gmail.com or become a fan of my author page on Facebook.

Warm blessings,

Barbra Annino

Acknowledgments

Thanks to Terry Goodman for his confidence and encouragement and for allowing this author to stretch her writer's wings. Thanks to Alison Dasho, my editor and the newest member of the Thomas & Mercer team. Here's to the start of a beautiful friendship. Big applause to the T&M team and my author relations liaison, Jacque Ben-Zekry, for all they do for me and my work.

Much appreciation goes to my sharp beta readers, who make suggestions and comments and tell me straight-up how it is. George Annino, Leslie Gay, and Selena Jones, your feedback is invaluable.

Finally, thank you to my husband for convincing me that Tisi's voice needed to be heard. You're my Archer.

About the Author

Photo by George Annino

Barbra Annino is a native of Chicago who currently lives in Galena, Illinois. Her past occupations include bartender, humor columnist, and bed-and-breakfast owner, but she now writes fiction full-time. You can find out more about her by visiting www.barbraannino.com or Facebook.com/AuthorBarbraAnnino or by emailing her at authorbarbraannino@gmail.com.